COLD
ISLAND

OTHER TITLES BY PETER COLT

The Andy Roark Mysteries

COLD ISLAND

A NOVEL

PETER COLT

THOMAS & MERCER

Text copyright © 2025 by Peter K. Colt
All rights reserved.

Published by Thomas & Mercer, Seattle

www.apub.com

Amazon, the Amazon logo, and Thomas & Mercer are trademarks of Amazon.com, Inc., or its affiliates.

EU product safety contact:
Amazon Media EU S. à r.l.
38, avenue John F. Kennedy, L-1855 Luxembourg
amazonpublishing-gpsr@amazon.com

ISBN-13: 9781662530388 (paperback)
ISBN-13: 9781662530371 (digital)

Cover design by Caroline Johnson
Cover image: © Chris Hackett, © Kirill Rudenko, © Chris Clor / Getty

Printed in the United States of America

For Steve Bender, one of two men I called my uncle.
The world is an infinitely duller place for his passing.
Also Cathy, Henry, and Alder, without whom there'd be
little point in any of this

October 1981

The day had been warm. It had been a lot of fun playing with the other kids in the neighborhood, and they stayed longer than they should have. It would mean trouble when he finally got home. It was early October, when the days were warm but at night, when the wind came up, it turned chilly. Especially without a jacket. He was wearing just jeans, ragged at the knees, a T-shirt, and a grubby sweatshirt.

It had grown dark, the sky having gone from bright blue to pink with india-ink clouds. He rubbed the palm of his hand along the underside of his nose and then on his jeans. He was a big boy, too big at eight years old to be scared of the dark. He kept telling himself that. The wind rustled the trees, and the cold as much as the sound made him shiver. He heard a twig snap and dry leaves moving somewhere behind him in the bushes.

"A dog. It must be a dog," he told himself. Except he knew it wasn't a dog. He was afraid of dogs, but he would never admit it. He shivered and decided he should start moving again. His knee hurt from where he banged it up earlier, scraping it, ripping through his jeans. He knew it would scab over, but right now it stung when the cold air hit it. He got up from where he was lying, hiding behind a bush just off the road.

His side hurt as he started walking down the road. He rubbed his palm against his nose again to wipe away the dampness there. His other arm hurt, too, but that was all right. He would be all right when he got home. It was warm there, and Mommy—he wasn't too big to call her Mommy—would *make him some tomato soup or maybe a grilled cheese sandwich. That was his favorite.*

The car glided up to him. He hadn't heard it until it was right there next to him, tires crunching on loose gravel or scallop shells. He hadn't seen its headlights because they were turned off. The passenger door opened, and the man leaned over.

"Hey, little man."

"Hi," the boy said, his voice uncertain.

"You look cold." The man smiled. The boy nodded.

"Come on, hop in. I'll run you home." The boy stood there; his feet were made of stone, it seemed. Then the wind picked up, and he shivered again. He heard a dog bark in the distance. He had to pee, and he wanted to go home.

"Come on, little man, you don't have to be scared." The man's smile never seemed to move—it was just all teeth, almost like a dog when it growled. The boy didn't want to get in the car with the man, but he was cold. He wiped his nose again, then wiped the moist palm on his thigh. Then he made up his mind and climbed into the car onto the seat next to the man. The car was warm, hot air pouring out of the vents, and the radio was playing soft music about a girl with faraway eyes. The boy's side hurt, he was hungry, and he was tired. He eased his head back against the seat. He didn't take notice of the man reaching across him to push the door lock down.

CHAPTER 1

2016

Tommy Kelly leaned against the front of the Ford Crown Victoria. It was one of the last models, and he adored it. It was black with tinted windows and had a spotlight on a swivel on the driver's side; everyone in the troop called it Black Beauty. Everything about it screamed "unmarked cop car." He had loved that Black Beauty from the moment it was assigned to him as his take-home car when he first made detective eight years ago. He felt like he was king of the road when he was pushing it down the Pike at a buck ten. Kelly was determined to keep the old warhorse on the road as long as he could.

The same could be said of him. Kelly ran at least twelve miles a week and spent a minimum of five mornings in the gym, lifting weights. His partner, Jacques, referred to it as "beating on your pecs." Kelly couldn't stand the thought of losing a suspect in a foot pursuit or losing a fight because he was out of shape. He drank a lot of expensive protein drinks, drank his coffee black, and avoided the drive-through the way a vampire avoided garlic.

He twirled a coin absentmindedly in his fingers as he watched the white hull of the Steamship Authority ferry ease into the berth. It had made the trip over from Nantucket, and he would be taking it back to the island. He was not eager to go there. Only part of it had to do with the fact that Jeanie was already on his ass about it. She had left an angry voicemail in which she inquired if she was "expected to do everything to raise our two children?" Liam and Connor were good boys, but they were a handful. Then if you added in Cub Scouts, sports, and karate lessons . . . it was a lot for two parents, let alone one left to cope on her own.

Kelly had walked into the detective bureau in the Troop Headquarters a little after seven in the morning. He shared it with five other detectives. His cubicle was next to Jacques's, which had a framed photo of his family from two Christmases before and a small wooden cross as its only decorations. The rest of his cubicle was plastered with pictures from cases he was working on: a car dealership with a broken glass door, a body slumped over a steering wheel; a drug rip gone fatal. Each photo had accompanying photos of the crime scenes from different angles, all with the report numbers written on the bottom in Jacques's neat script.

Kelly's own cubicle had a picture of Jeanie and the boys from a trip to Edaville Railroad the summer before. He had a memorial prayer card from his father's wake tacked to the cubicle wall next to a printed-out photo of the detective squad from the Worcester Troop. His desk had a computer, keyboard, and monitor; a phone with more buttons than he ever seemed to need; and piles of Massachusetts State Police manila folders.

His dark hair was still damp from the post-workout shower when Jacques looked up from his computer and said, "Big Dick wants to see you. Now." Big Dick was the troop's head of detectives.

"Shit, I haven't even had a cup of coffee yet." Kelly went through the mental index of things that could have landed him in the hot seat with Detective Lieutenant Richard "Dickie" Savoy.

"That's your fault, man. There's only half a dozen Dunkin's between your house and here."

"I can't have coffee before I work out." He was tall, broad shouldered, with eyes that had served him well with women.

Kelly dropped his gym bag next to his chair and walked down the hall to his boss's office. Kelly had transferred from Worcester to Middleborough, Massachusetts, six months earlier. He was still getting used to his new boss and was unsure what was so pressing it couldn't wait until he at least had his morning coffee. He stopped, knocked on the open door, and went in.

Savoy was in his mid-fifties with an iron-gray crew cut and the lean build of a marathon runner. Kelly heard that Savoy had spent a long time in the gang unit, much of it undercover posing as an outlaw biker. Rumor had it that Savoy once had a ponytail and a ZZ Top beard. Someone had said that he carried a stainless-steel Colt .45 in his waistband and had pistol-whipped a couple of bad dudes with it. It was impossible to imagine that the wiry man with the impeccably pressed suit and marine corps tiepin could have passed for a "one percenter." Others said that a bike gang couldn't believe Savoy had been a trooper.

The story going around was that bikers had put a price on his head. Legend had it Savoy had met with the president of the club and told him, *Come after me. I get it. I'll bury everyone you send at me, or they'll bury me. It doesn't matter. Come near my family, and all the rules go out the window.* No matter what had gone down, Kelly was certain he didn't want to be on Savoy's bad side.

"Kelly. Good. Don't bother sitting down." Savoy was not one to say more than he needed to, but he was never curt with Kelly.

"Okay, why not?"

"They found a dead body on Nantucket. Construction crew found it as they were breaking ground for some millionaire's new vacation house."

"Sure, Lieu"—no one called the boss Big Dick to his face—"but I thought one of the closer barracks . . ." Kelly trailed off, treading lightly. He didn't really want to go to Nantucket, but he didn't want to piss off Dickie Savoy either. No one likes a whiny subordinate.

"There are other dicks, but everyone is shorthanded right now. So, you get to go. Plus, you had plenty of homicide experience in

Wormtown." Every city had a nickname, and Worcester, Massachusetts, was no different.

"Sure, Lieu, but something tells me this isn't a drug rip or gang feud on Nantucket."

"No, it's a kid."

"What?"

"Yeah, the backhoe managed to dig up a kid's grave. Local cops don't get a lot of dead bodies, much less kids . . . so go home, tell the wife one less plate on the dinner table, pack a bag, and get your ass to the ferry. If you hurry, you might just catch the next one."

"Sure, boss," Kelly said and walked back to his desk. Jacques looked up as Kelly came over. He was smiling broadly.

"You going to the island?"

"Yep, that's what Big Dick said. What, did he offer it to you first?"

"I can't help it if you have more experience with homicides than I do. Plus, he is worried that at the pace I work, I might never leave the island." Jacques had immigrated to Boston from Haiti as a boy. He was a meticulous detective who annoyed his superiors by working at his own pace, which was slow. His cases were rock solid, and he was unshakable on the witness stand. Jacques got convictions, and the bosses liked convictions. He and Kelly got along well and worked together when they could.

"Fuck. Jeanie's gonna be pissed."

"Yeah, but at least you aren't in trouble with Savoy. You shoulda seen the look on your face when I told you he wanted to see you right away." Jacques laughed.

"Yeah, there is that." Kelly sat in front of the computer and checked the schedule. If he hurried, he could make the next ferry and be on the island before lunch.

After a quick trip home to pack and a terse conversation with Jeanie, he'd driven with his lights on the whole way down Route 6 and made it to the ferry with minutes to spare. They'd been married for more than a decade. Being married to a trooper was hard enough;

being married to Kelly was tougher still. This wasn't the first or worst imposition that the Massachusetts State Police had inflicted on her. There'd been lots of long hours away from her and the boys, lots of last-minute calls involving overtime, crime scenes, or carnage on the highways of the commonwealth. There'd been many missed holidays and family celebrations. There'd been one bad car accident while on duty that sent him to the hospital for a few days. Jeanie had put up with it, and Kelly had worked hard to be there for her and the boys, often forgoing sleep to stay up after a shift to spend time with them. It had gotten better when he came off the road and went to dicks, but not much better. Jeanie was sick of it.

Kelly made it in time to see the ferry in the distance as he pulled up to the small, shingled shack in the parking lot. He showed the attendant his badge, and the man assured him that there would be room for Black Beauty on the ferry. Kelly pulled into the spot in line he was directed to and went to get his ticket. The bored clerk looked at his badge and took his credit card. The ferry service always kept a couple of spots open for things like police on official business or ambulances.

He went out to wait for the boat. It was mid-April and uncharacteristically sunny but cool and breezy. Kelly leaned against the grille of his car. The breeze pushed at his navy-blue fleece jacket, cutting away the warmth of the early-spring sun. Gulls wheeled overhead, making their plaintive, high-pitched cries as they rode the thermals. He loved watching them fly but always found their cries to be off-putting. Kelly could smell food cooking from the Dockside Restaurant, which was next to the terminal. It brought back happy memories from his childhood.

He got in the car and, when his turn came, eased it onto the ferry. He pulled up the car ramp and into the cavernous car hold, following the man who directed him to a spot as the sun was blotted out. Kelly felt a small knot of uneasiness in his stomach. There was no part of an investigation into a dead kid on Nantucket that could bring anything good into his life.

He parked and locked the car and made his way up to the passenger deck. The wooden heels of his dress shoes made a clonking noise on the steel deck plating. The ferry seemed huge to him, and he wondered if the crossing would be rough. It wasn't crowded, and he found a seat next to a window. It had a table, and he was able to lean against the bulkhead in such a way that his issued pistol didn't dig into his side. With a blast of the horn, the ferry pulled away from the dock, navigated through the breakwater, and was on its way.

He watched as the cape slid away and they made their way into the ocean. The ferry picked up a decided roll to it. Things got rockier in Nantucket Sound, the midway point. The waves were capped with white foam, and the ferry seemed to pitch a little more. Kelly sat watching the ocean, wrapped around his own thoughts about what he would find on the island—what he would find at the crime scene, what the local cops would be like. He couldn't imagine that there were a lot of homicides on Nantucket. Kelly wasn't a man overly endowed with imagination, and his success as a detective had more to do with hard work and attention to detail than anything else. He preferred to watch the Red Sox or Bruins play than to read a book. In fact, the last book he read had been for his master's in criminal justice a couple of years ago.

The snack bar had a cup of coffee and blueberry yogurt. He hadn't had time for his protein shake this morning, and he was getting that hollow feeling in his stomach. He usually drank a chocolate or vanilla one while reading reports in front of his computer. Savoy's marching orders had made sure that he hadn't done either. Instead, he contented himself with *The Boston Globe* and what his body considered rationed amounts of caffeine and protein.

The *Globe* was full of news about a mass shooting in California and North Korea preparing to launch missiles to remind the world that it was still relevant. The political news was depressing, not that Kelly followed it. He paid attention to local politics because that impacted his salary, either in terms of raises or taxes. That and the politicians at the statehouse passing laws that made life easier for criminals. That was of more interest.

Kelly read the paper, and when the rolling swells got to be too much, he went up on deck to get some fresh air. He stood at the bow of the lumbering, white, slab-sided ship as it thrust through the waves toward the island. The island was a flat line before him that grew taller and more textured as the ship pushed onward. He could make out water towers, church steeples of white and red, and white TV towers. As the ferry drew closer to the island, the gulls appeared above it, wheeling on thermals, shrieking their madman's shrieks.

It wasn't long before it was gliding between the stone jetties that marked the entrance to the harbor. The PA system crackled with instructions for drivers to go to their cars. Kelly looked at Brant Point Lighthouse, the coast guard station, and the two white church steeples, and whistled softly. A million-dollar view. He took one last look at the island and then went down to his car. His stomach tightened as he got into it.

Kelly watched as the big hatch in the front of the ship very slowly lifted upward, revealing a sunny early-April sky. The ferry was rounding Brant Point, turning into the harbor. Local legend held that when leaving the island, people should throw pennies overboard at Brant Point to ensure a speedy return. Kelly could picture little kids doing that, if they ever came out to the island. The big ferry eased into its berth, and when it was safe, the crewman lowered the chain barring their way.

Kelly put Black Beauty into gear and rolled off the ferry and down the docking ramp. He turned off Steamboat Wharf onto Broad Street. It was strange how little things had changed. The Whaling Museum was still there, all red brick, celebrating a brief but glorious history at sea. He passed the Sunken Ship, a shop specializing in scuba gear, diving needs, and tourist clothes. He passed the town hall, which could have been the redbrick sibling of the Whaling Museum. He took a left onto Federal Street and stopped briefly at the intersection with Chestnut Street.

He turned down Chestnut, thinking he would box around and head to the town hall. He was stymied by the small town's one-way streets. There was a small two-story building of red brick with a Ford Crown Victoria wearing Nantucket Police livery parked in front. The building had a large garage door flanked by two huge windows that had once been garage doors too. In the red stone insert above the garage door, he could make out the almost completely sandblasted words Nantucket Fire Department. There was a sign bolted to the side of the building that read Nantucket Police Department Substation. He parked, then walked into the building, up to a wooden counter. A young officer stood up from behind a desk with a computer and came over. He was in his twenties, tall, fit, and fair-haired.

"Can I help you, sir?" he asked with the professionally detached politeness that cops developed over time.

"Detective Kelly, State Police." He held out his credential case for the young cop to examine.

"Mike Dukowski. We've been expecting you. Detective Harris is out at the site now. C'mon, I was heading out there. You can follow me."

"Good. I'd probably get lost in all these one-way streets."

"You get used to it. C'mon. Jo will be waiting."

"Jo?"

"Detective Jo Harris."

"Aha," Kelly replied.

They went out to their respective Crown Victorias, and Kelly followed the younger man down South Water Street. They passed the Dreamland theater and the Atlantic Café, the Atheneum on the other side of the street, with its pleasant, hedge-lined park and strategically placed benches to take advantage of pleasant days. They drove by some real estate offices and the Opera House Restaurant, and the street turned from tar to cobblestone. There was a large fountain in the middle of Main Street to Kelly's right, probably left over from when horses were the mode of transportation.

They crossed the cobblestone Main Street, bouncing over it until they reached smooth tar on the other side. South Water Street curved and turned into Washington Street, and they passed the redbrick American Legion hall. Kelly noted that everything in town was made of either red brick or wooden clapboard. All of it seemed old and designed to elicit maximum antique charm. It reminded him a little bit of a movie set.

He had his window rolled partway down, enjoying the cool, fresh air. They wound their way away from Main Street, the harbor on their left. Then past the Cumberland Farms, the Marine Home Center, and the Island Home for the Aged. Orange Street led to a rotary and then out on to Milestone Road. Here the island seemed open and wild with brown scrub pines on either side of the road. It was early spring, and the rich greens and bright-yellow daffodils were a couple of weeks off. Kelly had seen flyers on the ferry advertising the upcoming Daffodil Festival.

When Dukowski signaled and turned down a road on the right, Kelly followed. They went past a few cul-de-sacs with their housing developments of new, uniform houses and yards. They drove past them, and the land opened again. The road was mostly dirt or packed sand, and the grass on either side mounded up higher than the road. Now the houses were few and far between, and they were getting closer to the ocean. They pulled up next to a few police cars parked at the side of the road.

Dukowski walked over. "I am afraid we're going to have to walk from here, sir."

"No problem." Kelly hadn't had time to change and looked at his leather dress shoes ruefully. This was going to be tough on them. They walked toward the lot of the construction site. The yellow crime scene tape that had been put up, cordoning off the area, fluttered in the cool breeze. Kelly shivered slightly as a chill found its way through his fleece jacket.

Another Nantucket cop checked Kelly's credentials and then added his name to the crime scene entry sheet. Methodical, these small-town cops. He was pretty sure the cops he worked with in Wormtown had heard of a crime scene entry log only when they were taught about it in the academy. As he wrote his information down, he looked over at a backhoe that was parked. A tent with a folding aluminum frame had been set up in front of it, and he could see people moving carefully around the pit.

As they got closer to the backhoe, Kelly noted that it was mostly yellow except for reddish-brown, cancer-like eruptions of rust on its skin.

"It's the salt air," Dukowski said.

"Huh?"

"Everything rusts faster out here. It doesn't take much."

"Oh, yeah. Must be tough on your gear." Kelly still had nightmares about polishing and adjusting his leather gear when he was in uniform.

"You have no idea." The last word came out as "eye-deer."

The tent, with its aluminum frame, looked as though it would have been more at home at a high school graduation party than covering up a pit with human remains. A ladder led down into the pit, and a figure in a Tyvek suit was taking pictures. In the back of what would be part of the foundation was a woman of medium height wearing jeans tucked into red gum boots, a black turtleneck sweater, and a blue windbreaker that had POLICE written across the back. Her hair was dark brown and pulled back into a ponytail.

"Jo, this is the State Police dick . . . detective. Detective Kelly."

She looked up at Kelly, her brown eyes taking him in, measuring him up. "Hey."

"What do we have?" As much as he tried not to, sometimes he sounded like a cop on a TV show.

"We . . . we have some bones. Kid's bones. Come on down." She said it pointedly, looking at his leather dress shoes. He'd gotten them on sale, but they were still expensive. Kelly climbed down the aluminum ladder into the pit, and his foot immediately squished into wet mud when he stepped off the ladder. He turned away from the ladder to see NPD Detective Harris smiling slightly.

"Construction crew was digging a foundation for a new house. They were just finishing up yesterday when the earth next to the remains slid off the side of the pit. We had a few rainy days, and the dirt and mud really just slid away from the skull. Construction worker found it and freaked out. We set up the tent, the crime scene tape, and had a cop out here watching everything all night. We just started working a little while ago."

"Okay. What do you have so far?" he asked, almost rhetorically. She had told him: a mostly done foundation with bones.

"A few witness statements, buckets of dirt that will have to go to the lab, and a small human skull. We're taking our time, Detective, trying to do it by the numbers."

"Of course. Why are you certain it is a kid's skull and not, say, a petite woman's?"

"Well, besides the fact that the parts of the skull, the sutures, where the sides join aren't fully formed?"

"Yeah, besides that." His voice didn't betray the sinking feeling in his gut, the irrational hope that it wasn't going to be a kid.

"Besides the small bones and the baby teeth?"

"Uh-huh." Kelly realized he probably sounded like an idiot, an empty suit of a detective. He felt his stomach tighten as he thought about baby teeth and small bones.

"There was cloth caught in the backhoe blade. The clothing is degraded, but there's a design or pattern on it. Maybe a cartoon character. Hard to tell right now. Or at least on the piece we have so far."

"Okay, that's good enough for me." Kelly felt the cold water seeping into and around his feet, one of two things making him feel foolish.

"We've been carefully removing the dirt with trowels and putting it in sterile buckets. From here, the soil will go to the gym at the high school. It will get dumped out through a screen onto a tarp. We'll sift through everything, take samples, and send them to the state crime lab. The bones will go to the pathologist. We're taking digital photos of each excavation before we move on to the next. I know we aren't the State Police, but we are professionals out here."

"Yes, I am sure you are." Kelly saw no point in getting into a pissing contest. A lot of smaller-town detectives resented it when the State Police detectives showed up. He couldn't blame them. No one wanted to have some outsider come in and tell them how to manage their investigation.

With the exception of Boston, Worcester, and Springfield, the State Police were technically in charge of investigating homicides in the Commonwealth of Massachusetts. The theory was that because all homicides were overseen by the district attorney's office, it made sense to have a State Police detective in charge of the investigation so that they could answer directly to the DA. It pissed off a lot of dicks from smaller towns. Kelly was used to it.

The person in the baggy white Tyvek suit clambered down the ladder into the hole. He—Kelly was able to figure out it was a smallish man—had two orange plastic five-gallon buckets with white writing on the sides, the types that usually held paint or the ice melt that people put on their driveways every winter.

"Home Depot," Jo Harris offered.

"Huh?"

"We buy stuff like that on the mainland. The Home Depot in Hyannis is a lot cheaper than anything we can buy on-island."

"Does everyone do that?"

"What, go off-island to shop? Sure. Everything has to be shipped here from somewhere, and the stores in town have to make money . . . Summer people can afford to pay, but the rest of us have to try and save where we can. Even the police."

"I guess that makes sense."

"Your fancy shoes are getting wet."

"Yes, they are." He looked down. They were beyond the "getting" stage. They were soaked. Wet and ruined.

"Look, we're going to be here all day. Why don't you go check in with Bruce Green at the local barracks. Change into something more practical, get a bite, a coffee, whatever you need, and come back when you're ready."

"Okay. I can do that. Where's the local barracks?"

"It's on North Liberty Street." She gave him directions that he was sure he would, at best, only half remember. He thanked her and squelched through the mud to the aluminum ladder. When he stepped up the rungs, water oozed out of the seams of his shoes. He got to the top and walked over to Black Beauty.

Dukowski was talking to another local cop near the pit. Kelly went to the rear of his car and popped the trunk. He went to the far side of his vehicle, away from the locals, and, as quietly as he could, vomited up the yogurt and coffee he had on the ferry. When he was done, he bent over the trunk, rummaged in his duty bag, and pulled out the bottle of bright-green mouthwash he kept in there next to a bottle of Jameson. He rinsed the bile out of his mouth and closed the trunk. He got in the car, backed down the dirt road until he found a spot where he could make a K-turn, and headed into town.

October 1981

Richie Sousa was pedaling furiously on his bike. Pumping his legs up and down, calves straining against his Toughskins blue jeans. He was riding his Rampar BMX bike with knobby tires that you braked by pushing backward against the pedals. It was red in color, with red-and-white-checkerboard pattern pads on the handlebars and frame. His pride and joy. Richie had got it for his tenth birthday, which had been in August. The bike gave him freedom. He was allowed to ride it to school and back. He could go almost anywhere in and around town on it. It also meant that he could leave a little later to get home, because he knew the best shortcuts and he rode fast. Faster than anyone he knew.

A couple of the other kids had bikes. Mikey Parker had a green banana seat bike. The paint and the seat looked like they had glitter in them, and sometimes they teased Mikey that it was a girl's bike. Mikey would get mad, but he didn't say much. He knew Mikey's dad had found it at the town dump and had cleaned it up for Mikey. Mikey always seemed to have some new/old treasure his dad found. Stuff that was broken and mended but still good.

Richie's dad was a fisherman on one of the big boats, the Gwendolyn. *Richie's dad always smelled faintly of fish and cherry pipe tobacco no matter how fresh from the shower he was. The* Gwendolyn *had come back in after a good haul, and Richie's dad had bought him the bike. It wasn't like his dad to get him an expensive gift . . . but Richie was ten now. Ten was a big deal, even to his dad. Richie had screamed with joy when his dad wheeled* it out. He caught his mother looking at his dad, who shrugged his shoulders at her. His parents smiled at each other, proud of their son's happiness.

It was almost dark, and he had to get home. Dad was out on the boat, and Mom would be getting dinner ready. His little sister Jessie would already be in the high chair, Mark would be helping set the table, and Mom would be balancing baby Kerri on one hip while stirring something on the stove. Mark was getting over a cold and wasn't allowed to play football with the gang until he was better.

They had been playing in the field on Mill Street. It was a big field that narrowed as it went uphill. They played football in a portion of the field that had a split-rail wooden fence all around it, making a rectangle. It was the closest thing they had to a real football field that wasn't at the Boys & Girls Club or school. They were a gang like the kids on The Little Rascals, but not fake like on TV. Richie, the oldest, was small for his age, but he was fast and good at playing sports. He was the gang's leader.

Mikey Parker was eight. He looked up to Richie and wanted to be just like him. Louie and Johnny were both nine but big for their ages. Taller than Richie, but not as fast.

There was Nick, who had just moved to the island from Connecticut. Nick was nine, but they were in the same grade. He wasn't as good at sports, but everyone liked him. He had an actual X-wing fighter toy and a matching Luke Skywalker. He also had a Millennium Falcon, and lots of kids wanted to be his friend because of it.

There was Albie, who had just started playing with them. Albie was chubby and wasn't good at sports. He always seemed to have a runny nose. He cried a lot and was kind of a pain. Sometimes there were younger brothers and sisters who were brought along to play because their parents couldn't watch them, or the occasional older kid who had nothing to do and was bored that day. They all played football in the lot on Mill Street.

Richie knew he was good at sports and wanted to play for the Whalers, the high school football team, when he was old enough. They seemed like gods, riding through town on floats and the backs of trucks before the big game with the Vineyard. That day, Richie and the gang had been playing with some older boys. *They played tackle football, and it was always rough on the smaller boys. Richie was fast enough that most of the time he came out of it all right. Albie had taken a hit and came up crying and blubbering. He was never going to be a Whaler. Richie didn't like him and was impatient with him because his blubbering had held up the game. He had wanted to run! To play!*

They started playing again. Richie had run into the end zone, marked by book bags and windbreakers on the ground. He had been fast enough to get by a sixth grader and caught the youth-size football against his chest, where his number would be. It had stung in the ever-cooling air, but he made the tiebreaking touchdown, winning the game. He didn't mind when the high fives, especially from the older boys, stung his hands. It felt like victory to him. Then it was time to go. They all started to head to their respective homes.

Richie lived on Vesper Lane, and it was almost dark. Some of the streets were busy with cars driving by in a steady stream with their headlights on, forcing him to ride on the sidewalks. Richie had to be careful, and he wanted to go faster. Instead of taking North Mill Street and then going down Vesper Lane, he could save time by taking a shortcut through the big cemetery. He rode up Mill Street, then managed to cross at a break in traffic on Prospect Street. He took a couple of smaller streets uphill. He turned into the gates of the cemetery as the sky got reddish purple.

Richie gulped. The cemetery during the day was okay. Like a garden of sculptures with old names and old-timey writing. Little American flags and brass stars on sticks that had turned black as they had weathered in the elements. He rode up the hill, trying to race the darkness. Shivering despite his pedaling furiously. He could hear cars on the nearby roads, but they sounded far away. In the cemetery, it was quiet. Spooky. It was like one of the movies they played on Creature Double Feature *at Halloween!*

He pedaled downhill on the hard-packed dirt road. He could see the street in front of him. He was almost out of the cemetery. Almost home. Headlights washing along the black tar and the nearby houses. He would feel better once he was out of the cemetery. He saw the open gates by Vesper

Lane. His house was only twenty or thirty yards from the gate. He pedaled faster. He shot through the gate, clearing it.

Then, without warning, there was a car right in his path. He heard the car's brakes. He tried to brake the Rampar, but he was pedaling too fast. Richie hit the side of the car and bounced off his bike. He hit the ground, and the wind was knocked out of him. He lay there, on his side, aching like he'd been tackled by one of the twelve-year-olds.

Richie never made it home.

CHAPTER 2

Kelly took a right instead of a left on Milestone Road, which took him out past the cranberry bogs. The left would have taken him back into town, but the weather was still nice, and he couldn't have asked for a more scenic drive. He was hoping it would help settle his stomach. Out on this part of the island, it seemed wild and wide open. Here the houses were few and far between, unlike the cheek by jowl clapboarding of town. This allowed the scrub pines and beach plum to grow in abundance, adding to the wild, wide-open feeling. The thin black ribbon of the bike path paralleled him as he drove. Even though it wasn't tourist season yet, there were the occasional people riding bikes or running.

Eventually he could see a water tower off to his right, a baseball diamond, and then the houses began to appear and form a cluster of a village. Signs referred to it as the Siasconset Historic District. There was something about the place that reminded him of the classic Hitchcock movie *The Birds*. Like any minute now birds would start gathering in the quiet streets of this part of the island. It was the perfect setting.

He took a left at the Sconset Market, a big clue that the locals didn't bother with the first syllable of what was most likely an old Wampanoag name. Sankaty Road led him to a red-and-white-striped lighthouse in the distance. He turned onto Polpis Road, which he was certain would take him back to town. Scary movies aside, this was a beautiful part of the island, he had to admit to himself.

Kelly drove back along the route that he had used to follow Dukowski through town out to the crime scene. He turned up Main Street, Black Beauty bouncing on the cobblestones, making him wonder about the last time the suspension and shocks had received any love. He made a few wrong turns and was frequently stymied by one-way streets, but he eventually found himself in front of a pleasant-looking house of weathered gray shingles and white trim on North Liberty Street.

In front was a flagpole with the American flag and, below that, the Commonwealth of Massachusetts flag. There was a quarterboard over the door with MASSACHUSETTS STATE POLICE stenciled on it. A bit of tongue-in-cheek humor on an island where people named their houses and proclaimed them to the world with a quarterboard above the door.

In the driveway was a two-tone, blue-on-blue State Police Ford SUV. This was the local State Police barracks. One trooper, with or without family, got to live in a house on Nantucket year-round. That trooper lived in the most expensive zip code in the commonwealth, mortgage-free for the duration of his tour. Ironically, due to the isolation of the island, it was considered a hardship posting, and the assigned trooper received hardship pay. Extra pay to live in a house no trooper could afford, in one of the wealthiest communities in America. That wasn't a bad deal.

Kelly backed into the driveway next to the SUV. He turned off the engine, and by the time he was out of the car, there was a man in uniform standing by the corner of the house. He was tall with reddish-gray hair and green eyes. Kelly figured him for his mid-fifties. He looked tanned and fit. Kelly stepped forward and extended his hand. "Tom Kelly."

"Bruce Green. Come in, Detective, I've been expecting you." He looked down at Kelly's shoes as they squelched on the driveway. "I take it you've already been out to the scene."

Kelly smiled ruefully. "What gave it away?"

"Well, I'm not a trained detective, but there are a couple of clues. Were those expensive?" Green nodded toward Kelly's once-elegant shoes, smiling impishly.

Kelly shrugged. "You know."

"They're ruined, Detective. Or at least they will be when they dry."

"Yeah, I didn't have time to change into more appropriate clothes. When I got to the scene, the local dick, a lady—"

"That'd be Jo Harris," Green interrupted.

"Yes, the lady dick invited me down into the hole. You know how it is."

"Better to ruin a pair of Johnston & Murphys than lose face with the locals."

"Yeah, pretty sure I did anyway, or at least with Harris."

"Don't feel bad. Jo's pretty tough. Most people don't impress her, let alone troopers, and especially dicks from off-island."

"Yeah, I got that impression."

"Well, come on in. There is a spare room . . ." Green's voice trailed off, showing his lack of enthusiasm for the idea. "Or if you want some privacy, the Oceanview Motel just opened for the season. They'll have plenty of rooms, probably the most affordable place on the island."

"I'll do the motel. I don't want to cramp your style. But I'd welcome a chance to come in and change my clothes."

"Sure, come on." Green turned with a *follow me* wave of his hand.

The back of the barracks was the residence portion, with a kitchen and small dining room on the first floor. In front was an office and a room with filing cabinets. In one corner was a large gun safe.

"Nice, where's the cell?"

"Don't have one. If I arrest anyone, the locals put them in their holding cell until they go to court or get shipped off-island as needed." Kelly followed the older trooper down a hallway and was shown to a bathroom. He changed into khaki cargo pants; black, tactical sneakers; and a blue polo shirt with the State Police logo above his right breast. His duty pistol went on his right hip, next to his badge, and on his other hip he placed a combination magazine holder / handcuff case that matched his holster. When Kelly first got on the job, troopers were issued SIG SAUER pistols, but the SIG's had been phased out in favor of Smith & Wesson M&P automatics in 45 ACP. The Smith & Wesson was a good gun, but it was like going from a BMW to a Ford. They were both good cars, but there was a difference.

Green was waiting for him in the kitchen.

"Wanna cup of coffee? I put the pot on fresh a little while ago."

"Sure, anything has to be better than the stuff I got on the ferry."

"Any word on the body?"

"You probably know more than I do. Harris said it looks like a child's skeleton. When I got there, they were slowly removing dirt from it. My guess is that it's been there for years." Kelly took a sip from his cup of java. It wasn't much better than the stuff on the ferry.

"Huh . . ."

"Yeah, too soon to say, only time will tell."

"Murder, you think?"

"Most likely. It didn't bury itself. But it is just skeletal remains, so there won't be much in the way of forensics." Kelly, like most detectives, was sick of the word *forensics*. Ever since the TV show *CSI* came out, everyone's expectations had been raised. Now your random civilian thought every crime warranted DNA testing or that every bit of debris near a crime scene needed to go to the lab. Even worse, juries had started to expect it too. Now perfectly good cases were being jeopardized in the courtroom because jurors didn't understand why cases weren't cleared in an hour by DNA.

"Let me get you some proper footwear." Green disappeared and reappeared with a pair of rubber boots with loops at the tops, what the British called Wellingtons.

"Thanks again."

"No problem. I use them when I go clamming." Kelly nodded as if he knew what clamming entailed.

Kelly gave Green his card with his cell number written on the back, unsure if he even had service out on the island. Green gave him directions to Oceanview, the island's only motel. There were hotels, guesthouses, B and Bs, and inns aplenty, but only one motel.

Kelly took a right out of the driveway and drove by houses that would have been at home anywhere in Massachusetts, the difference being that here they were worth a million dollars instead of a few hundred thousand. He crossed Cliff Road, and the houses got bigger. He assumed that the prices went up proportionately. A few lefts and rights, and then he turned down Cobblestone Hill and took another right. Oceanview Motel was a couple of hundred yards down the road.

To Kelly's untrained eye, it looked as though it had started life as a typical 1950s motor court–type motel—single story, doors to the rooms facing the parking lot. Kelly and every other cop he knew referred to them as "stabbin' cabins." In most other towns in America, that style of motel was associated with the fringes: meth, prostitution, drug deals, grisly murders. Probably not on Nantucket, he mused. He parked Black Beauty parallel to the office door and went in.

The office still had hints of the motel's 1950s origins, like an aluminum wall clock that looked like a sun with arms radiating away from it in narrow, brushed-aluminum spokes. It reminded Kelly of Sputnik. There was an old calendar that advertised island businesses from the 1950s. The rest of the office, and Kelly suspected the whole motel, too, had been given the Martha Stewart treatment. Everything was painted in soft blues or tans, all of it trimmed with glossy white paint. The floor had bamboo matting, with decorative bamboo plants placed here and there as well.

A pretty woman with curly blond hair who looked to be in her early forties walked out of the office. Her face was tanned and spoke of time spent outdoors around sailboats and salt water. She smiled at Kelly.

"Can I help you?"

"Yes, I need a room for a couple of nights, maybe more."

"Well, since you're our only customer, I think we can accommodate you." She smiled again. She had a nice smile, and he liked the way her eyes crinkled in the corners.

"A little early in the season?" he asked.

"Yep. You the detective? Bruce Green called ahead."

"Yes. That was good of him." Kelly felt mildly annoyed. He knew there was no harm done. Kelly just didn't like the feeling that locals were talking about him behind his back.

"He wanted to make sure that we gave you a discounted rate on account of your being here on business."

"Business?"

"The body they found out by Tom Nevers. It's a small island, gossip travels fast. You can only imagine what the gossip about local romance is like."

"Uh-huh." He handed her his credit card and driver's license. She took them and disappeared for a few minutes. She returned with his cards, a piece of paper, and a room key attached to a blue plastic diamond with a number.

"Room number seven. It's a couple down from the office. I'm Laura, don't hesitate to ask if you need anything."

"Thanks, I will."

He was relieved she didn't put him right next to the office. He had probably watched too many Hitchcock movies. He went back to his car and pulled forward into the spot in front of number seven.

The room was exactly what America had been taught to expect from a motor court. Two queen-size beds with the regulation three feet between them, a bureau, a closet, a table, two bentwood captain's chairs, a TV, and a bathroom. The only difference that Kelly could see was that all the wooden furniture was painted white. The table and the chairs looked more like they belonged in a seafood restaurant than in a stabbin' cabin. The bedspreads had anchors and lobsters on them, and the framed prints on the walls were seascapes or beach motifs. The

TV had a small paper placard on top of it, which showed the available channels and advertised HBO.

Kelly put his duffel bag down on top of the bureau. He could unpack later. He took his shaving kit out of the duffel bag and went to brush his teeth. The mouthwash had done only so much to wipe away the taste of the vomit. At least his stomach had calmed down some.

He thought about the Jameson bottle in his bag. He was thinking of the way the first sip of whiskey made him feel. The warm, reassuring feeling that spread outward from the center of his chest. The instant relaxation. He wanted a taste, but it was too soon. If he started taking a taste during the day, then he had a problem. If he kept to the evenings, then he was just a normal guy having a drink after work.

His stomach rumbled. He had seen a place called Henry's Jr. It was in the same lot as a gas station and liquor store. Conveniently, it was also on the way to the crime scene. He used his phone to look up the number, then called and ordered a chicken Caesar wrap. The bright voice on the other end told him it would be ready in ten minutes. Kelly's stomach rumbled again, as if to urge them to hurry.

He locked the room behind him, mentally trying to remember the crime statistics for the island. He had $300 in cash in the side pouch of his shaving kit, a State Police laptop, and his off-duty pistol—a Kahr 9 mm—in a holster wedged between T-shirts in his bag. He figured it would be safe enough.

He pulled out of the lot and turned toward town on North Beach Street. He passed Steamboat Wharf where he'd come off the ferry and realized he sort of knew where he was. Some cops have an innate sense of direction. Kelly wasn't one of them. He navigated from memory and landmarks. When he'd been working in Worcester, he'd gotten his hands on one of the map books Wormtown PD issued to their new cops. To him it was worth a small fortune. He made his way through town, across the cobblestone Main Street and on his way to Henry's Jr.

With the casual disregard of someone not paying for his own gas, he left Black Beauty running while he ran in and paid for his sandwich and a bottle of water. Back in the car, heading to the crime scene, listening to the classic rock station on Cape Cod play AC/DC, he unwrapped his sandwich partway. He ate it steering one-handed, trying not to dribble Caesar dressing on his shirt. He made short work of the sandwich, and it gratifyingly filled the hollows left as much by last night's whiskey as by being sick earlier.

The sandwich was a distant memory when he pulled up at the crime scene ten minutes later. There was the same collection of Nantucket PD cruisers, an unmarked that he assumed was Jo Harris's, a Nissan Xterra that had seen better days, and a beat-up Toyota pickup. The island, with its narrow one-way streets, high curbs, and cobblestones, was probably tough on cars. There was also a Volkswagen Jetta that was at least ten years old parked behind the Toyota. Leaning against the back bumper was a thin man, fair in complexion and hair. He saw Kelly and automatically picked up the long, thin notebook that reporters and detectives seemed to favor that was resting next to him on the trunk. He certainly wasn't a cop, not stuck that far behind the yellow crime scene tape.

Kelly got out of his car, and the man jerked himself upright from leaning against the trunk of the Jetta. He had a blond beard that bordered on scraggly and watery-looking blue eyes behind wire-rimmed glasses. Kelly stopped long enough to change from his sneakers into the rubber boots that Green had loaned him. They were two sizes too big, and Kelly felt like he was walking in clown shoes.

"Excuse me, Officer . . ."

"Detective," Kelly automatically corrected him.

"I'm sorry, Detective. You're with the State Police, right? Chris Piper, *The Inquirer and Mirror*. Locals call it the *Inky Mirror*." He smiled in a way that was supposed to let Kelly know that they were both men of the world, definitely more worldly than the locals. That they were supposed to be chums, pals and all that. Kelly took an instant dislike to the reporter.

"Yes." Kelly, like a lot of cops, was weary of talking to reporters. It tended to be more painful than talking to defense attorneys.

"Is this officially a homicide investigation? Is that why you're here?"

"It's too early to say."

"If it isn't a homicide, Detective, then why are you here?"

"Ask my boss. He sent me." Kelly kept walking, wondering if he looked like Bozo the Clown imitating a tough guy.

"Come on, man. Help me out. I'm a small-town reporter. If I'm lucky, maybe the *Globe* will pick up my story. Maybe it could lead somewhere . . . you know, a byline off this rock."

"I am sure the local police will have a statement soon." He couldn't be less interested in the reporter's career goals. Kelly had reached the yellow crime scene tape, which Dukowski was holding up for him.

"You changed your clothes," he said to Kelly, who refrained from pointing out to the young cop that he was detective material with such stellar observational skills. He'd already had an uphill battle with the local detective. He didn't need to further alienate the locals by being sarcastic to one of their guys.

"Yeah, I slipped into something more practical."

He walked to the tent over the hole in the ground. Jo Harris was still in it, and now there was a body bag laid out. As bones were exhumed from the foundation of a millionaire's future home, they were carefully placed in the body bag. *Like some sort of grim jigsaw puzzle,* Kelly thought.

Jo Harris photographed each bone as it was revealed. They would go to the island hospital for examination by the town's surgeon, who doubled as the local pathologist. They would be X-rayed, and the dirt around the bones would be sifted through and sampled. At some point, the pathologist would tell them what they all knew—that it was a homicide. The child's corpse hadn't buried itself; someone had to have done it. That usually meant murder.

Recovering the bones and documenting the evidence was a grim process, and only more so after it was officially declared a homicide.

Then the bones would be sent to the state crime lab for further analysis and testing. Kelly noted that the body bag in question was smaller than the standard size. *Somewhere,* he thought grimly, *someone thought to make a child-size body bag. Who the hell comes up with this shit? How the hell do you market something like that?*

He slowly and awkwardly clambered down the ladder in the too-big boots. At least his feet would be dry this time. He stood next to Harris, who, when she wasn't taking pictures with a digital camera or jotting down notes, sipped coffee from a cardboard cup with a plastic lid. Kelly was certain that it wasn't Dunkin'. The cup was all wrong, but also the island had only one franchise, and that was the local Stop & Shop. Everything else was locally owned and operated. He had heard that in the 1970s, someone wanted to open a McDonald's franchise on the island. Many hoops had to be jumped through, and finally the town approved it with the condition that the signature golden arches be shingled. McDonald's corporate balked, and that ended all dreams of Mc-anything on the island, much less anything with a drive-through.

"Hey, Detective Harris, how's it going?"

"Slowly. We've gotten to the point where we can get the skeletal remains out faster. We've found more pieces of cloth, but we're also taking out more dirt just in case there's anything of interest. But . . ." She trailed off.

"But?"

"We're going to lose the light long before we can recover all the evidence, and it's supposed to rain tomorrow. We need lights." She looked up at him.

"Don't you guys . . ." She was shaking her head, her lower lip sticking out, not quite pouting. "Shit, no one has lights on this island."

"Ours aren't working. Bruce Green has some tower lights, but you might have to ask. Or there's a local construction company, but they bill us, and our budget's tight after last summer. The only person who can okay it is the chief . . . but he's indisposed. Whereas the State Police budget could afford to rent them." He grunted at the thought of explaining to Savoy how he had agreed to have the state pay for the rental of lights for the local PD.

"When's the rain supposed to start?" Kelly asked.

"A few hours before first light," Harris answered.

"Shit. I'll call Green and have him bring what he has."

"Okay . . . good. Nice boots. Did you get them from your dad?" She offered the hint of a grin.

Kelly made a mock aggrieved face. Harris breaking his balls was better than stony resentment.

"Worse, they're Bruce Green's old ones." He turned away, tapping numbers into his phone. He had a short, broken conversation with Green. After many frustrating attempts to communicate through sudden bits of dead air, Kelly heard him say that he'd bring the lights. "Green will have them out here in about an hour."

"Good. Thanks."

"Where's your chief?"

"Tied up. I told you." Her chin rose defensively, pure instinct.

"I can't imagine you have more than a homicide a decade or two out here. The buried remains of a dead kid . . . that seems even more rare. Seems more important than reassuring the town council that there'll be adequate traffic control for your Daffodil Fest or whatever it's called."

"Selectmen."

"What?"

"Selectmen. We don't have a town council; we have a Board of Selectmen . . . they're just as much of a pain in the ass."

"A rose by any other name . . ."

"Exactly."

"So where's your chief?"

"Chief's busy. The lieutenant came out before, but he's busy doing chief stuff while the chief's busy. I'm busy overseeing the removal of the skeletal remains of a child, and you're worried more about who's here than what's here. Let's make sure the remains are recovered, the forensic evidence gets recovered, evidence is preserved, all of it documented, and then . . . let's take roll call."

Kelly took a half step back and raised his hands in the universal *I surrender* pose.

"Easy, Detective. I was just curious. Won't happen again."

They stood in silence for a time, listening to the scrape of hand tools against earth as the remains were carefully removed. In the distance, the surf pounded against the beach, and the wind ruffled the edges of the tent. The Motorola radio clipped to her belt occasionally crackled out a message. Gulls turned and people came and went. Finally, Harris said, without looking at him, "Chemo."

"Excuse me?"

"Chemo. He had to take his wife to the Cape for chemo."

"Oh. Okay. Sorry, I didn't . . ."

"There's no way you could know." Her teeth weren't exactly clenched. It occurred to Kelly that the island was a small town, a tight-knit community. It would be more so with the cops, with their families. If the chief was a leader, a father figure . . . then Mrs. Chief was likely a mother to the cops and probably even more so to the lone lady dick.

"I just got waylaid by a local reporter," he said, changing the subject.

"Chris Piper . . . our own paler, less-interesting version of Ichabod Crane."

"Not a fan?"

"No, not really. He thinks he's both Woodward and Bernstein but doesn't seem to realize how small his readership is."

"Oh. Big fish, small pond syndrome?"

"Exactly. Unfortunately, his personality has the same problem."

"That's no good. I've met a few like that."

She turned back to the work being done, sipping what was most likely cold coffee. They stood next to each other, watching as the remains were carefully unearthed. They didn't speak much, and when they did, it tended to be about the details of evidence collection. One of the figures clad from head to toe in white Tyvek was an officer just back from the forensic evidence-collection course offered by the state. The figure moved with all the careful deliberation of one who'd been lectured for hours and hours about how cases have been won or lost based on proper procedure.

Sometime around five, Bruce Green arrived with the lights. They set them up outside the pit, shining down. He brought a small generator and a red plastic can of gas. No one was exactly sure what they'd find beyond the bones or how long it would take. Green left, only to return an hour later with a box of sandwiches and cups of coffee. The Tyvek-clad humanoids took turns, one working, one eating. Kelly learned that one was a man in his mid-sixties. A doctor, Harris informed him. The other turned out to be a woman with a round face and pleasant smile. She was the island's other female cop.

The sky went from dark blue to bright pinks and oranges that battled their way through india-ink clouds. The sun soon went down, taking the mild warmth with it. They turned on the generator and the lights and drank their now-icy coffee. The wind picked up, and even with the rubber boots, Kelly's feet started to feel numb. He had his fleece jacket zipped up to his chin. He was glad that he always kept in one of the pockets a fleece watch cap, which was now pulled tightly down on his head, over his ears.

"What'll happen now?" Kelly asked Harris.

"The bones will go with the doc. He'll do a preliminary investigation—pictures, X-rays, etcetera. Then package them up to go to the crime lab tomorrow. The dirt will go to the high school." They both knew it was a homicide. There was no need to pretend it was anything but.

"The high school. Do they have a lab?"

"No, they have a gym. We can lay out the tarps on the floor and sift through the dirt. It'll be a controlled environment."

"Won't the basketball team object to not having a place to practice?"

"It's April vacation. Nothing's happening there. The dirt will spend the night there with an officer watching, and we'll go to work tomorrow morning. Early," she added, looking at Kelly to see if he'd object.

Around 9:00 p.m., Harris and the evidence people decided they had all the bones and dirt there was to get. Kelly was glad because the cold had settled deep into his feet long ago. They took it all up and out of the pit. An ambulance arrived, and EMTs carefully loaded the body bag into it as the cops stood at some version of attention. Kelly felt his chest tighten as he took his fleece cap off. Then they watched as the ambulance drove down the road of hard-packed sand, lights flashing but no sirens. Kelly silently wished the little bones a safe journey and shivered hard. Harris made sure the crime scene was still preserved in case there was something else to be found in the morning. Dukowski, who didn't mind time and a half, would guard the crime scene from the warmth of his cruiser.

It was closer to ten when they finished documenting the day's events. One by one, they climbed up the ladder and started for their cars. Kelly walked down the hard-packed sand, listening to the wind play against the grass and the surf rumble against the beach. Kelly shivered again as thick raindrops began to fall. As usual the weatherman had gotten it wrong. If he was being honest with himself, the shivering wasn't entirely because of the cold. Maybe it was the bones of the lost child, the rumble of the surf, or the dark, inky loneliness of the night. It all felt like something from a horror movie.

October 1981

They had been searching for Richie Sousa, but the search had gone from full-court press to a routine part of every shift. Now with another kid missing, Doug Talbot and the other officers had been back on the full-court press approach. Talbot had been ordered to check out the Jetties Beach side and make sure that Mikey or Richie hadn't somehow gotten trapped under a jetty.

As he slowly parked his Ford LTD police cruiser at the end of the parking lot, he decided to check the swings to his right. Kids liked swing sets, and if it meant he didn't have to walk through the sand and screw up the polished shine of his black wing tips—"low quarters" they called them in the army—then so much the better.

It was early morning, and Talbot had had the midnight shift the night before, which on Nantucket in the fall meant finding a place to park and hoping that the radio stayed quiet. There wasn't a lot of crime in the offseason, and other than the occasional alarm or guy beating up on his wife, there weren't a lot of calls on the midnight shift. Which was why Talbot's last act of his tour was to check the beach at 6:00 a.m. before heading into the station.

He got out of the Ford, its dark-blue-and-white paint scheme an effort by the small-town department to copy the big-city departments on TV. The wind gusted off the water, cutting through his jacket, but even the sudden blast of cold couldn't compete with the bone-crushing tiredness that he felt.

Talbot walked across the wooden duckboards to his right, toward the metal swing set nestled in a small clearing in the dunes. He saw a kid's Rampar bike in the bike rack, his tired mind not quite putting the piece of the puzzle in its place. The bike didn't look right, but he couldn't figure out what was off.

He looked over at the swing set, and there was a kid on one of the seats. That's odd, it's six in the morning, *he thought. The swings were creaking in the wind.* Christ. The town could spring for some oil for the chains.

He walked closer, absentmindedly noting that the kid wasn't wearing a jacket. He must be cold, *Talbot thought.* That's why his face is blue.

Talbot's mind was struggling to understand what he was seeing.

"Hey, hey, kid. You all right?" Talbot had reached out to touch Richie Sousa when he noticed his nose looked funny, misshapen. There was a little dried blood. The wind gusted from offshore, and Richie started, in slow motion, to topple off the swing.

Doug Talbot screamed as Richie Sousa's corpse landed in the sand with a quiet thump.

CHAPTER 3

Kelly was running. The rain had ended at some point in the wee hours of the morning, and now the sky was a mix of spring sunlight and clouds. He was tired, not having slept well the night before. He had woken with a start and for a second didn't know where he was. He couldn't figure out what had woken him from his whiskey-assisted slumber, only that he had been startled awake. The door to his room rattled. He was reaching for his pistol before he realized that it was just a gust of wind and not someone trying to get in the room.

The wind cut across the road, blowing ripples across the large puddles as he ran out toward Jetties Beach. Off in the distance he heard something like seagulls' cries, but the noise was discordant and just a note off to be gulls. He passed a playground with an old swing set made of metal chains. The wind was catching one of the swings just right, and it was making a regular creaking noise that Kelly couldn't ignore. On the opposite side of the road was some sort of building with plywood on the windows. He turned back just before the tar turned to sand. Even with all his effort and high-tech running clothes, the wind cut through to his core.

He turned back toward the motel; the creaking noise was growing fainter as he ran up Cobblestone Hill. He knew he wouldn't be able to put any weight up today, so he had to settle for a long run. Last night he'd eaten two ham-and-cheese sandwiches out at the crime scene. The other option had been tuna salad. Mayonnaise and mercury or processed meat with nitrates and cheese . . . ham and cheese had won. Now he was running it off. He was forty-three and worked hard to stay in shape. He didn't want to be one of those guys who let himself go.

He pushed up the steep hill. In his head, he could hear his father's voice. *Push it, Tommy, come on . . . don't quit. Don't be weak, don't be a sissy. You wanna be a wolf or a bunny?*

Big Tom Kelly had been a genuine tough guy, a carpenter who had his own small construction company. He had hands that were calloused and rough. Kelly had gone into the Marine Corps Reserve as a way to help pay for college, and, if he were being honest with himself, to earn his father's approval. Big Tom hadn't been as effusive nor as impressed when he'd graduated from the State Police Academy.

Kelly cleared the top of the hill and let his momentum carry him. He turned away from town and ran to the amoeba-shaped field in the middle of Lincoln Circle by Steps Beach. His pace and breathing settled into the normalcy of running on a flat surface. Whenever Kelly had to push himself running or put more weight up on the bar, he heard his father's voice in his head. Big Tom Kelly had been a stern man. He'd loved his son and felt he had to toughen Kelly up for an unforgiving world. He'd never hit Kelly, except for teaching his son to box, and then only with gloves, every punch pulled. Big Tom's disapproval was quick and cutting and far worse than any physical blow.

Big Tom Kelly had been in the marine corps in Vietnam. He rarely talked about it, but his service in the corps, his dead friends, his survivor's guilt . . . all those experiences had been as much a part of their home as the furniture. Big Tom survived the siege at Khe Sanh. A couple of times a year he got rip-roaring drunk and might let something slip out. Sometimes it was about his best friend who'd bled out in his arms, or another time sorting through the bits of a person caught directly by an artillery round. It was a rare occurrence, but even as a little kid, Kelly understood the gravity of what he learned. Back in Vietnam, Big Tom had lived in the mud, surrounded by the stench of death and hungry rats. Rats that would bite marines when they were trying to sleep. Rats that had a lot of corpses to feast on but still went for marines in their bunkers. He'd survived such terrors and more. He had made it home and started to live his life and raise a family, rarely complaining about anything.

How was Kelly supposed to measure up to that? Do anything but his best? The junior varsity squad was only good enough his freshman year. After that, it was varsity or nothing. Kelly kept working, running toward and away from his father's voice.

He couldn't admit to himself, or anyone for that matter, that he resented Big Tom for constantly pushing him. He didn't hold the man's long silences and emotional distance against him. Tom had seen bad things in Vietnam. Lost friends and taken lives. Big Tom loved him, but that wasn't something said often and shown even less. Kelly kept running, kept pushing himself, kept pretending that he had only positive feelings for his dad.

By the time Kelly was thirty and he'd figured out that Big Tom was scared of losing his son, Big Tom was in a flag-draped coffin. After years of soul-searching, Kelly was eventually able to let go of the resentment and instead reflect on the missed opportunity that was their relationship. He vowed he wouldn't make the same mistake with his own sons.

Kelly got decent but unremarkable grades in high school and managed not to get anyone pregnant. Then he was off to Parris Island and the Marine Corps Reserve to help pay for a criminal justice degree from UMass. Kelly had wanted to go on active duty, but his mother had been adamant about him getting a degree. If Big Tom had pushed his son to be tough and athletic, his mother had the tendency to be overly attentive and concerned. She wasn't happy about his enlisting in the marines but could tolerate his being a reservist.

Then he applied to be a trooper. She was very unhappy about that, and he was met with the most sincere form of Irish communication— stony silence. It took a few visits home for her to thaw. The first time he didn't get in, his mother tried not to show her relief openly. A couple of years later, on his second attempt at applying, he was accepted. She got used to the idea in time, and then when Connor and Liam were born, she seemed to forget all about it.

Big Tom had been proud at his graduation from the State Police Academy, but it wasn't the same as the parade deck of Parris Island after the ceremonies, when the parents could see their sons and daughters after their final graduation formation. On Parris Island, Big Tom had hugged him in a rib-crushing bear hug, only the second time in his life he could remember his father embracing him. Big Tom's eyes were shiny with the tears he was holding back. It was a dry-eyed Big Tom who stuck his meaty hand out to shake when Kelly graduated from the State Police Academy.

A few years later, Kelly had met Jeanie in the emergency room one night when he was checking on a prisoner, a DUI. The guy had taken out three football fields' worth of traffic cones before he smashed into the back of a State Police cruiser. The trooper who had been asleep in his cruiser during his overnight detail was taken to the hospital in an ambulance. His career was over due to his injuries, and he would get two-thirds of his salary, tax-free, for the rest of his life. It wasn't as good a deal as it sounded. Kelly had eaten the report and had to take the handcuffed drunk to the ER because he had bumped his head. The drunk would get bail, and a halfway decent lawyer would plead it down. At best, he'd be inconvenienced, and the trooper he'd hit, his life would never be the same again.

Kelly liked to think that Big Tom would have been proud about the wedding and the resultant grandsons, but he had succumbed to lung cancer the year before Kelly met the nurse in purple scrubs with dark hair, pouty lips, and a foul mouth. Kelly had chatted her up on what was—fortunately, for them—a slow night. She agreed to a date by the time his prisoner was released from the hospital. Kelly had had her number in his uniform pocket while he walked the drunk to his cruiser.

Kelly ran down Centre Street, passing shops and one of the island's many inns. He crossed the street by the stately redbrick Pacific National Bank, which stood at the head of Main Street. The air was chilly but not cold. He ran up the hill on Orange Street, past the white Unitarian church with its steeple and clapboarding. He ran about a mile down to the Cumberland Farms store, mentally noting its location as a potential source of coffee. He turned left down Washington Street, doubling back toward town.

Cars hissed by. Islanders, early risers heading to work or breakfast or wherever. Kelly suspected that in the summer months traffic, even this early, would be heavy. Now it was mostly pickups with toolboxes, ladder racks, and the dressing of the construction trade. He started to think about the bones. It was possible that it wasn't a homicide. Maybe it was an accident or misadventure? Maybe there was an explanation for the remains being buried several feet below the surface.

Kelly took a right across Cliff Road and ran down North Liberty Street. He passed the State Police barracks, took a left onto West Chester Street, and turned uphill into the town center, passing a white clapboard church and the brick Jared Coffin House. His breath was labored but not strained.

Tommy . . . you can't be weak. This world is hard, and you gotta push, son. The only time he heard his father's voice in his head and he wasn't working out was on a car stop on the Pike. He had pulled over a guy who had a warrant. The man was polite and cooperative, and when Kelly came back from his cruiser, after having run him and finding out he had an arrest warrant for felony assault, the man was compliant getting out of his car. He was cooperative when Kelly asked him to step to the rear of it to be patted down. He was even compliant when Kelly told him he had a warrant, but when he went to put the handcuffs on, the man pivoted and drove his elbow into Kelly's nose, flattening it. The man was fast, and as he was moving, Kelly's mind was registering what was happening a split second later. *An asshole is most likely to fight when you put the handcuffs on or take them off,* Kelly's field training officer had told him.

The man's fist connected with Kelly's face. He had speed that Tyson would have approved of. Stars erupted in Kelly's head, and he tasted

40

copper in his mouth as he stepped back. The man went to punch him again, but Kelly had gotten his left arm up, taking the punch. The man grabbed him, and they went down to the ground. They rolled, and he felt the guy hitting him on the head, glancing blows. Then Kelly felt the man tugging at his holstered pistol. Thankfully the hood of the retention holster did its job.

He heard cars hissing by and wondered why no one was stopping to help. He heard heavy breathing and couldn't tell if it was his or the man's. The man started to lift Kelly up and tried to smash his head into the pavement. He was strong, stronger than Kelly. Prison fit. Then he heard Big Tom Kelly in his head. *Get up! Get up . . . fight! Fight him! Don't be a goddamned bunny, be a wolf!*

Kelly managed to get one heel flat on the pavement. Get one hip up. He dipped it and rocked the man off him, rolling as momentum carried him over and on top of the dude. Then he started to punch the guy in the face. The handcuffs were still in his hand, and he used them like brass knuckles as he smashed them into the man's face. He kept hitting him until he stopped trying to fight. Kelly gave him one or two more for the effort and stopped.

He rolled him over and got the cuffs on the man. Panting, he dragged him to his cruiser and stuffed him in the cage. Later, driving to the barracks, pieces of napkins from a drive-through stuffed up his nose to stop the bleeding, he heard the dude whining in the back seat. "Man, you fucked up my face . . . my face, man, you fucked it up."

For the first time in his life when he spoke, he heard Big Tom's voice saying "Motherfucker, you're lucky that's all you got" to the asshole behind him. Kelly knew that he was a cheap imitation of a legitimate tough guy.

He rounded the Lincoln Circle and headed back toward town, taking a right down a long block by homes whose landscaping cost more than his mortgage. He soon turned left onto Cliff Road and made his way to North Beach Street. Kelly passed the Oceanview Motel and slowed to a walk. Steam coming off him, breathing heavy, lungs straining a little but not hurting, he walked away from the motel. He passed Cobblestone Hill and kept walking. A ways down the road on his left, he noticed a path of duckboards that had been hacked into the overgrowth of vines.

He started up the path. It wasn't overgrown now, at the beginning of spring. He could see easily, but he imagined that in the summer it became a dark, dank, mosquito-infested tunnel leading up to Lincoln Circle at the top of Steps Beach. A shortcut, but at night the type of place that kids dared each other to walk down. A scary tunnel of vines and briars, monsters hidden just out of sight. The type of place where you would hear someone or something breathing heavily behind you. Real Stephen King territory. Kelly abruptly turned back to the motel. He needed a shower and a cup of coffee.

He let himself in, grateful for the sudden wash of heat. The morning had started chilly, hovering just above forty. He turned on the TV and watched the morning news out of Boston while he drank the thick concoction that was allegedly supposed to taste like chocolate.

There was nothing on the news of note and no voicemails on his phone. He was still thinking about his call to Jeanie the night before. He had called to say good night to the boys. That had gone well. Talking to Jeanie afterward had not.

"Tommy, it's late. I was just about to put them to bed." She sounded pissed.

"I know, Jeanie, I was just . . . I just wanted to talk to them. It's been a long day."

"This is gonna mess up my schedule."

"Jeanie, please."

"The day couldn't have been so long that you didn't have a couple of drinks."

"Jeanie, this case . . . this one's different."

"All right, boys . . . your father's on the phone."

Connor came on: "Dad, Dad! I scored a goal today at my soccer game. I was so fast, I ran past the other boys."

Then it was Liam's turn: "Dad, we have a new class pet. Wiggles, the guinea pig. He's really soft, Dad. Connor, I'm talking, stop trying to grab the phone!"

Kelly kept seeing the small bones when he closed his eyes and just wanted to hug the boys as they spoke. Crush them to his chest and just hold them. By the time Jeanie came back and had started in on the litany of his parental and marital failings, Kelly was on his second big Jameson.

"Jesus, Tommy, I'm doing it all myself. You're just an empty suit. An empty spot in the bed."

"Jeanie, I'm trying. I didn't ask to come out here, I was ordered. You know what it's like. A trooper goes where he's ordered to go and does what he's told to do when he gets there."

"You know what I know, Tommy? I know that it feels like I'm raising two boys on my own. It feels like I work my shifts at the hospital and come home to referee their brawls. It feels like I'm a single mom."

"Jeanie, I'll be home in a few days. I'll be able . . ."

"Be able to do what? Even when you're here, it feels like you're not. You're always checked out, Tommy. Like you'd rather be working on a case than be with me. Even when you're here, you're somewhere else."

"That's not fair."

It had gone on like that for another ten painful minutes. By the time his wife had hung up on him, Kelly was slurring his words slightly. She made sure to point that out to him as well. He compensated by pouring another drink before crawling into bed, resting it on the bedside table while he surfed the channels on the TV.

He had woken up with a sour stomach and a headache nibbling at his temples. The legitimacy of Jeanie's complaints wasn't lost on him. He didn't agree with all of it, but being married to a state cop, even a detective, was not easy. When he was in uniform, he was on the road, working long shifts. Late arrests meant overtime, but it meant time away from the family. Then there were the overtime details, which meant spending more time away from home to earn extra pay. It also meant more of the parenting burden shifted to Jeanie, not to mention the stress that came from worrying about him getting hurt.

Then he got promoted to detective. That meant handling his cases but also going into the homicide rotation. If it was his week and a homicide came in, he might work several eighteen-hour days in a row. His old troop was busy, and there were plenty of homicides to drag him out of bed late at night. Jeanie was married to a man who missed holidays, family events, and social occasions, and when he was home, he was too tired to be much fun.

The run had cleared Kelly's head and had undone some of the damage done by the ham-and-cheese sandwiches. He felt limber when he stepped into the shower. He washed under the hot water, thinking about the small skeleton. In his mind he was going over the mental list of questions he had. The biggest was cause of death. In the unlikely event this wasn't a homicide, he could go home. That led him back to Jeanie and the conversation the night before. He turned the water from hot to cold and stood under the spray as long as he could stand it.

The red light on his phone was flashing. Wrapped in a towel, hair still damp, he picked up the handset and stabbed at buttons with his index finger until he heard Jo Harris telling him to meet her at the police station and that they would head over to the high school from there. His cargo pants were muddy, and he opted for blue jeans and his State Police polo shirt over a white T-shirt.

With a stop for coffee followed by the inevitable wrong turns and one-way streets, he made it to the new-looking police station on Fairgrounds Road in about twenty minutes. Kelly parked in an open spot next to the attractive two-story brick building and went in the front double doors. He stopped at the glass. The clerk looked up.

"Hi, I'm Detective Kelly from . . ." Before he could finish, the door to his left made a buzzing noise.

"Yep, Jo's expecting you. Go on through. Detectives on the second floor."

"Thanks." Kelly quickly found himself in a hallway with a series of doors on either side. One of them opened, and Harris stuck her head out.

"Over here, follow me. How did you sleep at the Oceanview? Quiet this time of year."

"Not bad, thanks." He didn't tell her it was the nicest stabbin' cabin he'd ever stayed in, though he tended to avoid them. He followed her up a flight of stairs, down a corridor, and into a pleasant-looking office area with cubicles and new computers. There were posters on the wall, some identifying gangs and gang tattoos, others displaying common firearms and their characteristics. There were also informational bulletins about new types of fraud and a big poster with pictures of different types of illegal drugs.

"Everything seems new." Kelly could still smell freshly unwrapped rubber. The place looked more like an IKEA showroom than a detective bureau. There were no coffee stains, crumpled papers, or broken furniture being pressed back into service.

"Yeah, it's five years old but we try to take care of it."

"Very nice." He meant it too.

"I thought we might quickly go over the notes and then head to the scene to see if there's anything that pops out after a night's rest." Harris had dark patches under her eyes. Kelly was certain she hadn't gotten much sleep.

"Sure, sounds good. When can we take a look at the remains?"

"Doc needed to get some rest. Probably gonna need some time to look at them. Why don't we go to the high school after the scene and see if they've found anything in the dirt."

"Okay."

"We can circle back around with the doc during the afternoon sometime."

"Sounds like a plan." He took a couple of deep breaths. Kelly had to keep his impatience in check. He wanted to know if this was a murder. "Do you have any missing person reports that might fit?"

"Most of our missing person cases are adults. Usually it's stuff in the summer. Couples come out to the island, and after a couple of days of sun, beach, and booze, they end up fighting. One of them, usually the female half, takes off for the mainland. 'I'll show him' type of thing. The repentant, distraught boyfriend comes in to make a report after she doesn't turn up by midmorning."

"That's it?"

"No, we have the other summer missing persons. Those usually involve date rape and a desire to leave the island in a hurry. Friends contact us. It sucks but it happens. In the offseason, it's usually a teenager who longs to get off the rock and see what life on the mainland is like or a wife who gets sick of being an offseason punching bag. When fishing and construction slow down is when drinking and fighting pick up."

"Grim out here in the winter, isn't it?"

"It can be."

"Anything else?"

"It's a small community. Child abductions are unheard of, and we get a homicide about once a decade. If someone calls in a missing kid, it's more likely the kid is late getting home from school or a friend's house and the parent goes into panic mode. Usually we get a call within an hour telling us the kid is back at home."

"What if our kid was out playing. Falls into a hole or something. Hits his head . . ."

"Maybe, but it doesn't seem likely. There would be a report of a missing kid."

"True."

"Also, the remains were all more or less horizontal. Kids who fall in holes don't end up lying flat on their backs."

"No, they don't." Kelly was thinking aloud, working the problem with words.

"Also, there's this." Harris sat down at her computer and pulled a picture out of the file. It showed a small skeleton, arms clearly crossed over its chest, a piece of cloth pinned between small forearms and ribs.

"Oh fuck . . ." Kelly said it slowly, like the last gasp of the dying.

"Yeah. I don't know about you, but I've never seen an accident where the corpse crossed its arms before dying." She looked up at him and raised an eyebrow as some form of rhetorical question, but he knew she was right.

"Fuuuuuuck." Slower and quieter. He had a thing about dead kids. No cop he ever heard of was okay with it, but it hit him hard, especially after the boys were born. There were a lot of reasons why he'd been happy to make detective. Not going to car accidents where children had been in the car had been high on his list of them.

"We still have to wait for the doc to confirm it, but this is what it is." She sipped from her own cup of coffee—gulped it, actually. Kelly was sure she'd bought it while he was out running, having imaginary conversations with his dead father, and now it was cold.

"First priority for us is trying to figure out who this kid is."

"Yeah, that might be a problem. We started doing all our reports on computers just after everyone realized Y2K was a whole lot of worrying about nothing. Before that . . . all missing person reports would have been written by hand or typed. The good news is that they scanned everything from 1985 on a few years ago."

"And reports before 1985?" Kelly inquired.

"There are a few that are in boxes somewhere here. We are still unpacking a lot of stuff. As for the rest, they're gone. They were in a storage unit out by the airport, but a lot of water leaked in during a bad nor'easter in the early nineties," Harris said.

"Great. Okay, what about someone from off-island?"

"What do you mean?"

"What if a family comes to the island to vacation, say from New York or someplace. Something happens to the kid, and no one reports it . . ."

"Local school and social services wouldn't know anything, so it wouldn't be reported here."

"Okay, so we have to also check the National Crime Information Center. Widen the net. Is there anyone on the job now who was here before 1985?" Kelly asked.

"Just the chief. Why?"

"Being thorough. In case our bones are from the time before computers and dry storage units."

"I see where you're going. Yeah . . . that would be the chief."

"Before we do anything, we need to talk to the doc and narrow our timeline down. Otherwise, there could be hundreds or thousands of kids on that list."

"True. Also, we'll need the doc to get DNA from the bones if he can. Run that against all the databases to see if we can ID that way too. Jesus . . ."

Kelly allowed himself a grim smile. "Turns out to be a big mystery you got out here on your island after all, Detective."

"Yes, it does . . . it surely does," Harris said dryly.

November 1981

Halloween had come and gone, and it had been fun but weird. This year it had felt different. Nick's mom had outdone herself making his costume. He had gone as Luke Skywalker, his hero. Not The Empire Strikes Back *Luke . . . but* Star Wars *Luke. She had found a white bathrobe his size, the fuzzy kind, that went over a T-shirt and his tan sweatpants plus an old leather belt of his mom's. His hair was blond and shaggy, just like Luke's, especially after Mom had ruffled it with her hand. And she had taken a Wiffle ball bat and used silver-painted carboard to make what looked like the handle of a lightsaber—the best part of the costume! Somewhere she found some light-blue spray paint for the rest of the weapon. It looked pretty good. Nick had jumped and ducked and dodged while making* whaaawhosh *noises.*

They had gone out as a group. Nick, Louie, Johnny, Albie, and a bunch of other kids. They moved in a large gaggle. Some other kids were being driven around by their parents. Some houses had big metal pots filled with candy outside the door with handmade paper signs telling kids to take some candy. It was a little different from last Halloween. Some houses were just dark, and no one was home.

Albie's dad was with them. Mr. Parker, Mikey's dad, was too. He kept saying that he was sure Mikey would turn up soon. His eyes were bloodshot, and his breath smelled like he'd been drinking. Mikey hadn't been at school for a while, and the adults, the teachers who talked about it, did so only in whispers. Nick had wanted Mikey to come back to school. He liked Mikey, liked him enough that he had let him take his Luke Skywalker action figure home to borrow. Mikey didn't have new toys like that. This one was Luke in the tan suit and not the one in the white snowsuit.

One of the other kids' dads was with them. He was carrying a wooden axe handle. Nick was pretty sure that he had seen the handle of a gun sticking out of Albie's dad's pocket. Nick couldn't describe it, but the adults seemed jumpy. Like they were thinking of things but not talking about them, just sharing looks with each other. Either way, it hadn't been a bad night. He had filled up his pillowcase—they all carried pillowcases because they held the most—with a good assortment of candy.

Nick had also noticed that there were police cars out. They cruised slowly around, circling like big, fat, blue bugs. Now and again, a bright spotlight would reach out into the darkness, lighting up a corner or shady area like it was daytime. It was cool to see the cops out, like it was a scary movie on TV, like something they would show on Creature Double Feature *on Saturdays. Later they walked to Nick's house, and his mother let him in. She hugged him, kissed him, and locked the door behind him. When Nick and his mom had moved to Nantucket, no one locked their doors. Now his mom locked the door all the time.*

A few days later, Nick and his friends finished playing football in the field on Mill Street. They were allowed to play in the field as long as they were together and all got home well before dark. Nick's mom didn't want him hanging out, playing ball with the gang, but she was at work, and she told him she knew he'd play anyway.

Nick's mom worked in town at the Pacific National Bank. It was the big brick building that stood at the top of Main Street, looming over downtown. Nick loved the red stone steps that led up to the heavy oak door that he had to lean against with his full weight to open. Inside, the bank always smelled old and dry but not unpleasant. Nick's mom was a bank teller. Nick's dad and mom were divorced. Nick didn't know why, but he knew his mom was mad at his dad. She would take the phone from Nick after he was done talking to his dad and he would hear her whispering angrily into the handset. He wasn't sure what it was about, but he thought he heard her talking about money sometimes.

He and Albie were walking down Candle House Lane. Albie lived on Orange Street, and Nick wanted to walk down to the bank to surprise his mom. Nick was telling Albie about Star Wars. *Nick wanted to be Luke Skywalker when he grew up. Albie wanted to be Han Solo and fly the* Millennium Falcon. *Albie knew Nick had the toy version and desperately wanted to play with it. He was hoping for any chance to introduce such an idea. Nick, not being stupid, knew exactly what Albie was up to and changed the topic. He told Albie about the* Star Wars *action figure that he had loaned to Mikey and how he hoped Mikey would come back to school soon.*

They walked down Silver Street and said goodbye at Fair Street. Nick watched Albie go. Albie looked back at him, and his moon face lit up in an uncertain smile. Nick thought, He must be scared. *Nick raised his hand and turned onto Pine Street. He would be surprised if Albie didn't run the rest of the way home. Chubby arms and legs pumping, clouds of steam from his mouth. Nick smiled at the thought of it. Albie wasn't known for his bravery. He was always the last kid to finish any dare.*

The sky was getting darker faster than it should have. Clouds. Nick soon felt the first drop of rain, and then another fat drop splatted on his head. Then a few more on the pavement, and it began to pour down. Nick started to run. The rain was cold, and he wanted to meet his mom at the bank.

He was fast. Nick was a good runner. He might not have been the best football or basketball player, but he could run. The occasional car drove by, headlights splashing on him, but no one stopped. It was like he was invisible. Nick was running up a slight hill, lungs heaving. He didn't have far to go. He got to the top of the small hill. He was wet, and his feet squelched as they slapped on the pavement.

It didn't take much. A fraction of an inch. Nick's foot caught on some pavement displaced by a root. Just a fraction of an inch of his foot caught the pavement and snagged it. Nick's torso and head kept moving forward but his foot didn't. He hit the pavement hard, knees stinging with the impact, palms stinging and skinned.

He sat there trying to catch his breath, hoping his mom might drive by and see him. Pick him up and give him a ride in her nice warm car. He lay there for a minute, his breath coming back, rain soaking into his clothes. He heard a car stop and the door open. He never made it home.

CHAPTER 4

They had, after a brief discussion, agreed to take Harris's car. It was a newer, unmarked, tan Ford sedan that did no better hiding the fact that it was a cop car than Kelly's Black Beauty did. It was immaculate inside—no fast-food wrappers, no half-empty coffee cups. The interior smelled faintly of some sort of air freshener that wasn't pine.

"Is this car new?" he asked.

"No, it's a few years old."

"It looks as new as your station."

"Thanks, I try to take care of it." Which, in Kelly's mind, translated to *I have OCD and wipe everything down with Lysol wipes many times a day.* Kelly knew guys at work who paid more attention to their work cars than they did to their wives.

Her raid jacket, what cops called the ubiquitous blue windbreaker with POLICE stenciled on the back, was draped over her chair. She pulled out of the lot and turned onto Fairgrounds Road. He was beginning to notice that the island was a mix of really old construction, as in colonial old, and newer stuff from the seventies and eighties mixed with new buildings built to fit in with the island vibe. It reminded him of some sort of New England–themed ride at an amusement park.

Jo Harris was a good driver, and traffic on the island in the midmorning was sparse. Even so, Kelly was uncomfortable being driven anywhere. The job had ruined that for him. When he worked the road, there were a lot of pursuits, oftentimes hair-raising, driving well over a hundred miles an hour, bombing down the Pike or one of the other highways. Pursuits on the highway were bad enough, but the country roads or city streets were downright scary, with less room and all sorts of things to crash a police car into. He knew if he was going to buy it in a car crash, it would be on city streets and not the highway. One hand on the steering wheel, one on the microphone, trying to broadcast to the other troopers where they were and what was happening. Feeling the road vibrate up through the steering wheel to his arms, his brain.

That was a rush. It was a giant needle of adrenaline spiked in his vein, his own lights flashing. He had, over time, learned to broadcast between the wails of his siren or his airhorn. Only a rookie would switch to the siren being constantly on instead of just hitting the toggle switch to make it go off for a few seconds. After doing that, it was hard to drive with anyone else at the wheel. But Harris knew the island, and he was there to help. So he had reluctantly climbed into the passenger seat.

At the end of Fairgrounds Road, she turned on to Surfside Road and headed into town. They eventually cruised into the high school parking lot. Kelly could picture her during her days in uniform, making this same drive.

"What?" she asked him pointedly.

"Huh?"

"What are you grinning about?"

"When you pulled in here. Started slowly cruising through the parking lot. I pictured you in uniform, on patrol. Looking for criminals out and about."

"Ha. Yeah, this was my beat for a while. Midnights. Do you have any idea of how slow midnights are out here in the winter?"

"Where'd you sleep?"

"Other side of the football field. They park the school buses up against a hedge. I'd back between two buses."

"Good spot."

"Yeah, it was okay. How about you?"

"When I was in uniform, usually just one of the cut throughs on the road. People expect us to be out there, setting up speed traps. It wasn't like anyone was going to come up to the car and check to see if I was asleep." That had been an advantage of being a trooper. People just blew by while only his running lights were on. They assumed that they'd gotten lucky and beaten a speed trap.

She pulled up to the back of a building with a couple of cars parked by a set of double doors. The building seemed to be two stories tall with a row of windows high up on the second floor.

"The gym?"

"Yes, the doctor can't see us just yet. This was on the way. I wanted to see what progress they're making and to make sure they're doing everything by the numbers."

She strode up to the handleless fire doors, the kind that had push bars on the inside but were designed to stymie teens up to no good by making it hard for them to sneak into the gym. She knocked. Shave and a haircut . . . universal code for *Hey, it's me, not just any old random person knocking*. They waited for a while, and then as Harris raised her hand to knock again, someone pushed the door open.

"Hey, Jo." This from a woman in a Tyvek suit with a respirator pulled aside from her face.

"Hey, Holly. How is it going?"

"Slow but steady. C'mon in." She stood aside to let them pass. They stepped inside onto a beautiful parquet floor.

"Holly, this is Tom Kelly, he's a State Police detective." Then to Kelly she said, "This is Holly Taylor, the island's other female cop and one of our trained evidence people."

"They figured they could get two minorities for the price of one by hiring a Black female," Taylor said with a smirk. She stuck out a hand, and Kelly shook it. Her grip was firm, and she looked him in the eye when they shook, then pushed some stray black curls back under her NPD baseball cap.

"Troopers would have snapped you up in a heartbeat." He smiled to let her know that he was in on the joke.

"Naw, I'm too short and the hat looks silly. Like you're all supposed to be in the trenches in World War One or something." They walked across the parquet floor with its lines and different colors denoting all things important in basketball until they stopped at a series of blue tarps on the floor. There were piles of dirt on each tarp, and next to them were buckets. On the folding tables next to each tarp were small piles of paper bags for collecting evidence.

"This is what we have been working on." Taylor gestured with a sweep of her arm. There were two other cops in their white Tyvek suits. They carefully picked up a bucket of dirt and poured it into a wooden square in the middle of a tarp. Then two of the officers picked up the wooden square and proceeded to shake it back and forth. Dirt fell through onto the tarp. When they'd shaken all the dirt out, they looked at what was left on the wire screen stretched across the wooden frame.

"Find anything?" Jo asked.

"So far not much. Some pieces of cloth, some coins, some glass marbles. There isn't a lot left. It looks like the remains were interred for some time," Taylor said.

"What are you doing with the dirt after it's been sifted through?" Kelly was curious to see how methodical they were.

"Each bucket is numbered. Each number relates to when and where the dirt was shoveled out and will correspond to a picture Jo took of us doing it. For instance, the first bucket was number one. Anything that was recovered from the bucket would be bagged and a letter added to the number and put on the bag. If we found something in the first bucket load, it would be One-A. If we found something else, it would be One-B, and so on. We take a few grams of soil from each bucket, which will be sent to the lab for chemical analysis and whatever else the boys at the state crime lab think is important. Everything is logged and documented and will be part of the report. We small-town cops aspire to the approval of the State Police," Taylor explained.

"Just doing my job," Kelly said dryly.

"I didn't dig him up. The big hats sent him out to me. If I had my way, I wouldn't have a state dick looking over my shoulder. No offense."

"None taken." He couldn't blame her—there was often tension between local cops and the State Police—but Jo's candor had been delivered with a little too much enthusiasm for Kelly's taste.

"Ha! Trudat. Gotta gooooo. Be back." Taylor walked away from them, laughing. Her laughter echoed in the mostly empty gym.

"C'mon, let's get a closer look." Harris sounded annoyed. They'd crossed the gym and were standing closer to the tarps. They watched the cops sift more dirt. Now and then they would take things from the screens. Part of an old shoe, the rubberized heel. Small in size. A scrap of cloth. A small lump of dirt that turned out to be a plastic windup robot. Kelly remembered them from when he was a kid. A glass Coke bottle. A crushed beer can. A couple of bottle caps. A couple of cigarette butts too.

The challenge would be trying to discern evidence from litter. That was always the case with evidence collection. Most of the scenes he'd worked were easy. A bloody knife at a domestic homicide. Clothes from a rape victim. Smashed-up pieces of once-nice cars. In Worcester, they'd policed up a lot of empty shell casings and discarded guns. This was different. Now every little scrap could be a clue. No one wanted to throw away the seemingly benign-looking cigarette butt that might have a killer's DNA on it.

"It's a lot to go through." Taylor was back.

"Seems like it," Kelly agreed. "Any chance of getting anything useful from it? DNA?"

"Some. It depends on how old it is. DNA is great, but this isn't *CSI*. The DNA doesn't last forever. Fingerprints don't always either. We'll be able to type the bones, that should help with the ID. But DNA from a suspect, probably not gonna happen."

"Sure, why would it be easy . . ." Harris seemed surly.

"Assuming that . . . there should be DNA in the samples. As for on the other stuff . . . it depends on how long it's been there. If there are plastics, their rate of decay might impact samples . . . It's just too soon to tell."

"Let me guess. We just need to be patient," Harris said pointedly.

"Jo, it is what it is," Taylor said.

"Shit, Holly. I'm sorry. I got about three hours of sleep last night."

"No worries, girl. No worries. We've all been there."

Kelly wondered how much sleep the Tyvek suit squad had gotten. Not a lot, he presumed. He was probably the most rested of them all. The irony of technically overseeing the investigation and knowing the least about it wasn't lost on him.

They watched the process for ten or fifteen minutes, but neither Kelly nor Harris had much to offer. The two male Tyvek spacemen, as Kelly thought of them, worked efficiently. Taylor photographed, bagged, and cataloged on her laptop anything that turned up in the sifters.

Harris's phone beeped, and she plucked it from its carrier on her waist. "Doc's up. He'll meet us at the hospital."

"Good, let's go." Seeing the doctor meant more information, forward motion. Anything had to be better than watching the Tyvek-clad crew sift through dirt.

They bid goodbye to the Tyvek squad and hit the push bars of the gym doors at the same time, making noises like pistol shots in the echoey gym. They got into Harris's car. She drove around the gym, took a left, went through a stop sign, and pulled into the hospital parking lot after a hundred yards.

"Well, that was some commute."

"There *are* some advantages to living out here."

She parked near the emergency room entrance, and they walked in. A security guard sat in a chair by the door, while a duty nurse was stationed behind a counter with sliding glass windows.

"Doc Redruth in his office or down in the basement?"

"Basement," nurse and guard said in unison, his Jamaican bass forming an odd chorus with her hard, clipped Massachusetts falsetto.

"Thanks, guys. Stretch here is with me," Harris said. They pushed through a door marked with pictograms for stairs and an EXIT sign above it. This put them in a stairwell painted in institutional green, and they skipped down the steps the way people do. At the bottom of the stairs, they went through a fire door, down an institutional-green corridor, and through a door marked MORGUE.

In the movies and on TV, the cops walk into the morgue and there is always a body being worked on. Or an eccentric, genius doctor making great deductions, usually doing something like eating to impress the audience with how hardened the pathologist is. The smell of death and formaldehyde don't do much for the appetite. Even though it was small, the morgue at Nantucket Cottage Hospital was just like its cousins in cities and counties across America.

The doctor was hunched over an examination table. The bones were laid out on the table. He was taking pictures of them with an expensive-looking digital camera.

"Hey, Doc." Harris spoke softly so as not to startle him. Redruth was shaven bald with broad but stooped shoulders. He wore a white lab coat, and Kelly could see blue jeans and thick-soled moccasins.

"Hey, Jo, thought I heard the door squeak." Doc Redruth never moved from his camera.

"Doc, I've got Detective Tom Kelly from the State Police with me." The doc took a couple of more pictures, straightened his back—rolling his shoulders and stretching his spine without raising his hands—then put the camera down and turned to face Kelly.

Kelly hadn't been expecting the mustache. It was thick and flowing and looked more at home on Wyatt Earp or some cowboy than it did on a doctor. He was wearing a blue-and-black plaid shirt under his lab coat and half-moon glasses on the bridge of his nose. He was in his sixties, fit. Kelly imagined he was the type who ran or sailed or something. When Kelly took the doctor's hand, it was rough and calloused, each finger like the gnarled roots of an oak tree. His grip made Kelly wince a bit and made him wonder how much time the doctor spent in the gym.

"Nice to meet you, Detective." The accent was all New York City.

"You too. What can you tell us?"

"The bones are of a male youth between five and ten years old. Big for a five-year-old, small for a ten-year-old. The sutures in the skull aren't fully fused. Judging by the bones, excluding any damage done by the construction crew, your little boy met a violent end. Most likely through blunt trauma to the head."

"All that from a collection of bones?"

"It's a preliminary cause of death. We'll know more after X-rays and other tests. But for now, yes. He was beaten to death. Probably with a hard object, but again, I won't know for certain until we do more tests."

"By an adult?"

"Most likely. But that's a guess at this point."

"Any idea how long he's been buried?" Harris asked.

"I would say decades more than years. There's no flesh left on the bones. The clothing is mostly gone. When putrefaction occurred, it probably encouraged whatever bugs and microbes there were in the soil to be more active. That and the soil was loosely packed, or we would have had compression and preservation similar to mummification."

"Okay . . . Can you tell us anything else?" Harris again. Kelly was looking intently at the collection of bones, trying to picture the little boy that they'd once been.

"Yes, your child here, he didn't have the best diet. He didn't see the dentist often."

"Like he didn't have access to a dentist because his corpse is so old there weren't any?"

"Probably not. Judging by the state of his teeth, he liked sugar, candy, soda . . . that type of thing."

"Doctor, can you tell us anything else at this stage?" Kelly was asking just to ask something, to still be involved in the investigation.

"Nope. We need to X-ray the bones. Take samples. We'll take a sample of DNA and try and find out who this poor soul was. It'll take some time, Detective. Then further tests will be done by the state crime lab. That will slow things down further."

"Okay, gotcha. Thank you, Doctor," Harris said.

Kelly just nodded his thanks.

"Detectives, give me some time. Why don't you come back tomorrow afternoon. I might know more then."

Kelly took one more look at the bones laid out on the table before he and Harris walked out back into the hallway. They didn't say much. It was a small island, and he didn't want their conversation to be overheard and repeated. Already there'd be plenty of idle gossip; a collection of bones and the presence of a State Police detective warranted it.

Once back in Harris's car, Kelly said, "Okay, what do we know?"

"Not a lot."

"Seriously, what little do we know?"

"Two days ago, a construction crew was breaking ground on a foundation. They found some kid's bones."

"What else?"

"The arms appear to have been laid across the chest postmortem at the time of burial."

"Indicating what?"

"Murder . . . possibly remorse on the part of the killer or familiarity with the victim."

"Possibly. Sure."

"We know that the bones are of a little kid, and they've been buried for decades."

"And we know that blunt force trauma was the likely cause of death."

"Sure, and that the bones have been there long enough that we don't have much to work with."

"There's not a lot of physical evidence from the corpse. Not much in the way of clothes, just some scraps that have been in the dirt for a long time. Anything else from the scene so far?" Kelly asked. Recapping what they knew was a good way of shaking off the mental cobwebs caused by too little sleep.

"Coins, marbles, a toy, a cigarette butt, and some trash. Not much. Chances of finding the killer's DNA looks shaky at best, same for fingerprints."

"Next steps?"

"You tell me, Mr. State Police Detective."

"Comb through missing person files. Try and narrow our search down to something manageable. Wait to hear from Doc Redruth and see if he can tell us anything more."

"Lots of time at the computer."

"You see a better way?"

"Nope, not until we get more from the scene or the doc."

"Exactly. We're exactly almost nowhere . . . Now we have to see if we can make something turn up or turn loose. Between local records and NCIC, there might be something."

"We don't know how many decades to go back. For all we know, the bones are from when the island was settled."

"Sure we do."

"Oh, how is that?" Her sarcasm rolled around the inside of her car.

"The coins. They should have the year they were minted stamped on them."

"There's nothing to say they were buried when he was."

"No, but it's a starting point. They would only give us a range at best, anyway . . . but it's something. And I have an idea."

"What's that?"

"We might as well grab a couple of coffees, maybe a sandwich or something, and head back to your station. There we can eat, enjoy expensive java, and start poring over files. If the techs or the doc come up with anything, we can always go back to the files later."

"That's some State Police detective–level thinking. You buying?"

"Sure. Why not?"

Kelly noticed her smiling as she dipped her head toward the steering wheel, hiding her expression from him as she put the car in gear. She pulled out of the hospital parking lot and headed back toward the high school.

"We have a plan. At least that's something," he said.

"More importantly, Kelly, you're going to spring for lunch."

November 1981

Albie was home watching TV. Outside it was raining the type of November rain that forced even the hardiest of kids inside. The rain beat against the windows, and the wind shook the house. Tomorrow there would be big puddles in the street with brown leaves floating in them. The ground would be too wet and muddy to play football.

Albie was sitting on the floor, watching cartoons on the TV station from Boston. Mighty Mouse *was on. It wasn't his favorite, but it was better than* Casper the Friendly Ghost. *His toy soldiers were spread out in front of him. Off to one side was a small plate with the crumbs of the Oreos his mother had brought him and next to that, an empty glass. His mother had snapped at him about something, and then later she felt bad and brought him some Oreos and milk. Lately all the adults—teachers, his parents—seemed jumpy and short-tempered.*

"Albie?" His mother was standing in the doorway to the living room. There was a man in a police uniform standing behind her.

"Yeah, Mom?"

"Albie, this is . . . this is Officer Almeida."

He looked up and saw a tall, powerfully built man standing behind his mother. Albie took in the blue uniform, the long black raincoat, the gun belt, the big revolver in its holster, and the badge on the man's chest.

"Albie, he wants to talk to you about Nick."

Albie looked down. Nick hadn't been to school for the last two days. Richie and Mikey hadn't been in school for even longer. It was kind of scary that his friends were missing. If the guys who ran fast or were tough or were good at sports were missing, it made Albie wonder what would happen to him if the monster came for him. Because it had to be a monster. What else would take kids except a monster or a witch?

"Hi, Albie. My name is Joe Almeida, and I'm a policeman. You can call me Officer Joe."

"Okay, Officer Joe."

"Albie, I need to ask you about Nick Steuben. You were with him a few days ago. Your friends said you guys walked home together."

"Yes, we played football at the field and then we walked home partway together, then he went to meet his mom at the bank, and I went home."

"That's the problem, Albie. Nick never made it to the bank."

"Oh." *The monster had gotten Nick. That meant that Albie had been close to the monster.*

"Albie, do you remember anything about that day, about Nick?"

"No, it was just a normal day. We played football in the field on Mill Street. Then Nick and I walked home together . . . well, most of the way home."

"Did you notice anyone or anything out of the ordinary?"

"No, I was just trying to get home. I didn't want Dad to get mad at me." *Lately his parents had been much stricter about getting home before dark.*

"Did you guys talk about anything?" *Officer Joe asked. Albie felt like he was looking for a specific answer but didn't know what.*

"We talked about stuff. You know, Star Wars, school, sports, things like that."

"That's it?" *Officer Joe seemed disappointed.*

"Well, I was hoping he would let me borrow his Millennium Falcon. You know, from Star Wars. His mom bought him one, and I wanted to play with it really bad, but he doesn't loan his toys out."

"He doesn't share his toys with his friends?"

"He used to. He loaned his new Luke Skywalker action figure to Mikey. It was the new one with Luke in the tan suit."

"Oh." Officer Joe wrote in his notepad. "Do you know when Nick loaned that to Mikey?"

"Sure, the last time we saw Mikey playing football at the field."

"That was nice of him. What if Mikey had kept it or a bigger boy took it?" Albie smiled at the police officer. He wasn't smart like Kojak.

"Nick wasn't worried about that. He always scratched his initials on the foot of his action figures. That way he can always prove it's one of his," Albie said triumphantly.

CHAPTER 5

For Kelly, it was another grilled chicken Caesar sandwich. This time instead of a wrap, it came on a disk of pita bread. Instead of cutting it in half to make a pocket, the good people at the deli cut the pita bread into two flat disks. Kelly's was packed with romaine lettuce, an extra chopped grilled chicken breast, Parmesan cheese, and Caesar dressing. He passed on the offered croutons.

Harris had ordered them. Everyone seemed to know her and be on friendly terms. When he'd been in uniform, he and his fellow officers had been careful about where they ordered food. There were a fair number of ex-cons who worked in restaurants. No one wanted something extra in their meal. Maybe it was different out here, or maybe she was universally well liked.

Her sandwich was roast beef, with dill-speckled Havarti cheese, lettuce, tomato, mayo, and creamy horseradish sauce. Kelly seriously had to consider if he had made a mistake. He liked grilled chicken well enough, but sometimes he craved red meat and mayonnaise. Then he thought of the calories involved and felt a little better. Harris also ordered some kettle-cooked potato chips that were dusted with dried jalapeño. The kid at the counter put the two paper tubes containing their sandwiches in a bag, along with Harris's chips.

They drove around the corner to the next block to get their coffee. There were half a dozen customers constantly rotating in and out of the coffee shop. Kelly knew that it did well enough to survive year-round on the island, where many of the businesses seemed to be seasonal. He noticed they offered regular baked goods and also gluten-free and vegan options. He also noticed that rose hip iced tea was on the menu. Kelly knew he was in a strange land, but he was the type who thought a coffee Coolatta from Dunkin' was exotic.

Kelly dutifully paid at each shop. He was handsomely paid as a State Police detective, but even in the offseason, the prices were eye-catching. He wondered how anyone could live on the island on a cop's salary . . . but when he tasted the dark roast he ordered, he had to admit to himself that it was worth the price. Maybe that was why Bruce Green needed hardship pay, so he could afford the rose hip iced tea and fancy dark roast?

They were leaving the coffee shop when a man in canvas work clothes was walking up the steps. He was big, heavyset, with dark hair.

"Well look at who it is, the lady detective."

"Mr. Delvecchio." Harris came to a stop because the man was blocking the steps down.

"Oh, it's *mister* now?" he said with sarcasm. "It wasn't *mister* when you were arresting me on those bullshit charges."

"Mr. Delvecchio, your wife made a complaint."

"Which she withdrew."

"So we have nothing more to talk about. Let us pass," she said in a voice that made Kelly think of *The Lord of the Rings* anytime Gandalf spoke with authority. Delvecchio waited for a couple of beats, then stepped aside.

"Go ahead, Officers."

They passed him and were at the car a few feet away when Delvecchio said, "Stupid bitch."

Kelly wheeled toward him instinctively. He had been taught by the troopers, reenforced by the cops in Wormtown, that you couldn't tolerate open disrespect. You couldn't let people challenge you on the street, not like that.

"The fuck did you say?" Kelly asked in his most un-trooper-like way as he closed the few feet between them.

"I called her a bitch because she is. What are you gonna do about it? It's not illegal."

Kelly grabbed Delvecchio's shirt at the collar, twisting, rotating his wrist outward, tightening it against his throat.

"Apologize to the lady, or I'll give you something to be sorry about."

"Fuck you. I know you. You're a guy who got bullied as a kid, grew up, became a cop, now you take it out on everyone. You think that badge makes you a guy. You're . . ."

He never finished the sentiment. Kelly applied more pressure, lifting the bigger, heavier man onto his tiptoes as he did so.

"That's right, idiot. Now apologize or I'll show you some real fucking bullying."

"Kelly! Leave it," Harris said.

"Not until he apologizes."

"Kelly, he's an asshole. He's not worth it. Let him go."

After what seemed an eternity, Kelly released the bigger man.

"Go on."

"Fuck you," Delvecchio gasped.

Kelly and Harris got in her car. He sat in the passenger seat, shaking with frustration. His stomach twisted in knots.

"Jesus, Kelly, what was that?"

"You can't be disrespected on the street. I can't let another cop be disrespected like that." He defaulted to the words his field training officer had spoken to him on his first night on the road. The mantra of cops everywhere.

"Yeah, 'cause this place is so street."

"It's the principle," he said, fists still balled, but the moment was over. He didn't know if it was the case or the place that was driving him nuts. Either way, the sooner they wrapped it up and he left the island, the better.

They pulled into the new police station parking lot a few minutes later. Like most places in New England, Kelly knew that fifty years after it was built this would still be called the "new" police station. Inside, Harris pointed Kelly to an empty cubicle a few spots from her own. Kelly set up his laptop and was able to connect to the internet while Harris waited for Taylor to send them pictures of the coins. Kelly scanned through his emails from work while he wolfed down his sandwich. The pita bread proved to be far tastier than a wrap.

He opened his private email. Nothing of note other than a nice message from his mother and a not-so-nice one from Jeanie. Kelly had noticed that since he was sent to the island, his mother had upped her quota of daily emails. She was worried about him. Mary Kelly was a nice lady, and they had a good relationship, but she had a tendency to nag. That got worse after his father died. She pointed out for the twentieth time that week that she could come and watch the boys. He knew what Jeanie's answer would be. He closed both emails without responding. He could reply to them later.

He switched back to the work account. He drafted an email to Savoy, bringing him up to date on where they were in the investigation. He clearly articulated to Savoy the points that led him to believe that this was a homicide and not an accident. Savoy would be thrilled at the thought of his detective being out on the island and not taking other cases for a few more days. Kelly didn't even want to consider what he would say about the overtime. Oh well, Jacques had his chance to come out here. He could take whatever came in while Kelly was on the island.

He tapped at the keys of his laptop one-handed while he kept eating his sandwich. He set the search parameters for missing juvenile males between five and ten years old in the State Police database. While the computer was thinking, Kelly opened the National Crime Information Center's search engine. NCIC was founded in the late 1960s by J. Edgar Hoover's FBI. It was a central clearinghouse for all sorts of crime-related data that was designed so that local law enforcement agencies could share information and coordinate their efforts. It was also where all missing persons were supposed to be entered nationally and thus be searchable. It meant that if a kid went missing in San Diego, they could know about it in Boston.

Kelly's search parameters were too broad for the NCIC search engine, and he had to try to narrow them. The State Police database spat out a disturbingly large number of files that would have to get narrowed down as well. The searches were further complicated because he couldn't narrow them by hair color, eye color, or race. He also couldn't narrow his search by year, at least not yet, so he really couldn't do more than watch as the hourglass on the screen kept turning and the number in the "files returned" box kept increasing. At least his sandwich was good.

Kelly looked over at Harris in her cubicle. She was tucking in to her lunch while tapping at her keyboard. She ate her sandwich and chips in small bites. She looked over at Kelly, who was holding his sandwich in one hand like an ever-shrinking scepter bejeweled with lettuce and chicken. She would take a bite, put the sandwich down, tap on her keyboard. Then she'd repeat the whole process. Kelly looked like he was in some sort of speed-eating contest. It wasn't that she was being delicate; it was just that compared to him, a ravenous wolf would appear delicate while eating.

Kelly figured that she was searching through the Nantucket Police files, at least the ones that had been digitized. Anything predigitization would mean going through dusty boxes, and he assumed she couldn't do that while enjoying one of the excellent sandwiches from Henry's Jr.

"How's it going?" Kelly asked between bites.

"Ugh, slow. Most of the reports are kids who stayed out too late, and a panicky mom called. There were a couple of custody issues where one parent was trying to stick it to the other when their child wasn't returned on time. There were another few custody issues in which one parent took a child off-island either before custodial orders were in place or in spite of them. There aren't any that seem sinister," she said.

"I am not surprised."

"The only one I could find in local records that involved a death was one where a twelve-year-old boy had gone to Surfside Beach while his parents were at work. He got caught in a rip current. That was 1997, and he definitely wasn't buried in Tom Nevers with his arms folded across his chest," she said definitively.

Her phone vibrated and beeped on the desk of her cubicle.

"It's a message from Holly." She put down her sandwich so she could look at her phone more closely.

"It's taking forever to open." She popped a potato chip in her mouth while she waited.

"Must be something important, or she wouldn't have sent it," Kelly offered.

"Kelly, come here and check this out."

Kelly got up and walked over to Harris's cubicle, where they both hunched over her phone.

On the screen Kelly could make out the top of a disk. Dark colored . . . it was a coin. Slowly, line by line, a very heavily patinaed nickel appeared. It was also corroded, and the only number of the year that she could make out was the 1. The next picture started the slow process of being revealed. Harris ate more of her sandwich. Carbs would help keep her frustration from getting the better of her, Kelly thought. Her foot was tapping unconsciously and impatiently. "Come on . . . come on," she said between bites. Jo Harris was many things, but patient wasn't one of them.

"Can you make out the dates?" Kelly asked.

"Yeah, three are decipherable. There's a 1979 quarter, a 1977 penny, and a 1986 dime."

"Okay, so our bones, our kid, went in the ground sometime between 1977 and 1986," Kelly said.

"Well, it could have been later. Coins stay in circulation for a while. We know the coins didn't go in the ground before 1977."

"Right, but there are coins that were minted in 1986 that are still floating around now."

"Sure, but Doc said the bones are decades old." She popped a chip in her mouth and chewed thoughtfully.

"Okay, so let's say between 1977 and 1991?" he asked her with a shrug and raised palms.

"It's a starting point. We can always refine the search as we learn more from the tests."

"Okay, I'll narrow my search of MSP records, and why don't you start with your local files, the computerized ones?"

"Already done. Nothing doing. What about starting on the local files that aren't on a computer?"

"Those will be more labor-intensive. Let's hit the stuff we can on our computers and then tackle the local files. If we get to a point where we need to go through the dusty boxes of paper, we'll both do it. Do you want to start on NCIC, and I will work it with you after I go through the returns from the MSP database?"

"Sounds like a plan," she affirmed.

"Good." Kelly rolled his chair back to his desk and started to refine his search. He heard her fingers tapping rapidly on her keyboard. They spent the next several hours hunched over their respective computers. Kelly was fidgeting with a coin, a half-dollar in his hand. Rolling it between his fingers. He looked up and noticed that Jo was watching him.

"What?"

"It's just funny to see you fidgeting."

"It helps me concentrate."

"Sure, sure," she said.

They went back to the task at hand. Occasionally one of them would get up to use the bathroom or get a drink of water. The doctor soon texted Harris with an estimate of the victim's height. He was between forty-six and forty-eight inches tall. Doc said that would mean the child could have been as young as five or as old as eight or nine.

Having a height range allowed the two detectives to narrow the field from tens of thousands of cases nationally since 1977 to a few thousand. That translated to a thousand in New England and a few hundred in Massachusetts alone. It was a lot to go through but not as much as it had been before Doc's text message.

They worked through the afternoon into the early evening. If they saw a likely file, and there weren't many, they would download it and then print it out. Many of the cases stopped being missing person cases by the discovery of the remains. In three-quarters of the cases, children were killed within the first three hours of their abduction, and half were killed within the first hour. Kelly hated thinking about the statistics. He didn't like how the numbers never did justice to the very real, very human tragedies they represented.

The sky showing in the windows of the Nantucket Police Department Detective Bureau had gone from blue to a dark shade of purple to an inky-looking black. Most families would be sitting down to dinner, most couples might be at a bar having a drink, but the two detectives were hunched over their respective computers. Kelly's back had started to ache and his eyes were dry and itchy. Harris kept rubbing her temples with the knuckles of her curled index finger. Kelly suspected she had a headache. Their once-infrequent breaks to stand and stretch or go to the bathroom were now a more frequent occurrence.

"Kelly?" Harris called him from her cubicle.

"Harris," he answered.

"I am toast." She drew the sentence out, giving it more emphasis.

"Me too."

"What's your stance on beer?"

"I like it. Cold. Not too cheap. Not too fruity or fancy."

"Good, me too."

"The bones aren't going to be any more or less dead tomorrow. Let's grab a cold one and something to eat."

"Now that's a plan I can get behind."

Without much discussion or prior agreement, they took separate cars. Kelly followed in Black Beauty. He could see the light from Harris's phone pressed against her ear as she drove one-handed all the way. He'd called the boys shortly before they left. He listened to them talk about their days and made silly jokes over the phone.

He and Harris turned up the same street where they had gotten their expensive coffee. She turned into a gravel parking lot bordered by a split-rail fence. As Black Beauty's tires crunched on the gravel, Kelly saw a sign that read KITTY MURTAUGH'S. He had a moment of panic wondering if she had taken him to some cat-themed place.

Harris was waiting for him, cell phone stowed in the pocket of her fleece vest. She had locked her duty pistol in the trunk of her car. Kelly had taken off his pistol holster and put that in the trunk in his duty bag. His pistol was stuck in his waistband under the untucked Red Sox team shirt he kept in his trunk for just such occasions. No one would think he was anything other than a cop wearing a Red Sox team shirt, but at least the pistol wasn't as obvious.

They went inside, and Kelly was impressed and surprised to find himself in an Irish bar. The hostess seated them, and Kelly saw that almost all the seats at the bar were taken and most of the tables too. Not bad for a weeknight during the offseason, or maybe the reward for staying open in the offseason was guaranteed patrons. They settled into a hard wooden booth, and their waitress arrived with two menus.

"Start you off with a drink?" she asked brightly.

"Guinness," Kelly answered.

"Cisco," Harris said.

"Let me get those, and I'll be back to tell you our specials."

"What's a Cisco?"

"Cisco brewery. Right here on the island. They make some pretty good beer. Most of the local bars and restaurants carry it, and you can find it off-island."

"I'll have to check it out." They looked at their menus, and the waitress came back with their drinks. Kelly was pleased to note that his Guinness had a proper head on it. She told them the specials and asked if they needed a minute. They didn't. Harris ordered a bacon cheeseburger and french fries. Kelly ordered fish tacos and a side salad.

The waitress whirled away with a friendly smile and a word of thanks. Kelly took the first happy sip of his Guinness. He could feel some of the day's tension slide away with the first taste, that slight unwinding of the tightness that always seemed to have a home in his chest.

"How long have you been a detective, Harris?"

"Four years. I was in patrol for seven, and then I was able to move up. You?"

"Eight years. Before that, two years in the Violent Crime Task Force, and before that, eight years on the road."

"Where were you posted?"

"Springfield for most of my time on the road. A lot of time on the Pike, then task force and detectives in Worcester. I just transferred to this area six months ago."

"Worcester. Busy, huh?"

"Yeah, most of the time." Worcester PD's detective bureau was good, and the State Police dicks were only involved in some cases—anything on the highway or state land, joint task force cases, and officer-involved shootings. Still, there had been plenty of serious crimes for Kelly and the others to investigate.

"Why'd you transfer?"

"For the family. My in-laws live in Carver, so this is a better fit. My wife wanted to be closer to them. You know what they say?"

"Happy wife, happy life," she answered.

"Yep, exactly." Though he wouldn't really describe Jeanie as happy. "Are you originally from Nantucket?"

"Me, no . . . I'm from New Hampshire, a small town not far from Dartmouth. I went to college in Boston, wanted to be a cop, and had been out here a few times visiting. They have such a hard time getting cops out here that it gave me better odds. I figured that once I was in the state civil service system, I could transfer somewhere else."

"How'd that work out?"

"It didn't. I like it here." She shrugged. "It's slow in the winter, and there isn't a lot of sexy crime. No one will ever make a cop show about being an officer out here. But it's a community and I'm a part of it. Probably sounds silly."

"Not at all. Don't we all secretly, when we aren't trying to act all world-weary, want to belong to a community, to make a difference?"

"Sure. It just sounds so corny."

"No, I think it is what a lot of us aspire to but just don't want to admit." He'd joined the troopers because they were the best of the best. Kelly wanted to be one of the best.

He'd loved stopping cars and finding drugs or guns or someone with a stolen vehicle. Kelly loved putting handcuffs on bad guys. It was as simple as that. He'd hated writing tickets, and even though the MSP didn't have "quotas," they had goals and expectations. He did his best to meet them, but stolen cars, drugs, and guns . . . that was police work. That was probably why he ended up in the task force.

That had been a thrill, working with cops from the different cities and towns, guys from his agency. Instead of the blue polyester uniform and glossy leather gear, it was sneakers and jeans, Maglite stuck in a back pocket, body armor outside his shirt, and a raid jacket over that. They spent most of their time kicking in doors, looking for fugitives. It was dangerous, and the adrenaline dump was massive. Kelly loved being the first guy in the stack, using his size and time on the weight bench to kick a door or swing the ram into it. Being the first guy in and rushing headlong into the fight . . . there had been some close calls, and he'd had more than his fair share of luck. Kelly's mind drifted to the last time he had gone after a fugitive in Worcester.

They hit the apartment in the projects, Kelly booted the door, and there was the target, a little guy sitting on his couch. He sprang up with a pistol in his hand. Kelly's mind had a hard time processing what he was seeing. The little guy fired four rounds in Kelly's general direction before the gun jammed. Kelly should have shot him, but he hesitated. The guy started vaulting over furniture, making for the back door like he was competing for a track scholarship.

Kelly hesitated for a split second and then started after the track star. Kelly followed but realized he was a little extra careful going around corners and by doorways. He wondered why he hadn't returned fire. That would have solved the problem of the corners and doors right then and there.

Kelly made it up to the walkway on the roof. The metal roof sloped away from the railings; it wasn't an extreme angle, but it was a long way from flat. It was also winter in Worcester, Massachusetts. The track star was frantically tugging at the door in front of him.

"Turn around. Show me your hands!" Kelly had his pistol up and pointed at the track star. "Lift your shirt up and turn around slowly."

He turned around and faced Kelly, his hands raised.

"Okay . . . okay, just be cool, Officer."

The track star was complying. Kelly felt his own inner tension uncoil a little bit. He could hear other cops coming up the steps. Then the track star did the damnedest thing. He grabbed the railing and vaulted over it onto the sloped metal roof.

For the second time that night, Kelly was caught off guard. The track star landed and started running toward the other side of the building. Kelly pivoted, watching his progress. The track star was fast, until he hit a patch of ice. He fell, sliding off the roof. Kelly watched the track star's bare feet briefly face him as he tumbled, letting out a bloodcurdling cry. It was cut off by a sickening crunch of bone and flesh into the frozen pavement fifty feet below.

By the time Kelly and the rest of the task force got to him, the track star was breathing his last spasmodic breaths. Blood and brains were on the cold pavement, and though he was still breathing, it was at best a technicality, his body having not yet received the message that it was well and truly fucked.

Later, when his time on administrative leave was almost over, his boss came by the house. He wanted Kelly to know that he was being cleared. Not only was Kelly getting cleared, but he was also getting a promotion to detective.

He didn't say that Kelly should have grabbed the guy in the apartment or that his hesitation had put them all in the shit. Kelly wasn't being promoted; he was being sidelined with a pay raise. Kelly was just happy when he had stopped seeing bare feet tumbling ass over teakettle in his dreams every night.

"Yeah, you're right," Harris said, dragging Kelly's mind back to their conversation about wanting to make a difference.

"Well, once in a blue moon it happens." He was pretty sure that Jeanie wouldn't ever admit it.

The waitress brought their food in a metal rack. Kelly's fish tacos were composed of battered, fried cod in flour tortillas with a pinkish, creamy sauce and some shredded lettuce. His salad was a bunch of greens and vegetables in a bowl with a vinaigrette.

He looked over at Harris's burger. She was just taking a bite. He was instantly envious, and his mouth began to water. Her burger was about an inch and a half thick with orange cheese that was clearly not American cheese but rather an expensive sliced cheddar. On top of that, there were two strips of thick-cut bacon. He could smell the smoky aroma across the table from her. The bun was made of potato bread, yellow and grilled. Underneath the top, he had spied mayonnaise, a slice of red onion, lettuce, and tomato. She took a big bite and put the burger down to wipe her mouth in one pass of her napkin. Harris's jaws moved and Kelly could hear faint but distinct noises of happiness coming from her side of the table.

She took a big sip of her beer and picked up a large steak fry. She bit it in half, and steam poured out from the half that was held between her thumb and forefinger. She stabbed it into the small ceramic dish of ketchup and then popped the whole thing in her mouth. She ate with gusto, and Kelly wondered if she ate like that on dates or with a little more restraint. He hoped it wasn't the latter.

His fish tacos were excellent. The cod was fresh, the batter light, and they were just golden brown, not overcooked. The sauce seemed to be a mix of Mexican-style crema and chipotle with adobo. The sauce added the perfect amount of tang to the crispy, hot fish. He shouldn't have been surprised the seafood on an island would be fresh or cooked well.

They sat and ate, not saying much, just allowing the food and beer to help ease tired eyes, aching shoulders, and cricked necks. Harris ate a little slower than your average marine in basic training on Parris Island. Kelly's tacos were a dim memory and his salad half gone by the time she popped a last wedge of potato in her mouth. The waitress walked up to their booth.

"Get you guys another beer?"

"Yes, please," Harris said.

"Me too," Kelly said.

The waitress whisked their plates off the table and whirled away with a flip of her ponytail. The booths around them were empty, and the crowd at the bar and at the high-tops near the bar was getting louder. Harris leaned in, but there was no need to be quiet with the background din.

"Who do you think the little boy was?" Harris asked.

"Too soon to tell."

"Have you worked many cases like this one?"

"To date?"

"Yeah."

"No. This is my first one like this." He put a little extra emphasis on the last two words.

"Really?"

"Sure, most of the homicides I dealt with were part of a joint task force in Worcester dealing with drugs and gangs. Those are straightforward, Player A shoots Player B. Sometimes it's over territory or revenge for a previous killing. If I wasn't working those types of cases, I would be in the rotation to investigate officer-involved shootings. If not that, then it was homicides in the towns outside Wormtown."

"What was that like?"

"Kind of like this. I would be sent out to assist the local dick while they investigated a domestic homicide or some other type of killing."

"But nothing like this, right? A pile of old bones belonging to a kid with no real physical evidence."

"Nope, nothing like this," he said.

The waitress arrived with their pint glasses and halfheartedly asked if they wanted dessert. Kelly didn't, and Harris clearly did but said she didn't. The waitress glided off.

"I can't keep wondering who he is . . . was? Wasn't his mother worried? Shouldn't there be a missing person report?"

"Yeah, me too. Exactly, there should be something. Something to go on." He took a large sip of Guinness.

"We might not even be able to ID him."

"No, we might not, but it's too early to throw in the towel. We don't have much, but we're doing what we can do."

"This is my first homicide."

"This is a tough one. Most are easy. Mr. Man gets sick of Mrs. Man's shit and, after using her as a punching bag, strangles her or stabs her or beats her to death. Or the Player A and Player B scenario. Maybe a robbery goes wrong, and a gun goes off. Most homicides, the only mystery involved is figuring out who the kid in the dark clothing is."

"So I'm not missing much being single?" she asked with a bit of a grin.

"No, and if you ever asked her, my wife would tell you never get married. Especially to a cop."

"Never easy being married to a cop."

"I get the feeling she would feel the same way if I were an insurance salesman."

"Ha! What does she do?"

"She's a nurse. RN."

"Jesus, Kelly, are there any cop clichés you don't fall into?"

"Um . . ."

"Let me guess, you met in some ER somewhere?"

"Yeah, I was on the road then. Brought a DUI from an accident to be checked out. She was working that night."

"Oh Christ, Kelly. You probably wear all sorts of T-shirts and sweatshirts with the MSP logo off duty, don't you?"

"She's my first wife, if that helps. Most guys this long on the job are on their second or third by now. As for the shirts . . . no comment." As a matter of fact, Kelly had a large collection of MSP polos and T-shirts from a number of charity golf events and road races that he wore out and about when not on duty.

"Well, at least you don't live up to all the clichés." She smirked at him and sipped her beer.

"No, I don't drive a big pickup truck or a midlife-crisis-mobile either."

"Well, you've got that going for you."

"How about you? How many clichés do you fall into?"

"Oh, not too many. It is different out here. Everyone knows I am a cop. This is a small town thirty miles out to sea. It doesn't take long to ticket or arrest the same few people over and over again. In summertime there is some variety, but during the offseason, it is repeat customers."

"Is it tough living out here during the offseason?"

"It isn't too bad. Sometimes the boats don't run, and people get a little squirrelly in the winter, but I like the solitude."

"What is there to do?"

"When I first moved out here full-time and I was in patrol, I asked an old-timer that same question."

"What did he say?"

Harris comically scrunched up her face and proclaimed in an exaggerated New England accent, "Well, missy, in the summah we screw the tourists . . . in the wintah, we screw each oth-ah." Kelly guffawed, trying not to choke on his beer.

"There's a lot of truth in his words," Harris added.

"I'm sure."

"This place isn't as perfect as it seems."

"No place is."

"It's just that there's this image of the island as this wonderful community, but it's got very real problems. In the summer, it's the party scene, recreational drugs, DUIs, and the occasional sexual assault. In the winter, it's alcoholism, opioids, and domestic violence that keep us busy."

"Just like any other small town."

"Sure, just thirty miles out to sea. Out here, winters can be long, dark, and grim."

"Don't make it sound so appealing."

"Living here year-round definitely isn't for everyone."

They finished their drinks and settled the tab. Outside, their feet crunched on the gravel parking lot as they went to their cars.

"See ya tomorrow, Kelly."

"See ya."

He looked around out of habit, scoping the bushes, the shadows. There was nothing there to be seen. The wind gusted, shaking the trees back and forth across the light from the streetlight, making a sort of shadow puppet show. Kelly shivered. He unlocked Black Beauty, started the car, and turned the heat on. He realized his neck and shoulders were tight.

"Get ahold of yourself, Kelly, it's just another town," he mumbled to himself. He put the car in gear, the tires crunching on the gravel drive. Then he drove through the dark, empty streets, headed for the Oceanview Motel.

Early December 1981

Albie was sitting on the bus next to Louie Delvecchio. The bus was hot and had a smell not unlike wet dog. Twenty-five elementary school kids at the end of the school day in rain-soaked clothes . . . that was the smell. It had rained in the morning, stopping at snack time, leaving plenty of large puddles for the kids to splash in as they played outside during recess.

On the bus Albie and Louie weren't talking to each other. At recess they had played tag in the big grassy field between the two baseball diamonds. Louie had slipped in a puddle, skidding, sending up a spray of water. The kids all laughed, including Albie. It was funny, like something out of a movie.

Louie got up angry and red-faced. No one liked being laughed at. For Louie, it was worse coming from Albie, especially Albie. Albie who was slow, fat, and uncoordinated. Albie who was always picked last for kickball, for all the sports. Albie who was a sissy and cried all the time. They always saw it coming because his lower lip would quiver first, and then big fat tears were next. Being laughed at by Albie was too much for Louie.

Louie took two large steps, kicking his foot like a punter into a deep puddle. The water arched up into Albie's face, his nose, his open mouth, and his eyes. Albie was caught off guard, and the water from the puddle blinded him as well, making him cough and gag.

"Take that! You big fat baby!" Louie yelled. "Look, look at you! Allllbie peed his pants!"

Predictably, Albie's spluttering and coughing gave way to his quivering lip and tears rolling down his cheeks. Snot started running, and the other kids laughed. It wasn't that they didn't like him or that he was someone who got picked on regularly; that was just how it was on the playground. One minute everything could be fine, and then the next there could be a fight or an accident. You might end up the butt of a joke that lasted for months or days. Recess was a time of fun overshadowed by the dread of the unexpected.

The bell rang, and they all started running for the classroom. Albie shuffled in, his wet clothes suddenly not fitting quite right. The cold rainwater of the December storm made him shiver as much as the anger and frustration he felt. He hadn't peed himself. He hadn't. It was bad enough that he was crying, and they were laughing, but he hadn't peed himself like a baby.

Albie spent the last few hours of school sitting uncomfortably in damp clothes. He couldn't look at the other kids, especially the ones who'd been there. To make matters worse, Mrs. McDonough had told him to stop squirming and pay attention.

Louie's voice behind him said, "Yeah, Al-pee, stop squirming."

The other kids started laughing, and Mrs. McDonough glowered at Albie as if it was his fault. Albie's cheeks were hot with embarrassment. He bit his lower lip to keep it from quivering and managed not to cry in class.

Later, they lined up at the door for dismissal, and he kept his head down. The other kids were talking, excited to be going home. Albie didn't have anything to say to anyone. He got on the bus and sat down in his seat. Louie sat down next to him.

"Slide over, Al-pee."

"Don't call me that, Louie."

"Al-pee, Al-pee, Al-pee."

"Shut up, Louie!"

"Boys!" the bus driver called out. They both stopped talking and sat there in their seats, smelling like wet dog. Each one fuming and internally cataloging the insults and injuries to their pride, growing more and more

angry. When the bus stopped at Louie's stop, he got up and turned back to Albie.

"Goodbye, Al-pee!" he said mockingly.

Albie's face flushed as the kids around him laughed. Then he cried out as Louie walked away from him down the aisle toward the driver and the door: "I hate you, Louie Delvecchio! I hate you, and I hope the monster gets you!"

The kids on the bus stopped laughing, stopped chattering. They stared at Albie like he was the monster. Albie felt his face flush more, and his lower lip began to quiver. He hated Louie, the bus, the other kids, and the stupid wet dog smell. And he hated himself most of all.

CHAPTER 6

Kelly was sweating. Not the type of Hollywood sweating where the hero in the movie has some beads of sweat on his forehead and some damp patches under his arms. Sweat dripped into his eyes, stinging them. He stood at the bottom of Cobblestone Hill with his chest heaving. He'd spent the past half an hour sprinting up the hill and then jogging back down. He alternated doing burpees at the top of the hill and doing crunches at the bottom.

He could smell the alcohol leaching out of his pores. After dinner, he'd gone back to the motel. The Jameson bottle was there, and he had listened to his voice messages. Jeanie was still pissed off, and a coworker wanted to know if he was going to play in an upcoming golf tournament. Kelly had looked at the bottle but decided to call Jacques and check in.

"How's it look out there?" Jacques asked after they'd exchanged pleasantries.

"Not bad. Looks like the body's been in the ground for a long time."

"Not gruesome. That's always a bonus. How are the local dicks?"

"I'm working with a lady dick. She's young but seems to know her shit."

"I bet she's thrilled you're out there."

"Not hardly, but she's getting used to me. How's things there?"

"Not bad. Savoy is hoping you'll wrap it up quickly out there. Cases are piling up."

They spoke for a few more minutes, and then Kelly's thirst got the better of him and he ended the call. He had half a glass of Jameson and then another. *It's this place, the bones,* he thought.

By the time he turned off the TV, he felt warm, better about himself, and he barely noticed his tendency to hip check the bureau on his way to the bathroom.

Now it was morning, and he was exercising the toxins out of his system. He was sprinting up the only nearby hill he could find, chased by the ghost of his father. Big Tom, hero of the war that no one talked about. Big Tom, who wanted his son to grow up to be tough, to know how to take care of himself.

Kelly stood at the bottom of the hill, set his feet, and ran as fast and as hard as he could, growing a little more tired each trip up the hill, trying to outrun Big Tom's disapproving ghost. Finally, stomach hurting and legs feeling like JELL-O, he stopped. He wanted to be sick but instead went for a slow jog to cool down.

He jogged out to Jetties Beach. The flat, wide street would be crowded with cars, bikes, and mopeds in the summer but now was wide open. It was occupied by puddles left from the rain, and the parking lot was littered with all types of smashed shellfish. Seagulls were picking through the remains of shellfish they'd dropped from the sky.

He jogged out past a playground—swing sets and a round, metal jungle gym, products of the 1960s—on his right. It wasn't as windy today, but he heard the swing, making its creaking noise in his head, anyway. The sound was living rent-free in Kelly's mind, and it only added to the sense of creepiness that Kelly was feeling about the island offseason.

There was the boarded-up snack bar on his left. He jogged out onto the sand to the water. He looked at the stone jetties that formed the arms to the harbor and briefly contemplated jumping in the water. Then it occurred to him that it was April, and not a particularly warm one at that. Instead, he turned and jogged back to his motel.

Last night he and Harris had agreed to meet at the station and see if there was any news from Doc Redruth or the team at the high school. If there was, they would go there first; if not, then they'd pore over the missing person reports. Kelly was hoping to hear from the doctor. The reports were drudgery, and his neck and back ached at just the thought of another day in a chair bent over his laptop.

He was walking by the office when he spied Laura. He went inside.

"Hi. Do you need anything, Detective?"

"Are you the only person who works here? I never see anyone else."

"Well, we have a girl who comes in to do the rooms right now, and we'll hire a few more for the summer. But I'm here trying to get everything set up for tourist season. You might say I'm kind of chained to the place."

"Why's that?"

"My dad owns the motel. He's getting on in years, so I'm trying to keep it going."

"By yourself?"

"Yep, just me."

"No one to help . . . your husband . . ." Kelly trailed off, fishing for information out of habit.

She held up her ringless left hand.

"I haven't had one of those in years. The last was a lot more trouble than he was worth. Why else would someone my age still be living at home?"

"I'm sorry, I shouldn't pry."

"That's probably an occupational hazard."

"It is."

"Was there something you needed, or were you just trying to find out if I'm single?" She smiled her very nice smile, and Kelly was having trouble seeing her as being single for long.

"Yeah, I'm probably going to be out here for a few days longer than I initially thought. Is that okay?"

"Sure, we don't have anyone else staying here now. It won't start picking up until the end of next month, so you're fine."

"Thanks. Okay, I should go get cleaned up."

"Okay."

Kelly let himself into the room. There were no messages on his phone, and he was happy about that. He would call the boys in a bit before they went to school. He sat on the edge of the bed, watching the news from Boston while he drank his morning protein shake. There was nothing particularly interesting in the news. That was good in Kelly's line of work. No news was good news. He finished his shake and rinsed the shaker in the sink. He took off his shirt, turned on the hot water, and began to shave before stepping into the shower. He washed and then turned the tap from hot to cold and stood under it as long as he could stand. Between that and the PT, the whiskey cleared from his head.

He dressed in MSP casual: sneakers, khaki cargo pants, MSP polo shirt, Smith & Wesson .45 on his right hip, spare magazine and handcuffs in a case on his left. Out of habit he reached into his duffel bag to double-check that his off-duty pistol was still there. He slid his hand between the folded T-shirts and felt the butt of the gun, but it was facing the opposite way he remembered leaving it. He always put the pistol between the shirts on its left side. Now it was on its right side. Had he been messing around with it last night after too much whiskey?

He pulled the holstered pistol out of the bag. The leather retention strap was snapped closed. That was a good sign at least. Then he noticed that the magazine was sticking partially out of the grip. He knew he hadn't done that. He unholstered the pistol, double-checked there was still a round in the chamber, and slapped the magazine home. He reholstered it and put the pistol back in his bag.

Someone had been in his room, searching through his stuff.

He did a quick check of his wallet and spare cash, but nothing was actually missing. *Maybe a nosy chambermaid,* Kelly thought. He briefly considered going back to the office to ask Laura about it, but it probably wasn't worth the time. Nothing was taken, and it was likely just the local girl curious about what he was carrying around with him.

He put on his MSP fleece jacket, locking up behind him, and went out to where Black Beauty was parked. The morning was still chilly, and it took a couple of tries to get Black Beauty to turn over. When it did, he backed out of the spot in front of his room and started on the increasingly familiar trip through town.

Kelly mashed his home number into the phone and held it between his ear and his shoulder. Jeanie answered, sounding flustered. "Hello."

"It's me. Good morning."

"Oh, good morning." Then muffled, "Boys, it's your father. Come here."

"How's it going?"

"They've been fighting over everything from the TV to who gets the first waffle from the toaster."

"Shit. Sorry."

"Your being on travel doesn't help." Her tone was at the low end of recriminatory, and Kelly was grateful for that.

"No, I know. I'm sorry. The last thing I wanted to do was to come out here . . . but the lieutenant . . ." He trailed off. There was no point in explaining it. The damage was done, and like so many small injuries in marriage, it would just be added to the pile of other similar marital paper cuts.

"I know. I know. I just . . . you know, the boys are getting bigger . . . more to handle, with their constant fighting. You're never around anymore. It's hard."

"I hear you, but boys will fight. And I couldn't say no to this one."

"You're out on the island having a good time. I'm stuck trying to referee these two when I'm not at work or home, cooking, cleaning, taking care of everything." The plaintive edge in her voice was climbing.

"Maybe your mom could . . ." Kelly didn't finish the thought, knowing the suggestion wasn't popular. His mother-in-law was sweet, but she tended to point out to Jeanie how much harder she had it in her day, also working as a nurse with a trooper husband. The schedule was tougher for troopers then. They lived at the barracks when they were on duty, not at home. She never complained, and she managed to keep the house neat and orderly. There were never dishes left in the sink. Raise the kids, have meals on the table on time, make sure everyone is bathed without fuss.

Kelly was certain that his mother-in-law had come up with some revisionist-history version of her early marriage and child-rearing years. His father-in-law had spent a lot of hours on the road and doing details. Jeanie's mother worked, and there were plenty of dishes in the sink for a day or two. Jeanie's mom just had to one-up her whenever Jeanie started to complain about how tough it was being married to Kelly.

"Great . . . just what I need," Jeanie said over the line. "I'm not doing a good enough job; I have to bring Her Royal Highness in to remind me. Thanks, Tommy."

"Jeanie, you know that's not what I meant."

"Sure, sure, easy for you out there with the rich and famous."

"Jeanie, it's cold as fuck and rainy. I spent my first day here standing in a mud puddle up to my ankles and yesterday hunched over a computer all day. There's nothing glamorous about being out here. It might be nice in the summer, but right now this place is dark, there isn't much open. The whole place feels creepy, like something from a scary movie." Which was true. He didn't bring up the bones or the dead kid they'd eventually be linked to. There were parts of the job you didn't bring home.

"The boys are here." She sounded somewhat mollified hearing that he was mostly miserable. The boys came in excited, their chattering marked by bursts of verbs and occasional nouns, complaining about each other. It was worth every second of it to hear them, especially when they ended by telling him they loved him. He told them to have a good day at school and that he loved them very much too. Then the hollow feeling was back when he realized he was talking to the dead air.

He walked through the front doors of the police station, and the clerk behind thick glass buzzed him into the hallway leading to the detective bureau. Kelly, laptop case in one hand, hot cup of coffee that he had picked up on the way in the other, managed to awkwardly pull the door open. He wasn't surprised to see Harris at her desk, a yellow number two pencil clenched the long way in her teeth. She looked up at him, taking the pencil from between her teeth, and said, "Nice of you to join us, Detective."

Kelly grunted at her and went to the cubicle he'd used yesterday. He took his laptop out and turned it on. He sipped his coffee while waiting for it to connect to the Wi-Fi. In the next cubicle, there was a pastry box imprinted with the words NANTUCKET BAKERY. He smelled what was inside.

"Hey, Kelly, wanna doughnut? They were made fresh a few hours ago . . . they're good." Harris said it almost tauntingly. They smelled good. Very good.

"No thanks . . . I don't like perpetrating the stereotype about doughnut-eating cops. You've already pointed out I'm a walking cliché. Anything new from the doc or the team at the gym?"

"No, I thought we'd give him a call in a while. He was likely up late. The team at the gym is almost done sifting, and then they'll send the rest of the stuff over to the hospital."

"Okay, back to the files then," he said without enthusiasm.

Unlike on TV, most detective work was boring—taking statements, going through camera footage, conducting interviews, doing the paperwork. He hunched over his laptop and started to go back through the missing person results left over from the day before. He clicked on files, read the particulars, and then either saved or discarded them. It was drudgery, but Kelly waded through.

They worked for a few hours. Kelly's sour stomach from the whiskey had eased up a bit. He was just starting to think about giving in and having a doughnut when Harris looked up and over at him.

"Hey, Kelly?"

"Hey what?"

"Let's get out of here for a bit. Grab a coffee and head over to the hospital."

"Sure, sounds like a plan."

They grabbed their jackets and headed out to the parking lot to Harris's car. They drove over to the Green's to get their coffee. They compared notes on their progress so far. Kelly had some possible missing kids but not many. Harris had nothing.

"Maybe the kid wasn't reported missing?" She looked over at him.

"It's possible," he said doubtfully.

"What if it was someone who came in on a yacht? You know, one of the big ones."

"What, like the kid was a stowaway?" Kelly asked.

"Not so much that, but what if the yacht was from another country or . . ." She trailed off.

"Or what?"

"What if it was a kid who was abducted or sold by his parents . . . you know, crackheads."

"Jesus."

"What if it is a kid like that . . . say something happens. The kid gets sick or killed or something and the assholes on the yacht bury him out where we found him?"

"Wouldn't it be easier to just dump the body at sea? Go out deep off the continental shelf . . . some chain and weight of some sort . . . an anchor, maybe, and just dump him overboard?"

"That would be easier . . . shit . . . it's just a theory."

"It's as good as any we have. This is frustrating work. Painstaking."

"I know. I guess I'm just impatient."

"No, you're a cop." He put extra emphasis on the words. "That means you're a type A personality, always trying to resolve things, find the answer. A case like this . . . it's frustrating."

"Thanks, Kelly."

"And you're impatient."

"Asshole." She smiled at him as she said it.

"Come on, let's get our drinks."

The smell of freshly brewed coffee was in the air. There were a few customers ahead of them: a couple of guys who were carpenters on their coffee break talking about the Red Sox' prospects this year; a woman who—according to the name tag pinned to her blouse—worked at the bank nearby, checking her phone impatiently; and a couple in their sixties who seemed to be in no rush to do anything. Harris and Kelly waited their turn and then got their coffee. Kelly paid, and they made their way back to the car.

Harris navigated what little late-morning traffic there was, and they pulled into the hospital parking lot five minutes later. There were few cars, and the sun was punching through the clouds. In the distance Kelly could hear seagulls that were dancing and riding on the thermals.

They made their way inside, past the same security guard and nurse at the desk. They both nodded to Harris, and they exchanged hellos. Then down the same institutional-green stairwell and hallway. Doc Redruth was in the morgue, bent over a stainless-steel table that looked like the ones that had been in many of the kitchens that Kelly had worked in as a student.

"Hey, Doc," Harris said as they walked in.

"Hey, Jo. Morning, Detective Kelly."

"Good morning, Doctor." Kelly was the type of person who used people's titles. Today the doctor was dressed in work boots, khaki pants, and a flannel shirt under his white lab coat. He wore the same glasses, and Kelly wondered if he always dressed like an off-duty lumberjack.

"Well, Doc, do you have anything?" Harris asked.

"Whoever the boy was, he had a tough life." The doctor gestured toward one of the metal drawers, presumably the one containing the bones. "He was abused. Probably died from blunt force trauma. He was hit in the head with something that was slightly rounded, judging by the indentation."

"Like a bat?" Jo asked.

"Possibly, or a fish billy."

"A fish billy?" Kelly asked.

"A small wooden club, like the top of a baseball bat. When anglers get a fish in the boat but don't want to fight it, they hit it with a fish billy," Redruth explained. "His ribs had been broken and healed, likely without treatment. A couple of his fingers were broken too. Possibly defensive in nature," Redruth continued.

"Oh," Harris said slowly. Kelly clenched his jaw.

"His bone mass would indicate that he was malnourished, and I think I told you yesterday that his teeth had several untreated cavities."

"Most abusive parents tend not to take their kids to the doctor or dentist . . . no sense having someone see evidence of their abuse." Kelly heard himself speaking before he even realized he'd unclenched his jaw. His stomach was sour again, but this time not from last night's whiskey.

"Unfortunately, you're right, Detective. Due to the condition of the remains, it's hard to tell for certain, but I suspect that your victim suffered long-term physical abuse."

"There's no way that any of the broken bones and other stuff could have been caused, say, as the result of a child abduction? A sicko? That type of thing?" Harris asked.

"There's always a possibility. It is possible that his abuser and his killer were two different people. But that's for you two to figure out. I'm only here to present you with my findings.

"As I said, the remains aren't in the best shape. We don't have any other forensic evidence—skin, stomach contents, etcetera—which would tell us a lot more. All I can tell you is that he has injuries consistent with child abuse, and that based on the damage to his skull, he was most likely killed by blunt force trauma. Beyond having a time machine, there's no way to tell much more."

"Great. Thank you," Kelly said.

"Detective, please know we do have some material from the grave site. Some cloth that's badly damaged, a couple of things that are dirt encrusted and need to be carefully examined to see if there's anything to them. Otherwise, we just don't have much to go on."

"Any idea how long the rest of the stuff from the grave site will take to process?" Harris asked.

"That depends on the state crime lab and whether you can get your boss to rush it. We'll send it off by courier on the first flight to Hyannis as soon as it's ready to go. The DNA test should come back quickly, and that should help with the ID."

"Thank you. I will call my boss and see what he can do."

The detectives made their way out into the chilly, bright day. Kelly had to resist the urge to gulp in the clean-smelling air outside. By the time they reached Harris's car, the smell of formaldehyde no longer threatened to overwhelm him. There was nothing he could do about the bitter taste in his mouth from the information that the doc had shared.

He leaned against Harris's car. She got in on her side and then after a minute, realizing he hadn't joined her, got out again. He desperately wanted a drink of whiskey to wash away the taste of death. He was breathing deeply, fighting the rising bile in his throat.

"Kelly, you okay?" Harris said as she approached him.

"Yeah, I . . . the cases with kids . . . child abuse, molestation, abductions, murder, stuff like that . . . they're just hard for me to take. I've seen too many of them over the years. It got worse when I had kids of my own. You know, before that, I could keep it together better."

"I know what you mean. Hang in there. We'll get this guy."

"No, that's the fucked-up part. We probably won't. We don't have a lot to work with. These cases are hard enough with actual evidence. Also, nothing against the doc, but how much experience does he have with this sort of thing?"

"Forensics?"

"Yeah."

"I don't know. I know that he was an ER doctor in Providence, Rhode Island, during the crack years. He saw a lot of gunshot victims, a lot of stabbings. He's no small-town doctor."

"Okay, well that's something, I guess."

"Cheer up, Kelly."

"I just . . . this case is frustrating, and I don't see how we can solve it."

"Yeah, well, you've never worked with me before." She smiled and pushed a strand of hair behind her ear. "Come on, let's get back to work."

"Sure. My laptop is probably feeling neglected." He took a deep breath and got into the car. They rode in silence, past the Boys & Girls Club on one side and the high school sports fields on the other, then down past the local Stop & Shop, by the fire department, and back out of town.

"Jo, how many likely hits have you got so far from your search?"

"None that fit our parameters. You?"

"A few but not many."

"Okay. Let's keep at it. I figure we'll finish up tonight, maybe tomorrow, and hit the old paper files tomorrow."

"Sure, that should work." He watched her chewing her bottom lip. Kelly had to imagine that if Harris were lonely, it was more by choice than lack of opportunity.

"Kelly."

"Yeah."

"Maybe we should look at child abuse reports too."

"I was wondering about that. Are you thinking just the local ones, because . . ." He trailed off, not wanting to say what they both knew. Child abuse was local, part of every community and chronically underreported. He also wondered how many child abuse reports were filed on Nantucket during the time frame they were looking at.

"I know it's a long shot that might not solve the kid's murder, but we might be able to use it to ID him. Bring some closure to the family."

"It's worth a shot. Definitely. Who knows, maybe we'll be able to get lucky with the DNA. Maybe there's a familial profile out there somewhere. Something like that."

"You sound skeptical," she said.

"No, it isn't that. I think it's as good an idea as any."

"What then?"

"Child abuse often goes unreported now. I'm wondering how many reports there'd be from 1977 to 1991?"

"Who knows."

"It's just that a lot of departments didn't report on stuff like child abuse or domestics unless they were really bad. Maybe more so in small towns with small departments."

"Why?"

"A lot of that stuff was considered a 'family issue,' you know, private. Coming home and belting the wife was seen as a private matter between spouses. Also, the concept of 'spare the rod, spoil the child' was a lot more common. Back in the seventies, eighties, time-out wasn't a big thing."

"Are you saying that they'd have squashed reports of it?" She was offended at the implication that her department, even in the past, might do the wrong thing.

"Nope. Society was different then. It was acceptable . . . no, it was *expected* that parents would use corporal punishment. When I was a kid, a lot of parents spanked or hit their children. Some of my friends' dads were known for using a belt to punish their kids."

"Did your dad?"

"Big Tom . . ." He chuckled at the thought. "No. You'd think he did. Former marine, Vietnam vet, but no, Big Tom wasn't the type to hit. His words, his tone . . . that was enough. If I screwed up, he made me feel lower than dirt." He winced at the poor choice of phrase given why he was on the island to begin with. "Honestly, hitting would have been preferable; the sting wouldn't have lasted as long. Things were just different then, society was different."

"Or society just turned a blind eye more often."

"That too. I can remember one or two of my friends' moms who walked around moving stiffly or had a black eye hiding under their makeup. As a kid, I didn't know what was up."

"Jesus."

"You probably did too."

"No. I mean, I don't think so."

"Sure, maybe the week after the Super Bowl, you know, after a night of drinking, someone's team lost. Maybe money was lost too. Or during the winter when people got stuck inside for too long together. Kids aren't trained cops. They don't know a domestic violence victim when they see one."

"Okay, true."

"That's why I don't think there'll be much in the reports."

Harris nodded and they drove in silence for a bit, the police radio a constant in the background that they both ignored. That was one of the secrets of being a cop, the ability to have the radio on constantly, ignoring it until you were called. The radio was softly playing a pop music station from Cape Cod. It was some song that Kelly didn't recognize. Kelly was staring at the scenery slowly sliding by when Harris spoke again.

"There might not be police reports, but what about social workers, or . . . or what about the school nurse?"

"Probably retired by now."

"Probably, but worth a shot if you're right and there's nothing in the files."

"Definitely worth a shot."

"Let's keep wading through the missing person files, and we'll fold abuse reports in if we can find any."

"Works for me."

They reached the police department and went inside to their respective cubicles. Kelly sent a short message outlining his trip to the hospital and visit with Doc Redruth. He also asked if, when the time came, Savoy could see if the state crime lab could expedite their end of things. Kelly hit the send button, knowing that it probably wouldn't help much.

He started to go through the remaining missing person reports and flagged a few for further follow-up. The problem was that there just wasn't much that matched their criteria. They had to go through each report, and it ate up a lot of time. Ultimately, though, there just weren't a lot of matches with their collection of small, abused, malnourished bones.

Fruitless as it was for their investigation, it was also grim work, going through report after report of missing children, each one a recorded history of anguished parents and unimaginable loss. The only thing that was worse for Kelly to read as a parent were the reports that indicated that the parents just didn't give a shit. Big Tom Kelly and Mary hadn't been perfect parents, as if there were such a thing, but they'd been there, involved and caring.

Mom always made sure to greet him at the door when the school bus dropped him off. His dad was there to teach him how to throw a spiral or to play catch in the backyard. Kelly only realized how lucky he had been when he grew up and became a trooper and started to see the results of bad parenting or no parenting. Still, it wasn't all perfect. His parents argued at night when they thought he was sleeping. He never heard everything they were saying, just that their voices were raised. Sometimes he thought it was about money. Other times he got the feeling they were arguing about him. On very rare occasions, he got the sense that it was about Big Tom's drinking and Vietnam, or more likely the fact that Big Tom didn't talk about Vietnam. He'd just get moodier and moodier and drink more.

His own sons were the balm that soothed him after an awful night on the road or dealing with another homicide scene. After coming home from a bad tour, he'd hug the boys if they were still awake and instantly feel better. If they were still asleep, he would content himself by looking at them as they slept. It didn't matter how bad the tour had been; hugging them made it all seem to go away for a few moments. That was priceless.

Kelly dragged his mind back to the matter at hand. He spent the next several hours going through entries in the database, stopping now and again to get mediocre coffee from the pot or to use the bathroom. The only other thing that broke up the monotony was a couple of passive-aggressive text messages from Jeanie. Lunch arrived in the form of a bottle of water, a couple of tuna salad sandwiches on soggy white bread, and a small bag of potato chips. Somewhere around five, when his eyes were starting to itch, Harris turned to him. They decided to call it a night, and Harris turned off her computer and got up.

"I take it you can fend for yourself for dinner?"

"I am a grown man. I'll be fine."

"Okay. Cool. I'll see you tomorrow."

"Cool. I'm almost done with these. Why don't I stick at it for another hour, and then we can tackle the old files together tomorrow?"

"Sure, that works. Okay, gotta run . . . See ya tomorrow." Harris left.

Kelly stood up and stretched. He went over to the window and looked out at the sky, which was still blue, but the sun was making its way down slowly. It would be getting dark in an hour or so. Kelly stretched again and went back to his laptop. After five, the police station was a very quiet place. He imagined that somewhere in the building there was someone taking and dispatching calls for service. But here in the detective bureau with Harris and her portable radio gone, it was quiet except for the hum of the fluorescent lights.

He hadn't been wholly accurate when he'd told Harris it would be another hour. It was closer to two when he stood up from his laptop and closed the lid. The sky outside had gone from blue to the india ink of night. The parking lot was lit by floodlights, beyond which were deep shadows when he went out to Black Beauty. Kelly walked the short walk across the parking lot, scanning in front of him. Off in the distance he heard a dog barking repeatedly. When he went to unlock Black Beauty, he realized that he'd been unconsciously clutching the butt of his holstered pistol, ready to draw.

This case . . . this island's getting to your head, he thought.

He got in the car and his thoughts turned back to food. In their travels, Kelly remembered they passed a supermarket . . . Stop & Shop. More importantly, there was a liquor store next door in the same plaza. He could get something for dinner and some more Jameson. After all, he couldn't afford to eat out nightly in a place this expensive. His per diem went only so far.

It was a short drive to the small commercial plaza with the supermarket. He parked between the supermarket and the liquor store. Kelly went to the liquor store first and tried not to wince at the price of Jameson. Nantucket prices were comparable to high-end Irish whiskey on the mainland. Kelly used his debit card, internally dreading the thought of the inevitable conversation with Jeanie. He took his whiskey and the receipt and put the bottle on the seat of Black Beauty. Locking the car again, he went into the grocery store to see what there was for dinner.

The grocery store was mostly empty, and Kelly prowled up and down the aisles, trying to find something healthy to eat. He needed a break from grilled chicken Caesar wraps. Finally, under the unflattering fluorescent lights, he settled on premade salad in a plastic box, a bag of salted cashews, and a couple of foil packets of tuna.

Kelly walked down the aisles, plastic grocery basket banging into his leg, and as he turned the corner from one aisle to the next, he almost crashed into the woman from the motel: Laura.

"Oh, sorry," he said, feeling a slight flush in his cheeks.

"Oh, Detective Kelly. No problem."

"My head was in the clouds."

"No doubt thinking about the case."

"Exactly."

"How's it going?"

"Um, you know, about what you'd expect." One of his favorite nonanswer answers.

"I'm sure you're working very hard. You look tired." Her eyes twinkled as she spoke. She was a little older than he was and pretty, something Kelly found himself noticing again. Curly blond hair, pale-blue eyes, and a slim build that hinted at a lot of time spent in the gym or doing outdoor activities.

"Thanks, it's part of the job." He defaulted to his stock of clichés. "Nothing a good night's rest won't cure."

"I bet a home-cooked meal and sympathetic ear could do wonders for your outlook." She smiled at him in a way that made him think he was being invited for a lot more than a home-cooked meal. She brushed her curls away from her forehead.

"I really appreciate the offer, but I'm going to have to take a rain check."

"Disappointing, but the offer stands if you change your mind."

"Thanks. I appreciate it."

"You know where to find me."

With his dinner in a plastic bag, he stepped out into the parking lot. He crossed the darkened parking lot, eyes scanning from pool of light to pool of light, and then silently reminded himself he was on Nantucket, not in Wormtown. He got in and drove through the empty stillness of town to the Oceanview Motel. The island had an almost deserted, horror movie feel to it.

He noticed that there were occasional cars on the road, but he didn't see any pedestrians or bikes. But this was April, and the night had turned chilly. By June the island would be overrun with tourists, bikers and giant SUVs all crowding the streets. He preferred it like it was now, without all the traffic and people crowding the sidewalks. When he turned into the parking lot of the Oceanview, he had started to feel that the island was a lonely place in the offseason.

His headlights splashed on the door to his room as he pulled up. Even though the parking lot was well lit, it felt dark and sinister. The cold reached deep into his bones when he got out of his car. The wind had picked up and cut through his fleece jacket. He got his dinner, whiskey, and laptop case from the car, moving with slightly clumsier fingers than April weather should have brought. Kelly awkwardly juggled the bags, fit the key in the lock, and unlocked the door.

He dropped the food and whiskey on the table and slid the laptop case off his shoulder onto one of the chairs. He grabbed the ice bucket, locked the door behind him, and went to the office for ice from the ice machine. He thought that the chances of anyone sneaking in to steal his laptop would be low, but old habits died hard, and it would be just his luck to have his laptop or off-duty piece stolen.

The office was unlocked but empty. It was almost 8:00 p.m., and there was a note to call a cell number if someone needed assistance. He filled the ice bucket and went back outside into the chilly night. It was a short walk, but Kelly had the irrational feeling that he was being watched. When he got to his room, he realized that his hand was resting on—no, gripping—the butt of his holstered service pistol. He unlocked the door and went in out of the dark, thankful for the warmth and light of the motel room.

He knew it was silly, him a grown man, a detective in the State Police at that, getting spooked about the dark. He locked the door behind him and drew the curtains, more to keep the night out than to prevent anyone from looking in. Still feeling jumpy, his hand on the butt of his gun, he checked the closet and the bathroom. Nothing.

He turned on the TV as much to fill the silence as to be entertained. He took his holster off and put it, gun and all, on the table, then poured himself a healthy belt of whiskey on the rocks. His first sip was big, and he took it with all the gratitude that someone in the desert would have drinking water. Kelly felt the warmth from the whiskey spread through him. He wanted to call the boys, and however good it was to hear their voices, that meant a conversation with Jeanie first. That thought was enough to make Kelly take another large sip of whiskey.

He turned the TV down and took out his phone. He had one more large sip while he dialed. Jeanie answered and, as he'd predicted, she was in a foul mood. He listened to her litany of criticisms and took another pull on the glass of whiskey. He was tipsy when the boys came on the phone and with excited voices told him about their day. Sports and school figured heavily, followed by questions about the case he was on. They finished up by asking when he'd be home. By the time he answered as best as he could, Jeanie came on again. "I have to get the boys ready for bed." And then she hung up.

Kelly plugged the phone into the charger, drank some more whiskey, and turned his attention to the plastic salad container. He tore off the plastic strip in the front and then lifted the hinged lid. Inside was a slightly wilted collection of lettuces, shredded carrots, red peppers, pitted black olives, and feta cheese. He threw away the small plastic bag of fossilized-looking croutons. He poured the contents of the dressing packet that alleged to be Greek salad dressing on top of the salad. Kelly was certain it was just oil and vinegar with some spices mixed in. He opened the pouches of tuna and dumped them onto the vegetables. He tossed it all together by closing the lid and shaking the box vigorously.

He turned the TV to the sports channel and ate mechanically. Outside, the wind had picked up, and he sensed rather than felt the cold outside his motel room. When he finished the meal, he added more ice and whiskey to his glass and drank a quarter of it in one go.

He got up and moved to the bed, putting his holstered duty gun on the little bedside table. He sat propped up on pillows against the headboard, drinking whiskey, munching on salted cashews and channel surfing. His mind inadvertently wandered to the collection of bones; in his mind, they were starting to take on a personality. A malnourished, abused kid, buried in secret in the middle of nowhere on the island decades ago. A tragic end to what was likely a sad, unfair life. What little he knew of the kid's life was so different from his very own family life. Was it all just down to the luck of the draw, the birth lottery? Some kids get shitty abusive parents and others get loving ones?

After one last trip to the bathroom on clumsy legs, he climbed into the empty bed. Kelly unholstered his pistol and placed it back on the bedside table, grip toward him, muzzle facing the door. Then he turned off the light and tried not to think of the collection of small bones that had recently invaded most of his waking thoughts. The wind rattled against the motel room, and it struck Kelly that the island, while beautiful in the summer—all bikinis, beautiful people, Coppertone, and partying—was probably a much different place in the fall and winter. *Come for the summer fun and stay for the Gothic horror,* he thought. With the darkness, the wind, and the frequent rain, it felt like a sinister place.

Early December 1981

Albie was so upset, he missed his bus stop. He looked up when another kid said, "Hey, dummy, you missed your stop."

Albie got up, eyes blurred and stung by his tears. It seemed like the whole bus was laughing at him, calling him "Al-pee." He got off the bus with a couple of other kids and realized he hadn't missed his stop, but he had gotten off one before it. His house was down the street, around the bend.

His face was flushed with anger. He wasn't dumb. He wasn't a sissy. They had called him "Al-pee," but he hadn't peed himself. It was so stinking unfair. He balled his small, chubby fists in frustration. He wished he was bigger. He'd fight them. But Albie knew he wasn't a fighter. He wasn't very brave. If he was, he'd show them.

It was in that moment of anger and frustration that Albie had a flash of inspiration. He turned away from his house and started making his way up the hill to the top of Orange Street. None of the kids said anything. In fact, no one noticed. It seemed like that happened to Albie a lot. He walked up the hill as fast as his chubby legs could carry him. He didn't run. He thought that might make people notice.

When he got to Cobblestone Alley, he turned right, walking downhill away from Orange Street. Cobblestone Alley was flanked by the largest houses and lots of bushes. It gave the whole thing a dark, secretive feel. The cobblestones were wet, and he slipped but caught himself. When he got to the stone steps that had been there since the Revolutionary War, he didn't go down them. Instead, he stepped off the cobblestones and went around the fence that hemmed in the yard of the house to his immediate left. He was instantly in a small, wooded area and was out of sight.

He was on what local kids had called "the Indian trail" from time immemorial. Had he stepped to the right, he could have followed the trail on the underside of the old ridgeline of the hill that had been so attractive to sea captains when they built their houses on Orange Street back when there had been a whaling fleet. Every year in school since kindergarten they had been taught about the island's rich whaling history. Had Albie taken that right, he could have followed the trail, just out of view from the old, fancy houses, to within two streets of his house. If he had done that . . .

Instead, he made his way into the small copse of trees that provided so much shade to the house that abutted Cobblestone Alley, through the winter-bared bushes, angling downhill, slipping here and there in the mud until he found an old stump to sit on. He knew that he couldn't be seen by the house behind him, and there were too many trees for him to be seen by the house on the other side of the alley.

Albie decided he'd show them. He'd show the kids from school, that stupid Louie Delvecchio and the other kids. He'd show his dad, who never let him do anything. He'd show his teachers, who didn't stick up for him when the other kids were calling him "Al-pee." He was going to stay here on his stump until it got dark.

He knew that everyone was worried about the monster. They would all think the monster got him, and then they'd be sorry that they were mean to him. He could picture his mom and dad at home, worried. Maybe that policeman too. Maybe they'd be asking Louie questions like that policeman had asked him. That'd show Louie.

He sat playing games with a couple of rocks and twigs. He thought about his favorite TV shows. He made up stories to tell himself. Then, just before dark—because Albie didn't like the idea of being outside after dark— he'd go home. He'd walk in the back door to the kitchen and say something cool like, "Hey, guys, what's all the fuss about?"

He could see his mom and dad hugging him. The policeman would wipe his brow with a white handkerchief and say, "Boy, Albie, we're glad you're home. You must have been very brave."

Louie would give him a high five and say, "Albie, you can be on my team anytime."

That was the plan. It was a good plan too. Couldn't fail. To further prove his point, when he left his hiding spot a couple of hours later, he stepped out onto the granite steps and saw a shiny quarter. He picked it up and put it in one of the two pockets that were on either side of the zipper of his sweatshirt. Albie started to go uphill toward Orange Street but instead thought better of it and went down the steps to the cobblestones leading to Union Street.

It was darker than Albie realized, and he started to run. He was going downhill, down wet cobblestones. He saw lights on the street ahead of him as he neared the bottom of Cobblestone Alley. He skidded to a stop, or at least he tried to, but he was going too fast, and he slid, falling onto the brick sidewalk of Union Street. He landed hard, his palms stinging and his knees hurting.

The tears started immediately. He was wet, and his jacket was ripped. Mommy would be mad about that. He stood up, crying in sobbing hitches of his chest, snot coming out of his nose.

"Hey, little man," someone said. Albie looked up. There was a man standing next to the open door of his car.

"Hey," Albie said.

"You look like you could use a ride home."

"I'm not supposed to talk to strangers. Mom and Dad said so."

"Oh, it's okay. I'm a policeman. You can talk to me."

"Where's your uniform?" Albie watched a lot of TV shows.

"I'm an undercover detective. See, here's my badge." He held a shiny badge out for Albie to see.

"Oh." Albie's hand hurt.

"Come on, little man, let's run you home. It isn't safe out here."

"Sure, I guess."

"Get in." The policeman indicated that Albie should get in on his side and slide across the bench seat. Albie got in and slid over, and then the policeman got in. He put the car in gear. Albie noticed his cool hula dancer with the big bobbly head swaying on the dashboard. The policeman leaned across Albie, locking the door.

"Can't be too careful, little man. Now, let's get you home." The man took his next right down by the telephone company and started heading back toward Albie's house by way of Washington Street.

"Hey, little man?"

Before Albie could respond, his vision erupted into a bright shower of sparks and stars as he felt a sharp pain in the side of his head. Then nothing but blackness.

CHAPTER 7

Kelly woke up feeling a little rough but forced himself to go for a long run. He went to the bathroom and then pulled on workout clothes and sneakers, all of which were starting to smell and feel like they needed a wash in something better than a motel sink. Kelly's run took him away from town and toward Cobblestone Hill. He enjoyed moving through the quiet streets on the outskirts of town. A faint fog was still lying in the low spots on the ground, but it would be completely gone by the time the sun climbed a little higher. He ran past the State Police barracks and wondered if he could use the washer and dryer there. What would Bruce Green say?

He ran up Gardner Street and took a left on Main Street at the Civil War monument. Traffic was light, and he felt like he had the island to himself. He also felt like he was being watched. That the good residents, steaming coffee cup in hand, were standing in their front rooms, looking out the window as he ran by. He turned right onto Pleasant Street and ran past a large house and a mansion with a ten-foot brick wall. He had to be careful, because the pavement was uneven from the roots of trees that were planted before America was a country.

He ran by the high school, where Tyvek-clad cops and medical investigators would soon be sifting through dirt and packaging it up for the crime lab. Kelly turned around at the high school, then ran by the hospital and up to the Old Mill. The colonial-era windmill had its sails in and wasn't moving, but it was still an impressive sight. He then followed the road back down to Pleasant Street and doubled back on his route to the Oceanview Motel. No matter how he had felt about the island last night, he had to admit it was scenic as hell.

Upon his return to the motel, he walked past the office right as Laura strode out and leaned against the doorframe. "Detective, morning. Would you like a cup of coffee? I just put on a fresh pot."

"Sure, I'd love one." He didn't really want coffee right after a run, but he felt bad about turning her down in the supermarket.

"Come on in then."

He followed her into the office. She disappeared behind the counter.

"How do you take it?" she called out.

"Black, please."

Laura came back holding two steaming ceramic mugs with the motel's logo on them. She handed him one.

"Thanks."

"I'm sorry if I came on a little strong in the supermarket."

"No need. I was flattered, but you know . . ." He held up his left hand with the wedding band.

"Yes, of course. The nice guys are always taken."

"I find it hard to believe you have trouble meeting men."

"Meeting them is one thing. Meeting decent ones, another thing altogether." Her trademark smile was paler, a bit brittle now.

"Small town probably doesn't help."

"No, it doesn't. This place feels so isolated at times."

"You could move."

"I did once. I lived in Boston for years. Then my mother died, and my father needed help with the business. Now I'm here, taking care of my father, and sometimes it feels like I'll never be anywhere else. Just trapped here on this island with my memories and the ghosts."

"There's no one else to help?"

"No, I'm . . . I'm basically all he has. He's older now and has dementia. He needs me, and I'm stuck here for as long as he's . . . as long as he's alive. Have you ever had to care for an ailing parent?"

"No, I haven't."

"Well, it's all-consuming. You wake in the morning wondering what they're going to need today? Or what will go wrong today? You spend your days putting out fires, and then you go to bed thinking about them."

"He's lucky to have you."

"Thanks."

"I should get cleaned up and head to work. Thanks for the coffee."

"Sure, anytime," she said, looking at him in a way that gave him some insight to the weight she bore on her shoulders.

The thought of the poor kid's parents didn't go away with his protein shake breakfast or in the shower. His morning call to Jeanie and the boys offered some respite. Jeanie was in a rare good mood. She went so far as to tell him she missed him and, after a moment's pause, that she loved him. The boys were, of course, the balm to his unpleasant thoughts. He hung up feeling pretty good and wondered how long it would last.

He packed his dirty laundry in the grocery bags from last night's dinner, and then he pulled on his fleece jacket and loaded his laptop and dirty laundry into Black Beauty. He drove over to the local State Police barracks to see if Bruce Green was around and, more importantly, if he could do his laundry.

Green's State Police SUV was in the driveway. Kelly parked next to it and got out. Green opened the side door shortly after Kelly knocked. He frowned slightly at the two plastic shopping bags in Kelly's hand. They smelled like a high school locker room.

"Not a social visit then?"

"No, I was hoping to borrow a cup of laundry." Kelly smiled at the weak joke.

"C'mon in. I'll spot you a cup of coffee too."

"Thanks. I appreciate it."

"No problem. Wouldn't do to have a State Police detective's skivvies on view for everyone to see at the Laundromat."

"On this island, I probably couldn't afford the Laundromat."

"Naw . . . you're a rich State Police dick," he said, gently mocking Kelly.

Kelly laughed good-naturedly and followed Green through the kitchen, down a hall to a utility room where the washer and dryer were. They weren't the fancy front-loading types that Jeanie had insisted on having at home. Something led Kelly to believe that the people in charge of expenses weren't going to spring for high-end appliances. Also, they didn't have to face Jeanie's wrath. Kelly loaded his smelly clothes into the washer, added powdered detergent, and set the works in motion.

"How's the case going?" Green asked.

"Slow. And to be honest, frustrating."

"How so? Cup of coffee?" Green had already poured some into a chipped mug that advertised a restaurant called the Dory.

"Thanks." Kelly took a sip. "We have a collection of kid's bones that are decades old. They show signs of physical abuse. We don't have much to go on forensically. Jo Harris and I have spent days combing through missing person hits in from NCIC and state and local records."

"Anything leap out?"

"The usual combination of everything and nothing. We've gone through all the digital missing person reports. We came up with a list, but none of it looks good. Jo's gonna go through the old print ones, but they lost a bunch to water damage years ago."

"So what's next?"

"I will help her with what's left of the print records when I wrap up my searches. Doc Redruth is ready to send the physical evidence to the state crime lab. After that, Jo thinks we should interview retired social workers and school nurses on the island."

"That seems reasonable. Jo's a good detective." Green didn't add the unspoken admonishment that Kelly should trust Harris's judgment.

"I don't doubt that . . ." Kelly trailed off.

"Then what is it?"

"The fact is that this kid was buried for years. That somewhere out there are parents who've been missing their kid for decades, and I can't even ID him. There should be something, some indicator of who he was."

"DNA?"

"Waiting for results. That's only any good if there are family members in the system. We might not be able to ID this kid."

"You will. It takes time, patience."

"But then if we do ID the kid, if his parents are still alive, I'll have to tell them their kid is dead. This kid suffered a lot. That isn't something I want to tell the parents. On the other hand, they might've been involved. Doc says the kid was malnourished and showed signs of abuse."

"You don't have to tell them much, and when the time comes, you'll know what to say. This isn't your first rodeo."

"Thanks. This one's a little close to home."

"I get it. Listen, go link up with Jo. I'll throw your stuff in the dryer."

"You sure you don't mind?"

"Naw, it'd be a privilege for a lowly trooper like me to handle a detective's laundry," Green said.

"Thanks, I appreciate it."

"No problem."

Kelly went out to Black Beauty and started on his way to the police station. His phone buzzed. He fished it out and looked at the text with one hand on the wheel and one eye on the road. It was a message from Harris telling him to pick up doughnuts and she'd get them coffee. Kelly was starting to wonder if Harris was turning into his work wife. What would Jacques say? Kelly didn't think he was the jealous type.

After getting a dozen assorted doughnuts from the Nantucket Bakery, he drove down Orange Street on his way to the police station. The houses were all period pieces from the eighteenth and nineteenth centuries, or at least built and painted to look like they were. There was no such thing as modern or avant-garde architecture on Nantucket.

There were lots of high privet hedges and quaint buildings. Kelly was reminded of a trip to Disneyland he took a few years ago with the family.

The cars around him were new Fords, Toyotas, or Subarus, contrasting with cars that were at least ten years or older, all universally battered and rusted. It seemed like there was no middle ground. Either cars were new and nice, or they were older and weathered. Nantucket's salt air didn't favor any make or model, no matter how luxurious it once was.

A few minutes later, Kelly walked into the office.

Harris looked up from her computer. "Hiya," she said.

"Hi, how's it going?"

"You brought the doughnuts?"

He held up the box. "Yep. You got the coffee?"

"Right there." She pointed to two paper cups with cardboard sleeves and recycled plastic lids, from which small wisps of steam were escaping.

"You mentioned going through the old files today?" Kelly half asked.

"Yes, they aren't in the best shape. Some stuff was in a storage locker for a while. We noticed damage to a lot of the older files when we were getting ready to move to the new station. There was a leak during one of the big storms."

"Where are the files now?"

"The ones that we could salvage are in the basement."

"Sounds like fun."

"Sure, if you like transplanted mildew and cobwebs."

They spent a few minutes doing things like checking emails and, in Harris's case, eating two doughnuts. Kelly answered a few emails from the Bristol County DA about an upcoming case and a couple from his boss. Jacques had sent him a message inviting him to a function at his church, which he did regularly; Kelly just as regularly politely declined. Jacques was a true believer and felt that Kelly could benefit from some time in God's house. Kelly was afraid the roof would fall in on him if he went.

He quickly composed a mass email in Word, and then he cut and pasted it into messages to the few departments with missing children that might be a match for their collection of bones. He copied Harris on them and sent them out.

They went down two flights of stairs to the basement. The basement of the police station was well lit and clean. Harris pointed out things like the gym and the DNA evidence drying area. She opened a door to a room that contained a series of metal shelves.

"This is where we store the older files." Most of the shelves were full of cardboard boxes.

"You must be a busy department," he said, gesturing to all the boxes.

"Oh, no . . . these aren't all police files. The town uses this to store their overflow of records from town hall. Our files are back here in the corner."

She led Kelly over to a couple of dozen cardboard boxes. He wondered if they were moldy and how good the ventilation was in the basement. Harris pointed to a box.

"I think that we might want to start there."

"Sure." Kelly gingerly pulled a box off the shelf. Harris did the same.

"Let's go through them here. It shouldn't take long to see if there are any relevant files." She carried her box to an empty shelf, set it down, and pulled off the cardboard lid.

"These are what's left after they got rid of all the reports destroyed by the flood. That, and they didn't bother saving the noise complaints or the nuisance calls."

"At least that narrows the search down."

"Hopefully."

Harris had pushed her hair behind her ears and started thumbing through files. Kelly took the lid off his own box and began to do the same. Kelly's hands instantly felt like they were covered with a mixture of dust and mildew. He thumbed through the folders, looking for missing or abused children. It took them two hours to go through all the boxes one at a time, replacing each box back on the shelf before taking a new one.

They turned up two missing person cases and no files relating to abused children. Either no one was reporting it in the 1980s, or the files had been destroyed by the flood. They took two files back up to the detective bureau to see what they held. One involved a ten-year-old whose mother took him to Florida as part of a custody dispute in 1984. The case had been closed after the investigating detective made contact with the mother. The other was equally unhelpful. A twelve-year-old had gone camping on a remote part of the island in 1983. He hadn't told his parents, hadn't left a note. His mother had called the police on a Friday night in June. He walked in the door Sunday afternoon and didn't understand why his mother was so angry.

"Well, now what?" Harris asked.

"It'll take a while to hear back from the emails I sent out. I think it's coffee time. Wanna go for a ride?" They grabbed their jackets and made their way to Harris's car.

"Yesterday you mentioned social workers and the school nurse," he said.

"Sure."

"Would they still be on-island? I mean, we are looking at something that happened in the 1980s. They might be retired."

"I don't know. We can check it out. Let me call the principal." Kelly listened to a one-sided conversation from which he was able to determine that school was indeed closed, that the nurse hadn't gone on vacation, and that Harris was grateful for the information.

"The nurse lives out in Madaket."

"Okay, let's get coffee on the way."

In the Darkness,
December 1981

Albie slowly came to. He was having trouble breathing, and he hurt. He hurt like he'd been tackled a bunch of times by the bigger kids, playing football. He hurt inside too. Albie was scared. Scared like he'd never been in his life. He was in the Monster's lair. He knew that.

Albie was cold. It was damp in the Monster's cave. Albie realized he didn't have his jacket. His nose hurt a lot. When he touched it, blood and snot came away in his chubby hand. Slowly it occurred to him that he wasn't wearing pants, just his underpants. His throat hurt, and when he went to touch it, he felt the rope looped around his neck.

He heard the Monster snoring loudly near him, slightly above him. Albie realized the rope around his neck moved a little each time the Monster snored. Albie was lying on his side on cold, damp concrete. He was on the floor of the Monster's lair. Albie was scared. It was like a buzzing in his head, drowning out everything else. Even the pain.

Albie was too frightened to move at first. Then he thought of Bilbo Baggins. His mom and dad had taken him to the Gaslight Theater in town to see The Hobbit *when it was replaying last winter. He loved the Gaslight, which was the only movie theater open in the winter on the island. He loved sitting in the small, dark theater. His dad had told him it used to be a garage once.*

Albie especially liked that Bilbo was like him. Not tall, but pudgy. Not good at sports, not even very brave but brave enough. Albie suddenly wanted very much to be brave like Bilbo. He wished he had a magical dagger. He'd show the Monster!

Then Albie had a flash of inspiration. The Monster was asleep. He could escape while the Monster slept. Albie carefully worked his chubby fingers between his throat and the rope. He worked slowly, gently, loosening the rope until he could slip it over his head. Then he got into a crouch. He didn't dare stand up, because he might wake up the Monster. He knew that he couldn't let the Monster know he was free.

He looked around. He was in a cave dimly lit by candles. Music was playing, and the air smelled like burned spices. The cave was white with curved walls. In the middle of one of the walls was the opening of a tunnel. That had to be the way out!

But it was dark. Darker than night. Albie didn't want to walk down the tunnel. There could be other monsters. But he also knew that Mikey, Richie, and Nick never came back from the Monster's lair. He had to be brave like Bilbo Baggins. If only he had a ring that would make him invisible like Bilbo. Then he remembered the quarter he found in Cobblestone Alley.

He stuck his hand in the pocket of his sweatshirt. It was still there! He clutched it in his chubby hand.

I'm invisible now, *he thought.* If I'm quiet, I can walk away from the Monster and I can go home. I have the coin and I'm invisible now.

He clutched the coin in his hand. Hard enough to hurt. If I'm quiet, I can walk away from the Monster and go home. *He repeated it to himself over and over again, thinking of his home. His mother, who was warm, giving him hugs and kisses, cookies and chocolate milk whenever he needed it. His father, who was brave and strong and fought in a war, who would keep him safe from the Monster.*

Albie clutched his coin tightly and quietly shuffled off into the darkness on bare feet. He moved slowly and carefully with his left hand outstretched. He didn't dare let go of the quarter in his right. After what seemed like forever, Albie's left hand touched something. A wall. It was cold and damp.

He felt around, slowly, carefully, trying to be like Bilbo hiding from trolls. A short lifetime later, his hand found a handle of some sort. After another few minutes of trying, he pushed down on one part and turned the handle. It clicked.

The door was very heavy, and Albie had to lean his body against it to push it open. As the door cracked, he could smell the ocean air, which, after the Monster's dank cave, smelled like heaven. Albie pushed the door open enough to slip out. He slowly closed the heavy door behind him. Even though he was invisible, he didn't want to wake the Monster up.

He was outside with two walls rising on either side of him. He heard waves breaking on the shore. He was very near a beach. He started to walk toward the sound of the waves, the damp grass tickling his bare feet as he went. As he emerged from the walls of the cave, he saw that he was in a field, but it was foggy. Off in the distance, he heard a foghorn, but he couldn't tell where it was coming from. He could see ten or twenty yards in front of him.

I could be anywhere on the island, *he thought, giving in to despair. Then off to his left, he saw a flash of light in the foggy air high above him. A lighthouse! There were three on the island, he knew that. One was in the harbor by the coast guard station—Brant Point, where every time they took the ferry off-island, they threw pennies over because it was supposed to guarantee your safe return. That was what Mommy told him. But that was the shortest lighthouse on the island.*

He turned and looked to his right. There was another flash of light in the sky. "Think, Albie," he hissed to himself. Where on the island would he be between two lighthouses? He shook his head. He thought he heard a noise behind him. Get away from the Monster's cave, *his inner voice screamed. Albie started to run toward the sound of the waves, his chubby little arms and legs pumping. He stopped when his feet started to slap against the pavement.*

A road! He was on a road. That was good—roads, especially paved ones, would lead him to someplace he would know. But the Monster has a car. He would hunt for Albie on the road when he figured out that Albie had gotten away. Albie started forward again, the sound of the waves getting louder.

Then he took a step, and nothing was there. Albie tumbled, ass over teakettle, like his dad would say sometimes. He tumbled end over end in the sand, coming to rest on the beach ten feet below, breath knocked out of him. He wanted to cry, but he couldn't breathe, and he hurt in so many places. Slowly, he got his wind back and sat up.

Albie realized that he was still clutching his magic quarter! His ring! He was still invisible!

He got up and looked left and right. To his left was the higher of the two lights. That would be the Sankaty Lighthouse . . . but no one was in the lighthouses anymore. His dad told him that they replaced the people. He looked right. The lower light must be far away. Brant Point was a stubby lighthouse in town. Town would be far away, and people would be there. Mommy and Daddy would be there. Albie turned to the right and started to jog down the beach toward the farther light.

It was more of a shuffle than a jog. He hurt in too many places. He was cold too. The fog didn't help, and when he moved fast, he started to cough as he gulped in the cold, wet air. He kept the ocean on his left and kept shuffling forward, one painful footstep at a time. Albie knew he couldn't go back; the Monster would get him. He knew he could only move forward. He had to put as much distance between him and the Monster as he could before he woke up. That was what Bilbo would do. He clutched his quarter in one cold fist and kept going.

Albie kept walking with the waves breaking on his left and the big light at his back. He kept moving toward the low light, toward Brant Point. To his right the ground rose up and away from him. He didn't see any houses; he must still be far away from Brant Point. He thought for sure he'd see the red lights of the TV towers. They looked like something out of an erector set, painted in alternating red and white intervals as they rose to meet the sky. There weren't any houses close to the beach. He must be really far away from town.

Albie kept walking, feet and body aching, trying to be brave like Bilbo. Like his dad. His feet ached, and when the wind gusted, he trembled. His mouth was dry, and he desperately wanted a drink of water or hot cocoa. He imagined how good it would taste the way Mommy made it with milk and the little marshmallows. He could almost feel the cocoa warming him as he sipped it.

After a long time, Albie became aware of two things. The ocean sounded less angry crashing on the shore. The ground to his right that had towered above him was now level with his waist. He was closer to the light from Brant Point too. He kept shuffling forward. Albie knew if he stopped, the Monster would get him.

After what seemed like forever, Albie realized he was walking next to a chain-link fence. Albie thought hard. There was only one place with a light like a lighthouse and a chain-link fence by the beach. He was at the airport! He thought about trying to climb over the fence, but it was too high, and he was so very tired.

Then he saw it—there was an area under the fence where runoff from rainstorms had washed away the dirt. It left a gap under the fence that was big enough for Albie to squeeze through. If he could cut across the field and the runway instead of going around, he could get to the building sooner. There was a pay phone outside the building. Also, the Monster couldn't drive his car in the fenced area. Albie would be safe.

Albie got on his back and wriggled his shoulders, pushed with his aching feet, and managed to get under the fence. He ended up on the other side with a couple of scrapes from the bottom of the chain link. He stood up and the scrapes stung. He looked down and saw he was bleeding. Albie said "Fudge" in a tired voice.

He didn't care about a little more pain. He started walking in a straight line for the airport building. He knew it had a proper name, like what they called the place where the ferry came in, but his tired mind couldn't recall it. He didn't like the gusts of wind that were blowing toward the ocean. They made him shiver.

He staggered forward. There were lights on, but he didn't hear any planes or any cars or anything. He had no idea what time it was. But planes might not be flying because of the fog. When you live on an island, you become attuned to the weather. The fog didn't help Albie's feeling cold or hurt or tired. But as he drew nearer the lights of the building, his spirits rose.

He crossed the runway, bare feet dimly registering the cold tar. Then back on the grass, shivering and shuffling. He set foot on the tarmac again, this time in the big area near the building where planes dropped people off. He got to the back of the building. He'd made it! He noticed that there were some lights on, but they were on the outside of the building. The windows were all dark. It was closed. It must be late at night. Now he had to walk around it to find the phone to call Mommy.

Albie went around the corner of the building, and there was another chain-link fence, taller than he was. "No," he wailed, as the hot tears coursed down his cheeks. "No. I was brave. I did everything . . . everything I was supposed to do." He stopped and sat down against the wall, his chest racked with sobs. He'd been brave. Like Bilbo. He'd met every challenge. He should have won. It wasn't fair!

He thought about waiting till the airport opened. Someone would find him. He could just close his eyes and wait for them to find him. His head started to dip. He could just take a nap, and he would wake up and they would find him.

But the wind was cruel. It gusted hard, the cold, knife edge of it snapping him to. Albie pushed himself up against the building. He didn't want to be cold anymore. Albie looked at the fence. It wasn't as high as the one by the beach. It was taller than him, but not so much he couldn't get over it.

Albie put the quarter in the pocket of his sweatshirt. He grabbed the fence, pulling with his hands and digging his feet into the chain links. He slowly started to climb. He got to the top and painfully rolled over the sharp twists of wire. He hung by his hands for a second and then crashed to the ground. His feet hurt, a lot.

Albie was in the front of the building and limped over to the doors. He remembered there were benches in front, metal and wooden ones that looked old-timey. But there was also a pay phone with its gray, wooden enclosure that you were supposed to lean into. Albie hobbled over to it.

He pushed more than lifted the handset out of its cradle. He stood on tippy-toes to put his special quarter in the slot. He wasn't invisible anymore, but this was better. Still standing on tippy-toes, he started to dial, two-two-eight . . . when he finished, there was a pause, and then he heard ringing.

"Hello," she answered.

"Mommy."

"Albie! Where are you?" She sounded scared and relieved at the same time.

"I'm at the airport, Mommy. I'm cold." Hearing his mother's voice made him want to cry with relief. She would make everything better.

"Albie, you just wait there. Your daddy and Mr. Parker are out looking for you. They've been calling home every fifteen minutes. He should call any minute now. Just stay there, sweetie. Daddy will be there soon."

"Okay, Mommy." The phone went to dial tone.

Albie was too tired to hang it up. He sat down on one of the benches. He was too tired to move.

He had run out of steam, and he curled up on the bench to wait. He was too tired to care about anything. If the Monster came and got him, he'd reached the end, didn't have any more fight left in him. He'd been as brave as he could be.

Albie closed his heavy eyes for a minute. If he could just rest for a minute . . .

CHAPTER 8

The detectives got in Harris's Ford, made their way to the high school, and turned up by the windmill. Kelly recognized some of the route from his morning run. They passed the Quaker cemetery, which was devoid of headstones, as the Quakers had felt that headstones were ostentatious. They turned left onto Madaket Road, and Kelly was struck by how quickly the houses thinned out. The surrounding open space gave Kelly the impression that the island was bigger than it really was.

They drove down Madaket Road, and Kelly noticed the bike path paralleling the road. He'd noticed them on the major roads to the various beaches. Nantucket had clearly invested in its tourist infrastructure.

"What's the nurse's name?" he asked.

"Carol Lavesque, retired a few years ago."

"So she was most likely here in the 1980s."

"Should've been."

"Hopefully she doesn't have dementia."

"Ugh, just what we need."

Kelly took a sip of his coffee. Harris turned right off the main road and up a dirt driveway to a small ranch house on a slight rise overlooking the road. Kelly thought there was something odd about the house, and he couldn't quite put his finger on it. Then it came to him; he hadn't seen many ranch homes on the island. Most of the residences were clapboard or shingled Capes. There was a detached garage next to the house, all of it surrounded by scrub pines.

Harris parked in front of the house, and they both got out. Kelly noted that the Wormtown cops would never park directly in front of a house, but he assumed the threat was pretty low from a retired school nurse. Their knock on the door was answered by a trim woman in her sixties. She had a graying pixie cut, her face showing the effects of decades spent in the sun. She wore a lavender-colored flannel shirt and faded khaki slacks.

"Yes, can I help you?"

"Carol Lavesque?" The woman nodded. "I'm Detective Harris. This is Detective Kelly of the State Police. Can we come in and speak with you for a moment, ma'am?"

Harris had fallen back on the script written and used by cops for years, reinforced by cop shows and movies. *No need to mess with a classic,* Kelly thought.

"Yes, of course, Detectives." She led them inside. "Come into the kitchen. I was just making some tea. Would you like some . . . or would you like coffee?"

"No, thank you, ma'am, we don't want to take up too much of your time." Kelly fell back on his scripted line.

"How can I help you?" she asked while pouring water from the kettle into a mug. Kelly noted the paper tag attached to the teabag said Red Rose, the same brand of tea his mother drank.

"Mrs. Lavesque, you were the elementary school nurse?" Harris opened.

"Yes. I retired last year."

"When did you start?" Kelly asked.

"In 1978. I moved to the island after the blizzard." The Blizzard of '78 was still spoken of reverently in New England, the same way that people in Washington State spoke of Mount Saint Helens.

"We've found a set of remains. A child's remains, and they appear to be several decades old. We think they may be from some time in the 1980s." Harris again. She and Kelly hadn't consciously decided to alternate who asked the questions; they'd just naturally fallen into the routine. They clicked.

"Oh no . . . that's horrible. Poor thing. But I'm not sure how I can help."

"We were wondering if there were any children you tended to in school who showed signs of being abused?"

"Abused?"

"Physically abused, bruises, spiral fractures, that sort of thing."

"Or if there were any children who were out of school for long periods of time with little explanation," Kelly added.

"Wouldn't you have reports of that sort of thing?" Lavesque asked while stirring sugar into her cup of tea.

"Yes, we are looking at those, too, but we are trying to look at all aspects of the case."

"I see . . ." Her tone made it clear that she didn't fully see. "I moved out here in 1978 and became the school nurse at the high school. In 1991, when Mary Fallon retired from the elementary school, I ended up moving to that school."

"Oh." Harris sounded mildly disappointed.

"Yes, I'm afraid if you aren't here about teenagers smoking pot or getting STDs, I'm not much help."

"Is Mrs. Fallon still . . ." Kelly paused, wanting to say *alive*, but instead said, "On-island?"

"She is, but not in a way you'd find helpful. She's been out by Vesper Lane for the last fifteen years or so."

"Vesper Lane?"

"In the cemetery there. She passed away shortly before 9/11."

"Oh . . . thank you very much for your help, ma'am. We shouldn't take up any more of your time. If you think of anything, please give us a call," Kelly said, holding out his card.

"Of course."

"Thank you, ma'am," Harris added politely.

"Oh, no worries. I have never been interviewed by detectives before. I can't wait to tell the girls." Lavesque showed them out.

The detectives got in Harris's car. Kelly looked back and saw the retired school nurse standing in the bay window, looking at them. She was holding a cordless phone against her ear. He couldn't tell anything from her facial expression. He didn't like being watched.

"She wasn't kidding. She's already on the phone."

"That's life on the island. By the time we get back to the station, half the island will know we were here and what we were asking her about."

"Gossip much out here?"

"It's a local pastime, more entertaining than anything on TV. Out here it's a twenty-four-hour gossip cycle."

"Must be hard to be a female cop here. I imagine that every little thing turns into fuel for more gossip."

"You have no idea. It's like being on one of those reality TV shows without having ever signed up to be on one."

"I can't even begin to imagine."

"That and half the older women in town always manage to let slip that they have a brother, cousin, son, or daughter who's single."

"I bet that gets old in a hurry."

"Yes, it does. Probably not a problem you have in the troopers."

"Only before I got married. The wives of senior guys were always looking to play matchmaker. They always seemed to have a niece, little sister, or friend who they wanted to share the misery of being married to a trooper with."

Harris steered her car into town. The police radio crackled now and again while, in the background, the car radio was playing country music too softly for Kelly to pick out any specific song. He had often thought of all the things that Jeanie had to put up with because of the job. Most of the time when he thought about it, he came up feeling inadequate in the face of her sacrifices for their family. The few times when he didn't feel bad about it, she was quick to remind him.

Harris's phone made a series of electronic chirps. She took it off her belt holder, tapped a button, and held it up to her ear. Kelly heard a muffled voice at the other end but couldn't make out the words. "Uh-huh . . . okay. Yep, we're on the way. Can you also send the pics to my email? Thanks." She dropped her phone into the cup holder. "That was Doc Redruth."

"And?"

"There was some sort of accident. One of the boxes of evidence was damaged. They called him, and he wants us to head out to the airport."

"Doesn't sound good."

"Sure doesn't."

"Fuck a duck," Kelly said.

"Exactly. Fuck a damned duck."

They didn't say much on the ride over. It didn't take them long to get there. Like everything on the island, it took fifteen minutes to get anywhere. Kelly watched the scenery glide by, all scrub pines and new houses. Then Harris pulled into the parking lot of Nantucket Memorial Airport, and Kelly had to fight his sense of impending dread, the ever-tightening sensation in his chest. Harris, like most cops do, pulled up in front of the terminal and parked in a spot that was clearly marked No Parking.

"Jesus, Kelly . . . you look bad. We don't even know the extent of the damage to the evidence yet, but I am pretty sure your career in the troopers will be okay."

"I know, I know . . . it's just . . ."

"It might be nothing; we'll work it out."

"You're right. Let's go see," Kelly said with more resolve than he felt.

They went into the terminal building, Harris greeting people she knew and leading him through to the freight area of the local airline. A sign overhead read Nantucket Passenger and Freight Service. Harris led him through to the freight area of NPFS where Doc Redruth was waiting with a man dressed in industrial work clothes, the type that come with the sewn-on bits of reflective tape.

"Hey, Jo."

"Hey, Doc . . . How bad is it?"

"Not great, but probably not the end of the world. I felt you should know." They walked over to a pile of boxes that were scattered by a garage-style bay door. One unlucky box was partially flattened and had a tire mark from the forklift on it.

"Nobody's touched it. We figured you might want to see it as is," said the man in the reflective work clothes.

"Okay, thanks," Harris said. "Well, who wants to do the honors?"

"I'll do it," said Redruth, putting on a pair of latex gloves.

He picked up the box, took it over to a nearby table, and put it down. Then he pulled out a pocketknife, opened it, and carefully cut away the tape on the box. With that done, he pulled back the carboard flaps and opened the bag inside.

"This one looks to be dirt and rocks from part of the search area directly next to the remains," Redruth continued.

"Hold up, what's this?" Redruth held up a clump of rock or dirt that had two tiny feet sticking out of it. They were faded, but the feet were unmistakably brown and the pants tan.

"What is that, a G.I. Joe?" Harris asked as Redruth began carefully scraping dirt from the action figure back into the box. Kelly watched as Redruth methodically worked and realized that he was holding his breath in anticipation. Redruth held up a tan-suited figure with yellow hair.

"No, it's not G.I. Joe. It's Luke Skywalker . . . the one from *Empire* . . . *Empire Strikes Back*. You know, the real second movie," Kelly said. "I used to have one. I think every kid my age did. Jesus."

"I should take this back to the hospital and photograph it. I'll repack the box and send it to the lab."

Kelly watched the doctor, crumpled box in hand, as he walked away. He and Harris looked over the other boxes to make sure they weren't damaged. Harris took pictures of the boxes with her phone, and when she was satisfied that nothing else was damaged and that everything was adequately documented, she straightened up.

"You hungry?" she asked Kelly.

"I could eat," he said with false indifference.

"Let me guess, a grilled chicken Caesar wrap?"

"Don't knock it."

They made a quick stop for lunch and then headed back to the police station. They ate up in the detective bureau, sitting in their cubicles. Between bites of their lunch, they talked.

"Well, that should help narrow down our timeline a little," Kelly said.

"How's that?"

"*The Empire Strikes Back* came out in 1980. I doubt there would've been any merchandising released for it before then. Given the proximity of the coins, and the fact that the action figure was from the dirt removed from directly below the remains, I think that narrows our timeline down significantly." He couldn't bring himself to say *bones*.

"Okay, that makes sense."

"That also means we can get rid of any missing person files from before 1980," Kelly pointed out.

Harris's computer beeped, and she opened an email with several attachments.

"Wow, look at these." Harris pointed at a series of pictures of the Luke Skywalker action figure, faded but still in good condition. "The doc must have cleaned it up."

Kelly watched, fascinated, as she clicked through the pictures.

"Wait! Stop! Go back one."

"Sure." Harris clicked her mouse, and a picture of a small, brown-booted foot appeared.

"Do you see that?" Kelly asked quietly.

"Yeah, it looks like something is scratched into the bottom of the foot."

"It looks like letters . . . N . . . S," Kelly read out slowly.

"Are you sure it's an *S*? It looks kind of like *N5*."

"No, it's *NS*."

Kelly swayed on his feet and quickly sat down in his cubicle. He was about to say more, but the door opened and a statuesque man walked in. He was in his sixties, olive complected, with dark, swept-back hair that was just beginning to streak with gray. He was dressed in jeans and a flannel shirt, and Kelly picked up the bulge of a small gun on his right hip.

"Chief!"

"Hi, Jo." He turned to Kelly, and after the slightest of pauses he said, "You must be Detective Kelly. I'm Joe Almeida."

"Yes, sir."

"Jo, Doc Redruth called me and told me about the action figure. I thought I should head over."

"Okay, I don't understand. It's something, but we still aren't any closer to identifying the remains."

"Jo, the last person to have that action figure was little Mikey Parker. He borrowed it from a friend named Nick Steuben but never had the chance to return it."

"Sir, I didn't find any missing person reports for a Mikey Parker."

"No, it's an old case. The files got moved or were damaged with the rest of them."

"I see," she said, clearly not seeing. "Well, can we go talk to Nick Steuben? He might know something that can help."

"No, you can't. He's been gone for thirty-five years."

"Off-island? We can find him on the mainland."

"No, not off-island, Jo. Dead. He was abducted and murdered. He and two other boys."

The Airport,
December 1981

He woke up when he felt rough hands lift him up. He almost screamed, but he heard his father calling his name. He opened his eyes and saw his father's face. He tried to say something, but his teeth just chattered. His dad carried him to his truck. Mr. Parker was inside, and it was warm, wonderfully warm. The heat from the vents bathed over him. In no time, his exposed skin started to itch as the feeling came back to him.

"Albie, what happened? Are you okay?"

"He looks like he's been through it," Mr. Parker said.

"Dad. I didn't mean to be naughty. The kids on the bus were teasing me. I thought I'd show 'em, and I hid. I was gonna be home before dark, I swear. But the Monster got me."

"The Monster?" his dad asked.

"Yeah, the one that got Mikey, Richie, and Nick. He's bad!"

"Albie, did he hurt you?" his dad asked, gripping Albie's biceps tightly.

"Can you show us where he is?" Mr. Parker asked.

"Jimmy! Not now."

"My kid . . . my kid's gone. I wanna find the son of a bitch who did this to your kid. To my kid," Mr. Parker wailed.

"Okay, but then we call Joe Almeida."

"Sure, but we get to him first. Knock the shit out of him before the law comes."

"Albie, do you remember where he took you?"

"It was a cave, Dad."

"Albie, there aren't any caves on Nantucket," his father said in frustration.

Albie wanted to cry all over again, hearing his dad sound so frustrated. Albie was always frustrating his dad because he was fat and not good at sports or anything. Now he couldn't even tell his dad where the Monster's cave was.

"It was a cave with white walls," he managed to say. "There was a long tunnel. Then when I got outside, I saw the cave was kind of hidden. It was near the ocean."

"Okay, was there anything else?"

"There was a field, and streets but no houses."

"How did you get to the airport?"

"I walked down the beach until I saw the fence. Then I climbed under it, walked across to the building, and called Mommy."

"Do you remember anything else?"

"Um, there were two lighthouses. I thought I was walking to Brant Point because I was walking to the low one."

"There was a tall one?"

"Yes, I kept my back to it."

"Albie, this is important. When you were walking on the beach, was the water on your left or right side?"

"It was on my left."

"It wasn't a cave."

"But, Dad . . . I swear."

"It was the old JFK bunker," Mr. Parker said flatly.

"That's what I'm thinking," Albie's dad said. "I'm gonna call Joe."

"Okay," Mr. Parker said.

Albie watched his dad get out of the truck and go to the same pay phone that he'd used to call home a little while before.

"Albie, did the Monster say anything about my Mikey? Anything at all?"

"I'm sorry, Mr. Parker, I don't remember him saying anything. He was hitting me and stuff."

"That bastard! He's gotta know something about my Mikey, he's gotta."

It occurred to Albie that he didn't want to think about what had happened to him, much less talk about it. His dad came back to the truck a few minutes later, letting in a blast of frigid air as he got in.

"Okay, I reached Joe. He's gonna meet us at the JFK bunker."

"JFK, like the president?" Albie asked. Even though he was a kid, he knew who JFK was.

"Yes, Albie. They built a bunker out here in case there was ever a war with the Russians. He could fly over from his house in Hyannis with his family. They'd be safe."

"It isn't much of a bunker, basically a Quonset hut with a long tunnel, covered in a few feet of soil," Mr. Parker added.

Albie didn't know what a Quonset hut was. He didn't really care what a Quonset hut was. It was warm in the truck, sitting between his dad and Mikey's dad. After so long, he finally felt safe.

CHAPTER 9

Later, when he was talking to Jo Harris about it, Kelly would say that it was as though all the air left the room. It was like Joe Almeida was a magician and that was his signature magic trick. Kelly felt like he was underwater, in the surf, and then suddenly he broke through to the surface. Harris took a few seconds to process the words. Then she said, "I'm sorry, what?"

"In 1981, three boys were abducted and killed," Almeida said in clipped tones.

"Jesus, sir. I never heard of it," Harris said.

"It was a long time ago."

"But sir, three boys abducted and killed . . . this is a small community, how come . . . ?"

Almeida gave her a look, and she stopped mid-question.

"What now?" Kelly asked.

"Mikey Parker's father and sister need to know we found him."

"They're still alive?" Kelly asked.

"Yes, Jimmy Parker is, and so is his daughter, Laura. They live in Wauwinet. I am going to drive out and do the notification."

"Sir, are we sure it's the same boy? We don't have DNA or even a dental match. We should wait until we have a good ID," Harris said. Kelly wondered if she was always the voice of reason.

"Jo, I'll show you the files, my copies, later. But right now, I am one hundred percent certain that those are Mikey Parker's remains.

His family has waited a long time for him to be found. For him to come home."

"Yes, sir," Harris said quietly.

Kelly stood there awkwardly, as though he were watching an argument between a father and daughter.

"Sir," Kelly interjected. "Instead of doing a full note, we could go out and get a swab. Kind of tell them what we found, but leave the door open until we're certain?"

Chief Almeida gave Kelly a hard look, then said, "Okay, Detective."

"I'll get a kit." Jo piped up like the kid in class who wanted to impress the teacher. She headed off.

"Come on, we'll take my car," the chief said.

The detective followed the chief outside to his blue Ford SUV. It was unmarked but had the blue town license plates. Even without those, no one would mistake it for anything other than a cop car. The spotlight mounted on the driver's side and the push bar made sure of that. Jo joined them a couple of minutes later with the test kit in a brown paper bag.

Kelly rode in the back with Harris sitting next to her chief. He listened, staring out the window at the scenery going by. The island's vegetation was transitioning from the brown and muted greens of winter to the budding, light green of spring. They were driving by too fast for him to notice, but Kelly was sure that there were buds on all the branches. His mind was unfocused, wandering all over the place.

"During the fall of 1981, three boys were abducted and murdered. They were all between the ages of eight and ten. They were all taken as they were heading home from playing with friends after school."

"Chief, I've never heard anything about this."

"No, Jo, you wouldn't have. While there's a lot of gossip on the island, this wasn't something anyone wanted to talk about. Not at the time, even less so after."

"But, Chief, there are no case reports. No news stories. Nothing on the web."

"In 1981, this was a much more isolated place. The local paper didn't write about it at the time. We didn't want to encourage the killer, play to his ego. It wouldn't have made a difference. Everyone knew what was going on. There was no point in the paper reporting on it." Kelly perked up. It sounded a little false to him. "Plus, when it was over, the chief at the time took the files and locked them in his safe."

"Why would he do that? Wouldn't they be needed for the trial?" Harris asked.

"No."

"But, Chief—"

"Jo, there wasn't a trial."

"But why not?"

"Because he was dead, wasn't he, Chief?" Kelly spoke up from the depths of the back seat.

"Exactly. He was shot while we tried to take him in."

"You got the guy?" Harris asked excitedly.

"Yes, Jo. I got him. He pulled a gun and I shot him."

"Chief, I had no idea."

"It isn't something I like to talk about. I don't know a lot of guys who like talking about it when they take a life. What about you, Kelly?"

"No, sir. I think most guys just want to move on from it. Forget all about it."

"Who was he?" Harris asked.

"He was from off-island, a laborer who was working out at the old navy base. They closed it in the seventies. Then in 1980, they hired some workers to dismantle it best they could. What didn't get dismantled got turned over to the coast guard. What the coast guard didn't get, the town got."

"Yeah, I heard about some of that," Harris said.

"It wasn't glamorous work, ripping out asbestos tiles and sorting through whatever the navy had left behind. It didn't pay as much as construction, but it kept a few guys employed. One of them was Randal James Hampton." Kelly noted that the chief used the killer's full name.

"Hampton was a drifter from Louisiana. He'd been in the merchant marine and then traveled up and down the East Coast. He would crew on boats, take odd jobs, work construction, that type of thing. In a cruel twist of fate, he washed ashore here. I wish to Christ he hadn't, but he did, bringing misery with him.

"He had a record for assault and a rape charge out of New Bedford that was dropped. He'd been in prison and most likely started his criminal career in reform school. Anyway, he came to the island and abducted, abused, and killed three boys. In my opinion, there isn't a fire in hell hot enough for his ass."

"How'd you catch him?"

The chief seemed to ignore the question. He sounded like he was lost in time. "We never found the remains of his first victim, Mikey Parker, but the second and third victims were recovered in town." He paused and seemed to shiver in his seat. "He left them for us to find . . . posed them. It was almost as though he was taunting us."

Kelly could see it all in his mind. He thought about his sons, but that just made it worse. He could feel his chest tightening, his stomach twisting on itself. He was glad that Harris was so focused on her chief that she didn't notice his discomfort.

The chief had turned off Milestone Road onto Polpis. The whole area had a quiet, almost desolate feel. It was hard to believe that in a couple of months the island would be teeming with beautiful people in bathing suits, smelling of Coppertone, basking in the sun, crowding roads and bike paths.

"Jo, we don't talk about it because it ripped the community apart. Over the course of the weeks while we were looking for the boys, for Hampton, the island was a dark place. Everyone suspected everyone else. Neighbors who'd been close friends eyed each other with suspicion. Some even got into fights. People locked their doors at night, and there were some who went around armed. On Halloween night, there were parents out walking around with their kids, trick-or-treating. I saw men with axe handles, and there were more than a few people with guns in their waistbands. Hampton did something ugly to this place. No one wants to remember that time, much less talk about it."

"I just don't understand how this stayed so far under the radar."

"The island in 1981 was a very different place. It was more isolated, there was no internet. No cell phones. In the winter the harbor might freeze over for a week, no boats in or out. Sometimes it felt like we were living at the very edge of the civilized world.

"It wasn't just that, the people were different too. There was a tight sense of community. We still had a fishing fleet. The island was still home to working-class families and not just a place where the rich came to summer. I am not saying that the killings literally ripped it apart, but it got pretty ugly."

Harris seemed like she wanted to ask another question, but they'd turned onto a driveway of crushed shells. They crunched up the driveway and parked behind a newish red Ford F-150 work truck and white Jeep Wrangler. Kelly saw that the truck had PARKER CONSTRUCTION painted in gold lettering on the side.

"Kelly, I'm sure you've done a note or two. Jo, I'm pretty sure you haven't. There's no easy way . . . no *good* way to tell someone you've found their dead child. Even though we're here to ask for a DNA swab, I think they'll assume we've found him. Grief is rough, everyone reacts differently. Sometimes they just sit there unmoving. Sometimes they scream and yell. They almost always cry.

"They've been seeing me since '81, delivering bad news or no news. I'll tell them what we've found, and hopefully it goes okay. Do the best you can to not get sucked into the mess and stay professional."

The chief's jaw was set when he pulled on the door handle and stepped out of the police car. Kelly followed and was immediately struck by the wind and the sound of surf pounding against the shore. Had they made their way to an even windier part of the island?

Wauwinet was a thin, sandy arm of the island that stretched up to the north and led to the island's northernmost point. Here the houses were sparse, the last few of which were on a thin spit of land with the harbor on one side and the raging Atlantic on the other. Unlike most of the mini mansions all done up in Martha Stewart colors and styles, the house in front of Kelly was just a large Cape-style residence, old but updated and well kept. The area around the house was professionally landscaped, and many of the bushes were budding in the early spring. Almeida stood at the door, raised a brass pineapple door knocker, and brought it down on the striker three times with a loud banging noise.

"Don't they have doorbells on this island?" Kelly asked.

"Shut up and get up here," Almeida hissed at him.

Kelly did as he was told, with Harris falling in behind him. Kelly stood next to the chief and mentally prepared himself for what was to come. He made his face a blank, emotionless slate. Faintly, through the door, he heard approaching footsteps. The door opened, and standing in front of them was the woman from the Oceanview Motel. She was neatly dressed in jeans and a dark-blue Parker Construction fleece vest over a white turtleneck. Her pale-blue eyes matched her outfit.

"Chief. I wasn't expecting you. What brings you out?"

"Hi, Laura. This is Detective Kelly with the State Police, and you know Jo Harris. We were hoping to talk to you and your father."

"Sure, of course. He's home, come on in." She nodded at Kelly with no hint that she'd offered him dinner and more when they'd met in the supermarket last night.

They followed her into the house. Kelly took in the framed family photos that were peppered here and there on tables and walls. He noted the tasteful furniture and various knickknacks. Kelly decided it had been decorated in what he thought of as Nantucket chic: seascapes, repurposed nautical tools like harpoons and binnacles, even the relief of a whale carved from wood on the wall. There were also pictures of Laura Parker through the years. Elementary school, some sort of recital, not quite a teenager, in the uniform of the Nantucket high school field hockey team, prom, graduation, and a wedding photo. There was one picture of a young boy, six or seven years old, with buck teeth and a shy smile. It was a school picture, the type with the blue background. Mikey Parker.

"He's in here, Chief." Laura Parker showed them into the front room. A flat-screen TV was playing highlights from an earlier baseball game. Here the decorations were less nautical and more about the holy trinity of Boston teams: the Bruins, Red Sox, and Celtics. The New England Patriots were well represented, which wasn't surprising, as they were New England's football team. The man sitting and napping in the late-afternoon sun on the couch was thin with pale skin and a shock of white hair. A copy of the *Inky Mirror* was open next to him on the couch. Kelly noted that his feet were in shearling-lined slippers.

"Dad . . . *Dad*."

The old man shook his head and looked up. Kelly's stomach was doing angry flip-flops. The room felt hot. He was dreading the next few moments.

"Dad, Chief Almeida and his detectives are here."

"Hey, Jim," the chief said. The old man looked up with watery blue eyes that matched his daughter's.

"Chief, can I get you and your detectives some coffee or something to drink?"

"No, Laura . . . you should sit down with your dad."

"Sure, okay." She looked at the chief with a puzzled expression and then sat down.

"Jim, we've found some remains out in Tom Nevers. They're a child's remains, old ones at that. Jim, I'm certain that they're Mikey's."

Kelly winced. The chief might be sure, but without DNA or dental records, *he* wasn't sure the chief should be so confident. Kelly could feel sweat in the small of his back.

"Mikey?" the old man asked in a strangled voice.

"Yes, a construction crew was digging a foundation for a house out in Tom Nevers. They found some bones. Among the things we recovered were items that we know Mikey had with him when he was taken. Something that only Mikey had. We need to be sure, though. We'd like to take a DNA sample from you."

"You found Mikey?"

"Yes, Jim."

"He's late. Late for dinner. His mom made his favorite, grilled cheese and tomato soup."

"Dad, Mikey went missing years ago."

"Mikey . . . you found Mikey."

"We're pretty sure it's him," the chief said.

"Susan, tell Susan. She's been so worried for him. She's been beside herself."

"Dad . . . Mom's been gone for a long time."

"Gone where?" Jim Parker looked up in a mix of confusion and fear.

"Dad, she passed away a long time ago."

"Jim, we're sorry for your loss," Chief Almeida said to his old friend.

"Susan's gone? Why didn't any of you sons of bitches tell me?" Anger pushed the confusion away.

"Jim, I'm sorry it's taken so long." Almeida tried again to push through the fog that clouded his old friend's mind, with no effect.

"You son of a bitch, Joe. You son of a bitch!" Spittle flew from the old man's mouth.

"Chief, I think you should leave," Laura said.

"Of course. I'm sorry for your loss."

Kelly wondered if he was exclusively referencing Parker's son. It must be brutal for the old man, to constantly relive his wife's loss and on top of that find out his son's remains had been recovered after all these years. Parker was living in a hell few men deserved.

The chief turned and the two detectives followed him, letting themselves out the front door. The trio were getting in the SUV when Laura Parker called out to them. They stopped.

"Chief, I'm sorry. It's the dementia. He has his good days and bad. Can you come back another day and get your sample?"

"Sure. It's okay, Laura, we understand. There's no way this was news he wanted to hear."

"No, it isn't. We've been waiting a long time for that knock on the door, but we've also been dreading it."

"I know. I'm sorry about that. We'll come back for the sample another day. We can't positively ID him without that or dental records."

"Can you tell me anything?"

"Just that we found the bones, and there was an easily identifiable item that we knew he had when he disappeared. We'll get a DNA test just to be sure, but I'm confident it's him. Detective Kelly is with the State Police, and, based on my conversation with his boss, he's a good detective. I can vouch for Jo Harris, who's a very competent detective too. If there is anything to be discovered, they'll find it."

"Thank you, Chief." She stepped into Almeida and hugged him briefly. "Thank you for finding Mikey and bringing him home to us."

She let go of the chief and, wiping her eyes, went into the house. They got in the SUV and started back into town. It was late afternoon, and Kelly thought of his boys, who would have gotten off the school bus and run up the driveway, eager to get into the house. Run inside making a racket and leaving a trail of school bags, sports equipment, and clothes from the door to the living room. Jeanie would be there to meet them, to offer snacks and milk, to hear about their day. Mikey Parker had probably done much the same until one day he didn't come home. Jesus, the thought of his boys and of what happened to little Mikey Parker made his stomach turn.

No one said much of anything while the chief drove them toward town. Kelly took in the scenery that flicked by, struck by the stark beauty of early spring on the island. Almeida steered the SUV into town, navigating the island's numerous one-way streets and crossing the cobblestoned Main Street. He pulled up to park in the small lot of the police substation that still bore the signs that it had been the Nantucket Fire Department, the one where Kelly had walked in a few days before. Long, bitter days that felt like a lifetime.

They crossed the street on foot and passed by the Rose and Crown, which was open year-round. Next to it, closed for the season, was a restaurant boasting of its Italian food. Next to the Dreamland theater, which had also closed for the season, was the very much open Atlantic Café. The chief pushed the door open, and they went in, out of the wind. It was warm and inviting and, not surprisingly, the decorative theme was nautical. There were oars and nautical prints, prints of fish on the walls. There were even a couple of canoes hanging from the rafters, not to mention a fair number of signal pennants.

The man behind the bar was polishing glasses with a bar towel, listening to without really hearing two men in their seventies enjoying late-afternoon mugs of beer. He nodded to the chief and said, "Hiya, Chief. Hey, Jo. Sit anywhere."

He gave Kelly an appraising look and a nod and went back to his duties. The chief led them to a booth in the back by windows that looked out over the picturesque harbor, Old North Wharf, and the Steamship Authority terminal. The late-afternoon sun was splashing pale light on the cottages on the wharf, and Kelly understood why people paid so much to live on the island.

A waitress in blue jeans and a red plaid flannel shirt came over. Kelly mentally noted the fact that the shirt's top three buttons were generously unbuttoned. "Hiya, Chief, what'll it be?"

"Hi, Sandy. Three Irish coffees, regular mugs, no whipped cream, please."

"Sure, Chief . . . anything else?" she said, looking around at the three of them.

"No, thank you, Sandy."

"Okay, be back in a jiff." She left with a smile at Kelly and a swish of her ponytail as she pivoted away.

Nobody said much of anything until Sandy came back with three steaming brown mugs. Kelly took a sip and felt the warmth of the hot coffee and Irish whiskey as it radiated through him.

"I was in the coast guard," the chief stated, because the story had to start somewhere. "My parents were from the Azores originally. They came here to work in the mills in Fall River. Even though I was born in Fall River, I hated the cold. It must be something in the blood. I loved the sea but hated the smell of fish. So fishing was out. I've been on a charter boat once in my life, and that was about two times too many.

"I wanted to see the world, and the coast guard seemed like a good idea. I enlisted when I graduated from high school. After my training at Cape May, New Jersey, I was stationed in Bangor, Maine. I'd been hoping for Hawaii or at least Florida. I would have been happy with the Carolinas, but no. Winter in Maine, on a cutter . . . that was cold. They told me if I reenlisted, I could pick my duty station. Ha! I put in for Key West and ended up on Nantucket. I guess one island was as good as another to the coast guard." He paused to take a sip of his coffee.

"I was stationed here at Brant Point. It was good duty. The summers were great, and most of the time the winters weren't that bad. My hitch was up, and I'd met a local girl and decided I wanted to stay on-island but not in the coast guard. The local police were hiring, so I applied."

"When was that, Chief?" Harris asked.

"That would have been 1976, forty years ago now. I told you the island was different then. It was smaller and bigger at the same time. There were parts of the island where, if you were out of town, all you could see at night was stars. At night, driving out on Polpis Road, it seemed so dark and desolate that you were driving through a pool of ink.

"There were a lot fewer houses, but there were more locals, families that lived here year-round. There were regular people, working people who lived out here. People could afford to raise families on a single income, and we looked out for each other. There was a real sense of community. Back then, the telephone company had workers who lived here. Now it's cheaper for them to come over on the boat and stay for a day or two in a hotel. Isn't that crazy? Back then, the police department was small, housed behind town hall and the fire department."

"Where the tourist information bureau is?" Harris interrupted.

"Yep, it was tiny. We were a small department; the island didn't need much in the way of police. You might break up fights between drunk tourists in the summer or fishermen in the winter. You might have to investigate a theft or some vandalism.

"We carried .38 revolvers, and the cops who fancied themselves tough guys might carry a billy club. There were no detectives, and if we needed anything serious, the local trooper would call for reinforcements from the mainland. There were people who smoked weed, but we didn't see much coke or anything else in the offseason unless someone brought something back for New Year's Eve or some other special event."

"What changed?" Kelly asked.

"Money," the chief said decisively. "Money changed everything. But the island was already changing. Progress is unstoppable."

"What do you mean, Chief?" It was Harris's turn to ask a question.

"When I first came out here, tourism was a source of income, but the fishing fleet was the big moneymaker. Cod, haddock, scallops were big, fishing was the industry. I know it's hard to believe now there's only one commercial fishing boat out of Nantucket, but in the seventies, there were a dozen or more boats. People worked ordinary jobs, and you could buy a house on your salary. There was no such thing as the housing lottery that we have today to ensure that normal people can have a shot at owning a home.

"Then something shifted, and tourism grew bigger, but real estate became king. Then slowly, very slowly, money from the mainland started to find its way here. It occurred to some wealthy people that they wanted to promote the unique New England history of the place. Make a perfect community, tasteful and classy. They bought houses and land. And slowly more money started coming to the island. It started in the seventies, picked up steam in the eighties, and exploded by the nineties. By the beginning of this century, it became obscene. A two-bedroom house on two-tenths of an acre lot sold for a million dollars last month. A million for a shack! Can you believe that?

"What I'm trying to say is that in 1981, the island was still a close-knit community where everyone knew everyone else. We worked together; our kids grew up together. If you drove by your neighbors' kid and he was doing something stupid, you stopped and told him to knock it off. That stupid saying 'it takes a village to raise a child' was actually true here. This was a small town surrounded by the Atlantic Ocean. Back then, the year-round population was a few thousand, and nobody on-island knew what a cappuccino or a latte was."

"Are you saying the real estate boom killed the sense of community?"

"No, Kelly, the boom was inevitable, but it changed this place. The island was already on a lot of radars as a summer resort, but things were changing. Fishing wasn't sustainable, and the beaches and the views here were too nice for the rich to ignore them for long. It made sense that people with money would want to own their own slice of it. In 1981, it hadn't taken root yet. Nobody was trying to make this into a smaller version of the Hamptons. But in the fall of 1981, the abductions . . . the murders tore into this community and almost broke it apart.

"Guys like Jimmy Parker and his wife always wondered why their son was taken and not someone else's. Jimmy's wife, Susan, she was a regular in church, Catholic. Then after Mikey went missing, she started going to church every day. Looking for answers from the very God that she believed had taken her son. Looking for an explanation that would never come."

"Jesus," Harris said.

"She wasn't the only one. There was no explaining what happened. Not in church or anywhere. It gutted this community. Other families left the island."

"Chief, you said three kids were abducted?"

"Yeah. Mikey Parker was first. We think that's why we never found him till now. The killer was new at it. Developing his technique. Maybe it was an impulse thing. Who knows? Richie Sousa and Nick Steuben came next. He left Richie's body out by the swing set over at Jetties

Beach. He was dressed, but it was clear that someone had dressed him after the fact. We found Nick Steuben over at Academy Hill."

Kelly heard the creaking of the swing set in his head.

"The senior apartments?" Harris asked incredulously.

"In 1981, Academy Hill was an abandoned elementary school. The new elementary school had been finished in 1978. The funny thing was, you'd think an abandoned school would be a target for vandalism or a place for teenagers to go party, but it wasn't. Maybe it wasn't private enough, being smack in the middle of town.

"A lady walking her dog found Nick Steuben sitting on the steps leading down to Lily Street one morning in November. She said at first she thought it was one of those oversize dolls. Then she got closer to him and realized it was a child. He was . . . he was wearing only underwear and a T-shirt. Rattled her pretty badly. It rattled all of us badly, but we had a job to do."

"Were there any forensics?"

"It was 1981, Jo, the Stone Age compared to now. Now everyone expects it to be like it is on TV, where we pull DNA and fingerprints off everything. That we find a hair or cigarette butt and it leads us right to the killer. In 1981, we were lucky to get pictures. Hand-drawn crime scene sketches were still a thing, and the only thing we knew about blood was that it came in types. That was it. We collected what we could from the scenes, but . . . well, it didn't tell us anything useful."

"Was there anything collected from either scene?" Kelly stopped himself from saying *dumpsite*. "Cigarette butts, bottles, cups . . . anything?"

"No, there was nothing of use." The chief sounded old and tired. "We searched high and low and found nothing. It was so frustrating. We knew there was a killer living among us, but it was like he was a ghost. He was just moving around unseen, unnoticed. There were a lot of people who wanted to believe it was someone from off-island or someone coming out from the mainland, committing the crimes and then going back, then returning to kill another child. After Richie

Sousa, we had an officer watching everyone coming off every boat. We were desperate."

"No one could blame you for that," Kelly said.

"We didn't know what we were doing. We could've asked for help from the State Police or even the FBI . . . but we didn't. The chief was Arne Svenson then. He said this was a Nantucket problem, and it would be solved by Nantucket cops, not a bunch of people from off-island."

"That seems nuts."

"I know it does now, but back then there was a sense that people from off-island wouldn't know the island, the people, they wouldn't know who to talk to or even how. There was a lot of distrust of people coming from the mainland, much less cops from the mainland. Plus, no one was going to argue with the chief. Then the fourth child went missing."

Kelly listened to the chief's explanation. He had his doubts, but this wasn't the time to air them.

"Who was the fourth victim?" Harris asked.

CHAPTER 10

"I quit smoking a couple of years ago. You ever quit smoking?" the chief said. Kelly couldn't tell if he was ignoring Harris's question or if he had a reason for changing the subject.

Kelly shook his head. "Never really started. My dad smoked." He had the feeling that the chief was stalling, buying time to arrange his thoughts about what happened then. Why else would he ask about his smoking?

"Me neither. We were taught from kindergarten on that it was bad for you," Harris added.

"Yeah, well, I was of a different generation. We all smoked. Started in high school, then in the coast guard. Everything they say about it being addictive is true. Lighting up becomes something that you build other habits around. Look forward to it. First smoke of the day, last smoke at night, lighting up and enjoying one after making love. All that, but the one that was my favorite was coffee and a smoke.

"I sat here when it was Cy's Green Coffee Pot in the seventies and would have a smoke with my coffee. Later in the eighties, it was the Atlantic Café, the Sandpiper, or the Dory, any place where I was having my cup of coffee. I'd have linguica and eggs, grilled English muffin, and a cup of coffee, black. I'd finish my food and light up a smoke. Simple joys. You'd go to a bad call. Accidents in summer, drunk kids wrapping their cars around a telephone pole on Milestone Road or some kid whose moped hit a patch of sand on the road, leaving a foot of skin behind on the tar. That type of thing. I'd light up, and it would instantly calm me down.

"The fall of 1981, I went from a pack a day to three. My voice was always hoarse like some blues singer, and my fingertips were stained. By Christmas, my wife convinced me to quit. She never smoked, but now she's going through chemo. How does that figure?"

"Ah jeez, Chief . . ." Harris said, and Kelly caught a glimpse of the girl from New Hampshire—cheerleading, 4-H, all wholesome and all-American.

"This case. Talking about it again. Christ, I could smoke a pack of menthols right now."

"It must have been hard," Kelly asked leadingly, slipping into detective mode.

"We were small-town cops, not State Police dicks, much less city cops. We'd get a car accident or floater out at the beach, but murdered kids . . . that was a first. Yeah, Kelly, it was hard." The bitterness was evident in the chief's tone.

"Chief, why didn't MSP take over the investigation? Surely the local trooper called the mainland?"

"Is that why you're here, Kelly? To second-guess everything we did thirty-five years ago? Because I have to tell you, I've done that enough for both of us over the last three decades."

"No. I'm here because human remains were found, and I'm the unlucky dick whose boss decided to send him out here."

"Shit luck, huh? Happens to all of us."

The chief's phone buzzed in his pocket and he pulled his phone out, flipping it open. He perched reading glasses on his nose, brow wrinkling as he read.

"I have to go. I have the old case files. If you need them, I'll drop them off at the station for you."

"Yes, please," Harris said.

"Okay, we'll talk more later. Call Dukowski for a ride back to the station." Then he got up, stowing his phone, and walked away.

"Jesus! What was that?" Kelly asked.

"I don't know," Harris said, clearly puzzled. "I've never seen him like that. He's always steady, positive . . . maybe this combined with his wife?"

"Maybe," Kelly said doubtfully.

"What?" Harris asked defensively.

"Jo, why didn't they turn the case over to the MSP, or the FBI, or ask for help? Doesn't that strike you as weird?"

"Of course it does. I mean, even in the Stone Age of 1981, they must've known they needed help. That they were out of their league."

"Sure, they would have. It wouldn't have been Almeida's call. He was just a uniform cop. They didn't have any dicks . . . it would have been up to whoever was chief then. That and the trooper who was stationed out here. Why didn't he call back to the mainland?"

"I don't know, Kelly. I'm not sure it's even important. They got the guy in the end. Isn't that the important thing?"

"Sure. No, of course it is. It's just funny is all."

"You don't think it would have made a difference, saved a kid's life?"

"Oh, Jesus, Jo. I can't say. Like you said, 1981 was the Stone Age. I'm not sure what the MSP would have done besides sending a bunch of dicks and extra uniforms out here. They might have scared the killer off-island. Maybe the local cops were in a better position to find the guy. They lived out here. Like you, they knew everyone on the island. Maybe they were right to handle it themselves," he finished.

"But you don't think that, do you?"

"Jo, does it make sense to you? Any of it?"

"No, none of this makes sense. A couple of days ago we found some remains. Today, a man who's a mentor and father figure to me tells me they're the remains of the victim of a serial killer that no one on-island talks about or acknowledges. No plaques, no memorials. None of this exactly makes sense."

"No, none of it does," Kelly agreed.

"I never heard of a serial killer out here, much less one of children. Shit, other than the Boston Strangler, I didn't even think there was one in the whole state."

"There was the guy killing and dumping prostitutes from around Fall River and New Bedford in the eighties," Kelly said. "That was a couple of years later, and they were adults, women."

"How many other serial killers can you think of in the state?"

"Gaynor in Springfield in the nineties, but he killed adult women as well."

"So this should have been big, big news."

"Front page on *The Boston Globe* and on the TV every night, that type of big news," he said.

"Instead, thirty-five years later, it's more secret than a CIA black site."

"Definitely, secret like some CIA, James Bond type of shit."

"You got that right."

"And the only guy who was here then was a cop who knows the whole story and just walked out that door."

"Leaving us with bubkes."

"Yep, a whole bag of nothing."

"So now what, mister big city, state dick?"

"Let's see what the case files have to say when he gets them to us. Circle back around and talk to him again."

"That doesn't sound like much of a plan."

"Nope, but I honestly don't know what we are dealing with here and don't have any better ideas. You?"

"We could check the Atheneum for back copies of the *Inky Mirror*. See if there were any stories in the paper," Harris said doubtfully.

"The chief said there weren't any stories in the paper. What about on the job? Any cops still around who'd know something about it, other than the chief?"

"No. This is the type of thing they'd still be talking about today. I would have heard about it when I joined the force. One of the old-timers would have said something, told it like a spooky ghost story to scare the rookie girl cop from New Hampshire."

"Okay, so there probably won't be any newspaper stories."

"Nope."

"But we should probably check just to do our due diligence."

"What about checking with the MSP? There was a trooper out here. Maybe he reported something?" Harris asked.

"Doesn't seem likely. If he reported it, it would have made the news. Something like child murders, there'd have been a file. I'm guessing whoever the Statie was, someone got him to keep it quiet. Otherwise, can you picture my guys, even in the dark ages of 1981, letting the locals handle a serial killer on their own?"

"When you put it like that . . . no. No, I can't. But what about the trooper assigned out here then? He might still be alive. He must've been involved. He must know something."

"Sure, if he's alive, if he doesn't have Alzheimer's or isn't living in Florida, he might be of use. Thirty-five years is a long time, Jo."

"It's worth a shot."

"Sure, it is. But we have a guy here, now, who was right in the middle of the whole thing. Except he's ducking us."

"The chief isn't ducking us, Kelly. He isn't." The last comment was in response to the face that Kelly made, the face that had been lied to by almost everyone he'd met professionally, cops and criminals alike.

"Maybe he isn't, but he isn't exactly helping us fill in the blanks on this one."

"No, he isn't. Technically, there isn't a case anymore. The remains have been ID'd, and they're part of a murder case they solved thirty-five years ago."

"Technically. It's also a case that someone apparently put the serious squash on. It might be closed, but it's shady as fuck."

"It doesn't look good," Harris admitted.

"No, it doesn't. On the other hand, we might know more once we see the case files."

"Sure. Of course."

"Jo, I'm not saying the chief did anything wrong."

"No, but you think he did."

"Not necessarily. We just don't know enough."

"Kelly . . ."

"Jo, we don't. We haven't seen the file, and we don't know who the players were. We don't know what the situation was like, we just don't know enough. We know that the chief just ID'd the victim before we had forensics, DNA, any of it, but that doesn't mean anything."

"What's our next move?"

"We can't look at a file we don't have. We don't know who's still on-island or still alive from 1981, or if they'd even talk to us. The Atheneum is probably closed by now."

"Okay, any idea what we should do next?"

"I think we get some dinner, maybe drink too much, and try and forget about the day."

"That's your plan?"

"Best one I've come up with in weeks."

"Okay, but on one condition."

"Sure, what?"

"Will you eat a steak or a burger or something other than a grilled chicken Caesar wrap? You're starting to give me a complex."

"I think I can manage that," he said, blushing.

Jo waved her arm at the waitress, who came over to take their order. Harris ordered shrimp scampi, and as requested, Kelly ordered a cheeseburger with bacon and french fries. They both ordered beers from Cisco, and then Kelly excused himself to step outside to call Jeanie and the boys.

Outside, dusk was crowding daytime to the other side of the world. Streetlights and the lights of downtown businesses were coming on. Kelly punched the number into his phone from memory. Jeanie answered and at least waited until they had exchanged greetings before she started in on him.

"You're probably out there with some girl right now."

"Jeanie, c'mon, don't be like that."

"That's why we're in this mess, Tommy. Because of you."

"This is my fault now?"

"Jesus, Tommy. When we first started dating, you were, like, the sweetest guy. You were thoughtful, always calling or bringing me gifts. You couldn't keep your hands off me. Remember we couldn't even go to the movies because when the lights went down, you'd be all over me. Later, it all changed; it's like I married the only trooper with a limp dick."

"Jeanie, our two kids didn't happen by accident."

"I'm not sure given all the times you . . ."

"All the times I what?" he asked in a tone with more acid than he wanted.

"You know."

"Jeanie, put the boys on. We can talk again tomorrow."

She put the boys on. He listened with a smile on his face as they told him about their days and made corny jokes. Then Jeanie came back on the phone, and his smile fled as she went on again about how he was coming up short as a husband and father. It was a relief when he pushed the red end call button.

Back inside, it was warm, and Harris put her own phone down and smiled when he joined her. "How's the home front?"

"Ugh."

"That bad?"

"Yeah, well, the other night when you were asking about how many cop clichés I fell into . . . ?"

"Sure, wearing MSP clothes off duty, that sort of thing."

"I wasn't being entirely straight with you."

"You and the wife?"

"We're separated."

"So phone calls home . . ."

"Ten minutes of listening to all the things I did wrong, all the ways I've ruined Jeanie's life, for five minutes of talking to my boys."

"Why'd it end? Were you screwing around?"

"Oddly, no. I somehow missed out on that cliché. She was. One of the doctors at the hospital."

"Ah hell, Kelly," she said sympathetically.

"It happens. I was working a lot of hours, but the truth of it is that was just an excuse. We had drifted apart, a little more each year until . . ." He made a motion with his hands like he was snapping a twig.

"The job is tough on marriages. If she cheated on you, why do you sit there and take all that shit from her?"

"I don't know. In part I don't even hear it anymore, but also, I just want to hear the kids' voices. If we get into it, she'll hang up and I won't get to talk to them while I'm on the road. It's much easier to tune her out until she's done and then talk to the boys. It's tough at home because we're still living together until I can find a place of my own. I don't want to fight in front of the kids, so I've gotten used to not engaging.

"I wish I could blame our marriage falling apart on the job, but in the end, I think we started to realize that other than the boys we didn't have anything in common. Then she went from complaining about all the normal things, like me working too much or being a slob, to complaining about how I had ruined her life or how she could have done better."

"And that's when . . ."

"Yep, Doctor Lover Boy showed up."

"Lover Boy?"

"He was an intern, younger than her and, well, you can figure it out."

"Jesus, Kelly, that sucks."

He shrugged. "You know, it hurt at first, but not as much as I would have thought."

"That's good, I guess. She still seeing the guy?"

"No, he didn't last long. She moved on to a middle-aged surgeon, and she's currently between doctors."

"Couples counseling?"

"We tried for a while, but it just turned into paying someone listen to us bitch about each other. We're trying to figure out how to divorce without hurting the kids or going broke in the process."

"That really sucks. I'm sorry."

"Me too."

The waitress brought their food, and they spent a few minutes in companionable silence while they ate. Harris eventually looked up from her scampi.

"Kelly, can I ask you something?"

"Sure."

"Are you mad at her?"

"About the cheating or the divorce?"

"Both."

"You know, at first it hurt. Like, why wasn't I good enough for her? Why'd she start screwing other guys? That type of thing."

"Then?"

"Then I realized I was just going through the motions of anger. Like I was angry because I was supposed to be angry. Then it occurred to me."

"What did?"

"She wasn't cheating on me because I wasn't there or because I wasn't paying attention. She was doing it because of something missing in her life, in her. She could blame the job, my working long hours, all of it. In the end, if I'd been a guy who worked a nine-to-five in an office, it wouldn't have changed a thing. She still would have been looking for something more."

"Aren't you angry about it?"

"I don't like that I won't see my boys all the time, that my time with them will be cut in half." Kelly left out the bit about how expensive it was to get unmarried.

"Are you guys, you know, amicable?"

"For the most part, if we aren't talking, texting, or emailing each other." He laughed. "Right now, we're at the stage where every conversation turns into Jeanie taking five minutes to list and elaborate on all the things I do and have done wrong."

"That's fucked up. Why do you put up with it? I am sure you know how to hang up a phone."

"Well, for one, I want to keep it from getting worse. It's easier to listen to her vent about me than have to listen to her lawyer. Two, she has to blame me for how it worked out."

"What do you mean?"

"Well, if she points out all the stuff I did wrong, all the ways I failed her as a husband, then she doesn't have to admit to herself that a lot of the problems with our marriage are things that she brought to the table. So it's easier, and cheaper, frankly, to let her vent. Also, it's not like I don't carry some freight for how it worked out. I could have done some . . . a lot of things differently."

"That's pretty understanding of you."

"It's not that, it's just about keeping my eyes on the prize. The boys are more important than anything else. I want to be able to see them, and going along to get along seems the best way."

"I can see that." They'd finished their meals and were on their second Ciscos.

"How about you?" Kelly asked her.

"How about me, what?"

"Any ex-husbands?"

"No." She laughed. "No ex or current husbands, no boyfriends. I dated a guy for a while when I first got out here. It didn't work out."

"The guy from the local paper?"

"No, he was the guy I dated after the guy that didn't work out."

"Oh, short-lived."

"Very. He was more interested in where I worked than me personally."

"Is there that much crime here?"

"No, but he thought it was nice to be able to write 'a source inside the Nantucket Police Department' in his stories."

"That seems like a poor reason to be with you."

"I thought so too. That's why I broke it off."

"Probably better off without him."

"Sounds like you're better off too."

"Cheers to that." They clinked pint glasses.

"Kelly, you want to get out of here?"

"You don't want another drink?"

"Small town. Everyone will know I'm here. Two beers are okay, but nothing more."

"Gotcha."

"Plus, we came here right from work," she said, nodding toward his right side, where his duty weapon was holstered. While neither of them was drunk or even close to it, drinking while openly armed was verboten.

"What were you thinking?"

"I've got some whiskey back at my place."

"That sounds perfect."

The waitress came by with the check, and Kelly paid. Then they slipped out the back door of the Atlantic Café, which faced Easy Street and the Steamship Authority terminal. Lights twinkled here and there.

Jo called Dukowski, who was on duty and came by to pick them up. Kelly sat in the cramped, clean back seat of the cruiser. It was hard molded plastic, separated by a clear plexiglass shield and molded metal partition below that. At the station, they collected their cars, and Kelly followed Harris back into town. He watched the two red taillights in front of him as they navigated through the series of narrow one-way streets. They turned past the Cumberland Farms and went a hundred or so yards until Harris turned into what looked like a lot with shrubs in desperate need of landscaping. He parked behind her and got out.

"It's this way," she said, leading him down a short path. Kelly realized that the shrubs had been planted in a zigzag pattern on opposite sides of the lot so that there was a path leading to a small patch of lawn and a two-story saltbox house. They went up the three steps leading to the door and went inside. Harris flicked a light switch as she stepped over the threshold.

"It's not much, but it's home, and it's mostly mine."

"Mostly?"

"Well, the bank owns more of it than I like, but still."

Kelly was standing in one room with a stairway that curved at a right angle upward, with a door that could only lead to a closet beneath it. A partially open door a few feet in front of him hinted at a bathroom, but the rest of the ground floor was one big room that was about fifteen or twenty feet across and deep. The floors were made of rough wood. In front of Kelly, the far wall was the kitchen area—refrigerator, stove, a series of cabinets in knotty pine, a sink—and the back door was set into the wall to Kelly's right.

Opposite the door, tucked into the corner next to the refrigerator, were a stacked washer and dryer. To his right was a small table and four chairs, and in the alcove that he realized was the protrusion sticking out of the side of the house was a small couch, a bookcase against one wall, and a small table with a TV. Between the couch and the table were two small wing chairs that faced the couch. The alcove seemed deceptively deep because there was a closet of knotty pine that extended the wall on one side. The overall effect was of a snug living space that would be warm and cozy during the stormy island winters.

"This is nice," he said.

"Thanks. It was my grandfather's. We'd come visit from New Hampshire, and when he passed away, I was new on the force. He left it to me, but the plumbing and the roof were in rough shape."

"Hence why the bank owns part of it."

"Exactly."

"Who did the paintings?" Kelly said, gesturing to the framed paintings on the wall.

"A couple of friends of my grandfather's. There was a time in the 1930s when the island was home to a sort of artists' community. My grandfather was a writer and hung out with a lot of them."

"That's pretty cool."

The paintings were mostly of the sea and landscapes, which were reminiscent of Edward Hopper. The other paintings were mostly portraits done in oil. These tended to be bigger, brighter, and in better frames. The smaller landscapes were very spare, done in flatter paint, but they were eye-catching for that leanness.

"I really like these," he said, pointing at the landscapes, thinking of his art history class from college.

"They're good. Drink?"

"Yes, please."

"Scotch okay?"

"Scotch is perfect."

"Make yourself comfortable." She'd taken off her jacket and hung it on a hook by the front door. He took off his own jacket, hanging it on the back of one of the chairs at the table, and then sat down in that chair. He watched her take a bottle of Famous Grouse out of the closet and two glasses from the cabinet. "Ice?"

"Yes, two cubes."

She went through the motions, getting ice trays from the freezer, popping cubes out, putting them in a glass, and pouring scotch.

"Here," she said, handing Kelly his glass.

"Thanks."

She sat down across from him and took a sip.

"You think you know people," she said with mild exasperation.

"Your chief, not telling you about this?"

"Sure, him. Your wife. Everyone keeping secrets, making you question who they are versus who they led you to believe they were."

"The chief probably had a very good reason for not sharing this with you. As for my wife, she never kept who she was secret, I just didn't want to see it. Admit it to myself."

"Kelly, the whole island—or at least the ones who were around then—kept this case secret. I've lived here, been a part of the community, for years, and no one mentioned it."

"Jo, maybe it was too painful for folks. You heard the chief say that it nearly ripped the community apart, turning neighbor against neighbor, friend against friend. Maybe, after they got the guy, they just tried to move on. Put it behind them."

"How? I don't see how they could do that."

"Who knows? You know how it is with the media and serial killers. Maybe they didn't want the island to become known as the place where a serial killer had murdered a bunch of kids. That type of thing would never go away."

"Maybe it shouldn't ever have gone away. It's like they erased the memories of those boys, of what happened to them. It just seems so wrong."

"I'm sure that things were handled a lot differently back then than now. DUIs that got squashed, date rapes that maybe didn't go too far because of whose son was involved, domestics that got ignored."

"Who knows why Chief Almeida chose to keep this secret. He might have thought he had a good reason for doing what he did, but that doesn't change how this was handled. It doesn't change that we seem to have a positive ID on the remains," Kelly said.

"So what now?"

"I don't know. Technically, my side of things is done or mostly done. I would like to see the original case files and talk to the chief, but I'll have to go back to the mainland in a day or two."

"It just doesn't feel like the case is done."

"I know. But unless there's something that indicates it isn't Mikey Parker or that his death isn't linked to the closed case, then we just ID'd remains involved in a long-solved case. It's at best a supplemental report. Right now the only mystery seems to be why this was kept so hush-hush thirty-five years ago."

"It just doesn't make sense that they handled it that way."

"No, it doesn't . . ."

"But?"

"Jo, you said Chief Almeida is a mentor, maybe a father figure to you. Is it possible that some of your problem with this is that you feel like he lied to you?"

"You a dime store psychologist now, Kelly?" Her tone reminded him of the woman he met standing in a muddy hole a few days before.

"Easy. I'm on your side."

"No, you're probably right."

"There's nothing more that either of us can do until we get a look at those files." He took a sip of his scotch.

"Nothing to do with the case," she said coyly.

"What did you have in mind?"

"We haven't finished the tour of the house. You haven't seen the upstairs."

"Is it interesting?"

"It is. It has a big bed."

"That is interesting."

They got up from the table, and she led him by the hand up the winding stairs, both of them eager for a break from the loneliness, from the disappointments that life had thrown them. For a few hours to push away the intrusions of a brutally uncaring world.

CHAPTER 11

Kelly woke up at five thirty when the alarm on his phone started beeping. He shut it off and eased out of bed, where Jo Harris lay snoring softly. He dressed quietly in the dark of the low-roofed second floor of her small house. When he was almost dressed, he heard her say, "Sneaking off, Kelly?"

"No, I was going to say goodbye. Also, I was pretty sure I was going to end up seeing you, like, all day."

"Well, that's good." She smiled at him from under an unruly tousle of dark hair. "It's a small town, Kelly, and there'll be a lot of gossip with your car parked in my driveway. Probably not a bad idea to get out early."

"I hadn't thought of that." He went over to her side of the bed, leaned down, and kissed her.

"I'll see you at the office."

"Yeah, see you there," she said, slightly preoccupied.

"Having regrets?"

"No, I was wondering which one of my colleagues is going to bring up your car parked out front all night?"

"Again, any regrets?"

"It was worth the gossip," she said.

"Good. I am glad to hear it." He kissed her again and said, "I'll see you at the station."

Kelly returned to his motel. After he shaved, showered, and dressed, he went to the office. Laura Parker wasn't there, just a note with her cell number for anyone who needed assistance. Kelly wasn't sure what he would have said to her, and it didn't seem like the right time to ask about the chambermaid poking around in his stuff. Sighing, he went off in search of doughnuts on the way to the station.

When he and Harris met at the Nantucket PD later, they exchanged greetings and made their way up to the detective bureau, where they settled into their cubicles. Fifteen minutes later, Chief Almeida stood in the doorway and said, "You two. Conference room. Now."

The two detectives stood up, exchanging a slightly panicked glance. Had the chief already heard about Kelly's having spent the night? Kelly wasn't surprised to see that the conference room, like everything else on the island, was decorated in a nautical theme—the wooden captain's chairs around a wooden table, a light-blue rug, darker-blue walls with pictures of Nantucket cops past and present. Color photos of the local cops at events contrasted with black-and-white ones from decades ago. There were two file folders on the table.

"You wanted the case files. There they are. I was up all night copying them for you. The originals are mine and stay with me."

"Um, okay, Chief," Harris said.

"You got any problem with that?" the chief asked Kelly pointedly.

"No, Chief," he replied, picking his battles. This wasn't how it was supposed to work. Kelly was technically in charge while it was an open investigation, but nothing about this was normal. He wasn't about to cut off his only access to the old files, even if the chief was holding on to the originals for some reason.

"These stay with you and no one else. No gossiping to friends and family. No other cops, Jo. No reporters. Kelly, I know you won't talk to Savoy until I get a chance to first."

"You know Lieutenant Savoy, sir?"

"I know a lot of people, Kelly."

"Yes, sir," Kelly said with mild discomfort.

He didn't like the thought of Almeida talking to Dickie Savoy. He wondered how the chief of Nantucket's small department knew Big Dick. Then he wondered if he really wanted to know the answer to that one. Dickie Savoy had been around for a long time and had probably made friends everywhere.

"This stuff"—the chief indicated the files—"it's hard reading. It was the worst case I ever had to work. We made some mistakes, but we busted our asses to find Randal James Hampton. We got him in the end, and no more kids were hurt. I'll stand by that."

"Chief . . ." Jo began.

"Jo, I've been up most of the night. I need a cup of coffee and to check on my wife. Read the files, we'll talk in a few hours when you're done." With those words, the curtain covering the chief's fatigue and worry about his wife dropped away. He turned into an old man in an instant.

"Yes, sir."

"Good. I'll catch up with you two." He walked out with his shoulders stooped.

"Jesus, what the hell was that all about?" Harris asked.

"I don't know. Maybe he thinks we're second-guessing how they handled the case?"

"Search me. I've never seen him like this. It's like he's seeing ghosts."

"Jo, it was a bad case. He knew the victims, their families, everyone involved. For the last thirty years, he's probably run into family members of the victims, people who knew what happened. He's probably never had any relief, and this must be dredging up a lot of bad memories for him."

"I guess. That makes sense."

"Can we work in here?"

"Sure."

"Good. Let me get my computer." Kelly headed back to his cubicle. When he returned, Jo was seated at the table in one of the captain's chairs, going through a file. Kelly took out his laptop. While it was powering up, he got his notebook, a ballpoint pen, and a highlighter. He took a deep breath before diving into the reports. Kelly started to fidget with his coin again while reading the reports. He twirled it between his fingers. Occasionally he would squeeze it in his palm, feeling the metal edges digging in. It hurt, but it also helped him focus.

The first page was a handwritten dispatch form. Susan and James Parker had called to report their son, Mikey, missing on a Sunday in mid-October of 1981. Mikey had gone out to play and disappeared without a trace. The Nantucket Police had searched high and low but found nothing. Mikey was small for his age and too young to be seriously considered a runaway, according to the next report. The prevailing theory was that he somehow ended up in the water around one of the numerous beaches and drowned, his body being taken out to sea with the tide into the cold depths of the Atlantic Ocean.

Richie Sousa hadn't come home from playing football with some friends. That was why an NPD officer named Doug Talbot found Richie Sousa posed on a swing set at the playground at Jetties Beach early one fall morning.

CHAPTER 12

Harris put the file down. Jesus. She could picture Officer Talbot finding Richie Sousa. Stuff like that just didn't happen on Nantucket. It was hard to imagine it happening today, much less in 1981. Talbot, who'd probably never seen a dead body outside of the Island Home for the Aged or a floater pulled out of the water. Then he found a murdered boy.

He must have known the family. The year-round population in 1981 was probably a few thousand people at most. As a cop, he'd interact with everyone. He'd see them during the Shoppers Stroll at Christmastime, at visits to the schools, during the Daffodil Festival, or at the supermarket. He'd see them when he was on and off duty. That was the problem with being a small-town cop: There was never any getting away from the people in your community.

She turned back to the file and read about the scene of the crime—or, in this case, the recovery. What Tommy Kelly thought of as the "body dump." She looked at the photocopies of the crime scene diagram, basically a sketch of the sandy playground where the body was found. There were photocopies of pictures of the body on the sand. Close-up ones of the bruising on the neck. The kid's broken nose, the dried blood.

Harris read the autopsy report in its clinical, horrifying detail, describing the indignities and pain inflicted upon poor Richie Sousa. She mentally noted the petechial hemorrhaging of the eyes. She boiled it down to his having been sexually and physically abused, then strangled after those indignities. She grimly noted that he would have died of his other injuries had he not been strangled.

She put the file down and looked over at Kelly. His face was ashen. His knuckles were white as he clenched the file.

"Hey, Kelly," she said softly.

"Huh," he grunted.

"You okay?"

"Yeah, it's . . . it's . . ."

"I know. Hard to read. Probably harder if you're a dad."

"Yeah, something like that," he said quietly.

"You need a break?"

"No, I'll be okay."

"You want another coffee or something?"

"No. Thank you. I just want to get through it."

"Okay."

"Thank you, though." He smiled at her, and she smiled, almost shyly, back at him. She liked him, in spite of his tendency to eat like a fashion model. She turned back to her copy of the file and marveled at the sloppiness, not that the Nantucket cops in 1981 were sloppy. They had been as thorough as they could have been. The crime scene methods were crude. There was no DNA, no digital photography. There was no such thing as profiling. No one considered or knew enough to consider the significance of the placement of Richie's body. No one considered the victimology. All of it was just attributed to the odd behavior of some "sicko." That was it in 1981.

She turned her attention back to the file. The next few pages were field notes from interviews with Richie's parents, neighbors, etc. There were interviews with a few locals who had records. One guy had a statutory rape charge out of New Bedford. They ruled him out when it turned out that his wife was the victim.

Harris followed the case's progress, noting that shortly after Richie was found, the NPD determined that Mikey Parker was a victim of the same killer. They had a dead boy and a missing boy; it was a small island, and it wasn't much of a leap. Had Mikey been older, they would have assumed he ran away off-island, but he was too young.

She read through the interviews with the Parkers. It was clear that Susan Parker was already coming unglued. She started off like any mother of a missing child would—worried, scared, entreating the police to do more. Beseeching God to bring back her Mikey in front of the officers. Then over time, it was more about God and his infinite plan. God had taken Mikey from them; it was his divine Providence, not for her to question. She'd gradually fallen apart, finding solace in extreme faith. James Parker was a rock throughout it, stoically answering questions about clothing, times, and dates, the things that every missing person investigation requires.

Harris couldn't blame Susan Parker for unraveling. She must have been under unbelievable strain. That type of grief, the uncertainty, it was a wonder that Susan Parker had held up as well as she did. Then Jo remembered what Chief Almeida had said about Susan Parker's going to church every day. How she was there looking for answers about her son from God. *Jesus, that poor woman,* Jo thought.

She came to the end of the Richie Sousa file. The file on Mikey Parker was just a few pages. They didn't have a body, there was no forensics; they didn't know anything other than when he disappeared. She flipped to the file on Nick Steuben's murder.

Steuben had been last seen near Pine Street. He'd been playing with friends at the field on Mill Street. The assumption was that he was going to meet his mother at her job at the Pacific National Bank at the head of Main Street. It wasn't far, half a mile at most. He should have made it there in ten minutes, fifteen if he'd dallied, but he never arrived.

Steuben's mother returned home, and her son wasn't in their apartment. She was divorced, and the boy's father was still in Connecticut. An hour later, she called the Nantucket Police Department, and they sent Officer Joe Almeida out to interview her. Harris couldn't picture the chief as a young cop with his .38 revolver hanging off his hip.

She looked at the photocopy of his typed notes. They laid out a bare timeline of events as well as the child's clothing description. Almeida had talked to the kids who Nick Steuben had played with, as well as interviewing the last of them to see him alive. The boy's name and address were redacted, and Jo made a mental note to ask the chief about it.

Like the chief had told them, Steuben was discovered on the steps leading up to Academy Hill School by a lady walking her dog two mornings after his disappearance. There was a fresh note on a Post-it next to the woman's name, stating that she'd died in 1988 of natural causes. Steuben was found in only his underwear and T-shirt.

Jo read the grim autopsy report. It was nearly identical to Richie Sousa's. Maybe finding Mikey Parker's remains thirty-five years later was a blessing in disguise. She didn't have to read about the bruising, hematomas, and ligatures, or the other stuff that really made her stomach turn. She noted the crime scene photos and the crime scene sketch. The body had been posed.

The killer, Randal James Hampton, like a lot of serial killers, was a creature of habit. He killed the victims and transported them to another location. He probably dumped the bodies late at night or very early in the morning. The parking lot of Academy Hill was positioned such that he could have driven over to the steps and backed to within a few feet. Because the steps were below the line of sight, with retaining walls on either side, he would've had all the privacy he needed to position the body. The victims' injuries were the same, and the kids all came from the same pool of acquaintances.

"Shit!" Harris exclaimed.

"What?" Kelly looked up from his own file.

"Jesus, Kelly. He watched them. He watched them playing football."

"Why do you say that?"

"Kelly, all these kids—Mikey Parker, Richie Sousa, Nick Steuben—they all played football together in the same field on Mill Street."

"Sure," he said slowly.

"It was a small group of kids. A small pool of victims to choose from. He must have been watching them as they played."

"Jo, it's a small island, even smaller then. All the kids here knew each other."

"But these kids, they all played together. Regularly. It was a small group of kids that the victims were all from. He sat there, watching them, stalking them . . . Kelly, he was hunting little kids. He followed them, and either an opportunity presented itself to him or he made one in order to snatch the kids. Jesus. Sick fuck."

"Yeah, now that you put it like that," Kelly said, stone-faced.

"Jesus, this whole thing is sick."

"Child murders are bad, something like this is unimaginable."

"I can't imagine what it was like for the chief back then. Living through this."

"Probably pretty rough."

"Are you through with your files?"

"No, not quite. You?"

"Yes. Do you need much longer?"

"No, give me a few minutes."

"Sure." Harris watched Kelly while he read through the files, his brows knitted, chewing on his lower lip while scribbling notes. After a few minutes, while her mind had drifted to the night before, he put his copy of the file down on the table. He sat back, eyes shut as he pinched the bridge of his nose, then sat up.

"What do you think?" he asked the younger detective.

"I think the bones are definitely Mikey Parker."

"Me too."

"In that regard, I think once the DNA confirms it, this case is closed."

"That eager to get rid of me?" he asked with a wan smile.

"No, it's not that," she said with a little more enthusiasm than she expected. She hadn't thought about it, much less given voice to it, but she'd grown used to him being around. Going to bed together had seemed like a natural extension of things. A foregone conclusion. Suddenly she didn't like the thought of him on the mainland instead of being here next to her. *Where'd that come from?* she wondered.

"What is it, then?"

"Kelly, this whole thing feels weird."

"Why, because Mikey Parker wasn't placed like . . ."

"No, it's not that. Not just that. There could be a hundred different explanations. Mikey was his first victim, and he was still figuring out his own technique." Kelly grunted at her use of the word *technique*. "Or there was something in his circumstances that made disposing of Mikey's remains different. But that isn't what I'm talking about."

"So what are you talking about?"

"Kelly, you've been a detective for a while, worked a few homicides."

"More than a few," he said.

"Have you ever seen case notes like these? It's like they're only partial files. There's a lot that's missing or been pulled out."

Kelly started to squirm in his seat, his eyes glazing over. "Like what?"

"Like the fourth victim. The one that got away. How come there's nothing about him in any of these files? How come what little there is, it's redacted?"

"That's because we were trying to protect the child," Chief Almeida said from the doorway. "Jo, this is a small town. In 1981, it was smaller and more . . . backward."

"How is that an answer, Chief?"

"You read the files. You know what Hampton did to those boys. Can you imagine the effect that would have on a kid growing up here? You know how people here gossip. Well, it was a lot worse when that was the primary form of entertainment in the winter. It wasn't just the boy; it was his parents too."

"You're protecting them . . . or you were?"

"Randal James Hampton did more than just abuse and kill those boys. He poisoned this community. Imagine how people felt. It was the offseason, the weather packing in, and the year-rounders felt like they were trapped on the island with a killer. No one knew who he was."

"I don't see . . ."

"Of course you don't. You can't because you weren't there. It hurt this community. But after we got him, after it was done, the family of the boy who survived, they weren't treated like heroes. Instead, all the worst parts of society in small towns focused on them. Why had their son been spared? Why did they get to be happy when three other families never would be again? It was like dumping poison in a well. All the questions turned to resentment. Eventually they were ostracized, and they left the island."

"Chief, was it really that bad?"

"No. Jo, it was worse than that. Much worse."

"Chief, who was the fourth victim?"

"He was a very, very brave little boy who got away."

"What happened, Chief?"

"The fourth victim, Albie, got off at the wrong bus stop. Some kids were teasing him, and he decided he'd show everyone by hiding. Making them think he had been abducted by Hampton."

"It didn't work out that way," Kelly said, his voice low.

"No, Detective, it didn't. Hampton must have seen him at some point. He lured the eight-year-old boy into his car and then incapacitated him." The chief spoke slowly, the strain of the memories rising to the surface after so many years.

"Then what?" Harris asked.

"He took the boy to the JFK bunker out in Tom Nevers. He assaulted him, and after a time, he passed out. We found any number of drugs at the scene that would have done it. The boy woke up and somehow managed to free himself without disturbing Hampton."

"That's when he got away?"

"That was the beginning of another sort of ordeal. The boy walked out into an unusually warm December night. It was probably in the low forties. He managed to walk down the beach two or three miles from Tom Nevers field to the airport. He somehow got under the fence and cut across the runway and made his way to the pay phone in front of the terminal."

"Gutsy move, crossing the runway at night. He could have been hit by a plane or something."

"It was late and foggy, but still very brave. It also saved his life."

"Hampton was chasing him?" Harris asked, ever the eager student.

"No, hypothermia. He was barefoot, missing his blue jeans and winter jacket. I don't think he would have lasted much longer in the cold. Crazy that he even made it to the pay phone. He did, though, and he called his mother. His father and Mikey Parker's father were out looking for him. Calling home from pay phones every ten or fifteen minutes, hoping for news."

"He must have felt like he won the lottery the last time he called home," Kelly said.

"He surely did. He and Jimmy Parker drove out to the airport, and there was Albie, curled up on the bench by the pay phone. He was asleep, and hypothermia was beginning to set in. It must have been a hell of a shock to see your kid like that. I can only imagine how they felt."

"Then what happened?" Harris leaned forward.

"He described where he was held to his father, told his father where he'd escaped from. He described his route, and his father figured it out. He called me and told me to meet him at the JFK bunker. Hampton had been using it to . . . to do things to the kids in private."

"How'd he know about it? You said he was an off-islander."

"He'd been hired to help clean up the old navy base. The bunker was part of the facility, and they were using it as temporary storage. He had access to it and, more importantly, he kept it locked up."

"Did anyone think to look there for the missing kids?"

"Sure, when we looked it was all boxes and crates, like some sort of haunted warehouse."

"So what happened?"

"I met them out at the bunker—Albie, his dad, and Jimmy Parker. They told me the guy who abducted Albie and hurt him was inside. I told them to take Albie to the hospital, and I'd go arrest the guy. They left with the boy. I called it in, and the sergeant told me to wait for backup."

"You didn't, did you?"

"No, Jo. It was five or ten minutes away at best, but I wasn't in the mood to wait. I remember walking up the tunnel, which was basically one long Quonset hut stuck to another one at right angles. I could hear music and smell burned weed. I remember thinking of how I felt and thinking of how brave Albie must have been to walk down that tunnel in the dark, no Maglite, no gun. Just a little kid clutching a quarter.

"I stepped into the main room, and it was clear that the boxes and crates we saw when we searched had been for show. There was Hampton, lying on an old army cot, naked from the waist down. I must have made a noise or startled him, because he sat up, pulled a revolver, and ripped off a shot that went by my head. You can still see the mark on the old door of the bunker where the bullet hit."

"What did you do?"

"I shot him between the eyes," Joe Almeida replied matter-of-factly.

CHAPTER 13

"You shot him."

"Yup. To be honest, I think I would have even if he hadn't pulled on me."

Kelly sat still, listening to the chief, trying to visualize it.

"I know you wouldn't have," Harris said, wanting to believe her own words.

"After that, the cavalry arrived, as they say."

"Chief, how come this was never in the papers, not even the local one?" Harris asked.

"Because they didn't want to blow it, Jo," Kelly said, shaking his head. He was trying to follow everything the chief was saying, to make some sort of sense out of it.

"What do you mean?" she asked.

"This place was different then. There were rich people, summer people, and yachts, but nothing like now. The year-round community was pretty tight. Then there was a lot of investment in the island. People started to sell land or houses for more money than they could make in ten years. They didn't want to scare the money away," the chief explained.

"That was it?" Jo said.

"It wouldn't have made a difference. Chief Svenson wanted to, but the Board of Selectmen urged caution. We were searching high and low for the boys, for their killer. It was only a matter of time, and we ended up getting him in the end."

"What about the local trooper? Why didn't he report it?" She kept digging.

"Someone talked to him."

"Who?" Harris asked angrily.

"I'm not sure exactly. It was either a banker or a real estate developer or both."

"What'd they say?" Kelly asked hoarsely.

"I don't know, Detective. I do know that the trooper in question wanted to retire on the island, run a little charter fishing business. His dream came true."

"Al Johnson? They bought him off?"

"They floated him mortgages and business loans that he never could have gotten with just his trooper's pension."

"Was he the only one?" Harris asked pointedly, staring at the chief.

"Are you asking if they bought me off?"

"Yes, that's *exactly* what I'm asking."

"No. I was happy to pay my own mortgage and work my way up from being a patrolman."

"But you're here," she said icily.

"Why'd you keep quiet, Chief?" Kelly asked, wondering how they'd gotten here. The whole thing seemed a little surreal when he heard Almeida talking about it.

"The chief at the time decided how he wanted to handle this. He wasn't a bad man nor a stupid one. The whole island knew what was happening, but no one from the outside was going to do much more than muddy the waters. That was the consensus. Then, afterward, after it was done, it didn't make sense to make a fuss about it."

"Not even an 'attaboy' or your picture in the paper?" Harris asked.

"No, Jo. I didn't want any of that. In truth, I never felt like I deserved any of it. I failed those boys. Every one of them. But in the end, I believe we caught Randal James Hampton as fast as it could have been done. If I was wrong, then I'll have to live with that for the rest of my life," the chief said quietly.

"But they took care of you, didn't they." She wasn't asking him a question.

"They did, Jo. I never asked for it, but I always ended up getting an extra detail or two when money was tight. Specialized training came my way. The department paid for two degrees and sent me to the FBI Academy. Promotions too. I never questioned it. I just went on with my life."

"What happened to the others? The parents?"

Kelly sat quietly, not sure if anything he could say would make things better or worse.

"Nick Steuben's mother drank herself to death. It took ten years, but she never heard of President Bill Clinton. Richie Sousa's parents stayed on the island until a few years ago. They moved away as the fishing fleet couldn't afford Nantucket as a port anymore. I think they're in Florida or something. And you know what happened to Susan Parker. She never got over losing her son. They say some people die of a broken heart . . . She died of grief. The grief of losing her son killed her. It took years, but it got her as sure as cancer. Jimmy ended up owning his own construction company. It grew rapidly, and he did quite well. He was a popular contractor, got a lot of referrals. He did well enough that when the owner of the Oceanview ran into some financial problems, Jimmy went in with him as a partner. When the original owner kept snorting his profits and got into more financial trouble, Jimmy was able to buy him out."

"What happened to Albie and his family?" Harris asked.

"Ah, that's a tough one."

"Tough how?"

"This was a great place to live." He paused as though he was carefully choosing his next words. "But it was also provincial, narrow-minded, and, at times, cruel."

"I am not following you."

"You would have thought that they would have rallied around Albie's family. Treated Albie like the hero he was. You would think that, wouldn't you? For some reason, it was like Albie and his family were marked by something. There were ugly rumors. Albie's dad got into a few fistfights. Their house was egged. People started saying that Albie didn't escape, but that . . . that he did what he had to do to get away. Instead of being happy for Albie's mom, the other women—the other mothers—shunned her. She was punished for her boy having survived. In the end, the family moved off the island. Driven away. Not with pitchforks and torches, but with whispers and cold, nasty stares."

"So then why not tell us who Albie was?"

Kelly felt like he was watching an interrogation more than three cops sitting around having a coffee, talking about an old case.

"Because I made a promise to his father after, and, more importantly, standing in that bunker, I made a promise to the boy. I promised to protect him for the rest of my life."

"Chief, they left. Thirty-five years ago. What does it matter now?"

"Jo, I can't imagine what that boy went through. I can only imagine how brave he had to be to get away. The ordeal he went through just getting to the airport. Then this town, my community, shit on him and his family. It was the definition of insult to injury. The least I can do is keep my promise. It won't make up for anything, but it's something. God knows I couldn't protect Albie before or after he was taken."

"Chief . . ."

"No. That's final, Jo. That's all I have to say."

CHAPTER 14

The two detectives watched the chief walk out. They waited in semistunned silence, listening to his footsteps moving down the hall, away from the conference room. The two detectives looked at each other.

"What the hell?" Harris asked.

"I'm not sure what to say," Kelly said.

"Did he actually say that they covered up the abductions and murders of boys because it would be bad for business?"

"It sounded a lot like it." Kelly was still processing everything he'd just heard.

"They really covered it up," Harris said.

"Did they? I mean, it's a small island. Everyone knew. They were still investigating, trying to find Hampton. It seems like they went overboard keeping it an island thing."

"But if they had help from the Staties or the FBI . . . they might have caught him sooner."

"They might, but I don't think so. MSP would have sent a detective or two for the first kid. The FBI wouldn't have gotten involved until the third at the earliest. I don't know how much difference it would have made."

"You make it sound like they were doing good police work. They got lucky. That kid, Albie, got away and somehow stayed alive long enough to call for help. That's how they caught him. Luck, dumb fucking luck."

"You know that most police work is being in the right place at the right time. Getting lucky."

"What if their approach cost some kids their lives or got that last kid hurt? What then?"

"I think that they were doing the best they could. Sure, there was a lot of pressure, but I don't think that hampered the investigation or trying to find the kids."

"So they kept a lid on it so that they could sell more houses?"

"And have a tourist season. Even in 1981, I have to imagine that it brought in more money than the fishing fleet did. Imagine what the summer of '82 would have looked like if people were afraid to bring their families out because their kids might get abducted and killed. Real estate would have tanked too."

"You sound like you're defending them."

"No, I'm trying to understand what went down. It was a bad decision, but that's the one they made."

"It reminds me of the mayor in *Jaws*. How he doesn't want Chief Brody to warn the people about the shark because it will tank the summer tourist business."

"Didn't Benchley have a house out here?"

"Yeah, in 'Sconset."

"Maybe Benchley was a visionary?"

"More likely he understood human nature," she said.

"Or he understood the small-town mentality."

"Yeah, more likely that."

"So they caught the guy but kept the murders quiet. Everyone on the island knew, but they didn't tell the MSP. Is that a crime or just sketchy?"

"I don't know, Kelly. I don't know how to feel about this. I hate thinking that the chief was a party to it."

"You know he's still the same guy."

"Same guy?"

"He's still the same guy you respected and looked up to before he told us about this. The same guy who gave you a shot and mentored you. The only difference now is that there's a little tarnish on him. It doesn't change who he is, and it shouldn't change your relationship with him."

"Kelly, I wasn't expecting that from you. You don't seem like a guy who's awfully forgiving."

"Jo, all of us make mistakes. Bad judgment or no judgment, we all have our secrets and have our share of sins."

If Kelly thought she was going to tell him angrily to mind his own business, he couldn't have been more wrong. She got up, bent down, threw her arms around him, and kissed him deeply.

"Thank you, Kelly. I needed to hear that." Then she started to walk out.

"Hey, where are you going?"

"I have to run an errand. Also, I don't know about you, but I'm hungry. You want the usual?"

"Please."

"You look like you didn't get much sleep last night," she said with a mischievous grin as she left. Kelly smiled in spite of the general mood that had fallen over him in the last couple of hours. He liked her and hoped that the previous night wasn't a one-time thing. He shook his head and went back to the files, going over them, looking for something in the pile of unpleasant details and ancient history.

At some point, while Kelly was going through it all, Dukowski walked in.

"Hey, Detective," he said by way of greeting.

"Hey, Mike."

"Have you seen Jo?"

"She stepped out. Said she had an errand to run. What's up?"

"Oh, I got a report from Doc Redruth about the bon . . . the remains we found."

"I'll take it, make sure she gets them."

"Sure, of course," Dukowski said, handing Kelly a manila envelope.

"Thanks, Ski," Kelly said as he tossed the envelope on the table, going back to his case notes.

"No problem. See ya," the young officer said as he walked out. It occurred to Kelly that Dukowski was probably the same age Joe Almeida had been when the killings happened. Kelly couldn't picture Ski walking up a hallway to face a serial killer without backup. Something told Kelly that Almeida had been a bit more world-wise at that age.

He went back to reading the reports from 1981, compiling a list of all the questions he had. He added notes about anything that stood out from the things that he'd highlighted. Then he made three columns in his notebook, one for each of the dead boys. In each of the columns he wrote down the characteristics of the injuries, of their dumpsites. He also wrote down the dates and times they were reported missing.

Kelly filled in the columns for Nick Steuben and Richie Sousa. They were very similar. Near identical would be a better way of putting it. They had both been missing for thirty-six to forty-eight hours. Both boys had died of strangulation after being sexually and physically abused. The catalog of injuries matched, as did the dumpsites. Both were in public but still out of the way, enough to allow Hampton to place the bodies without being seen.

Kelly's stomach was turning, going over it all. He was having trouble focusing, and the air around him felt charged with electricity. Like it is before a lightning strike. Kelly could hear the blood pounding in his ears, and his mind kept drifting. He kept thinking about the Rankin and Bass cartoon version of *The Hobbit*. He had to keep dragging his attention away from that back to his notes and the reports.

When he had written all he could about those two homicides, he turned to the envelope that Dukowski had dropped off. Kelly pulled out twenty or so pages of typewritten script. There were also a bunch of digital pictures of X-rays. Kelly started reading the files, going through everything twice. He kept hearing the orcs' marching song from the cartoon. It involved a whip instead of willpower.

Mikey Parker's remains, having been discovered thirty-five years after he was abducted by Randal James Hampton, didn't have anything to offer by way of forensics. There was no way to tell from his remains if he'd been abused by Hampton like the other victims. Redruth's report indicated that Mikey Parker was malnourished based on bone density. He hadn't received dental care. There were many indications that Mikey had been beaten: broken ribs, a spiral fracture of his right forearm. The spiral fracture hadn't healed, indicating that it had occurred near the time of death. Mikey's hyoid bone was intact, making it unlikely that strangulation had been the cause of death. Lastly, his skull showed evidence of blunt force trauma to the head, which most likely had been the cause of death.

Kelly felt like his skin was tingling. He kept looking up expecting to see someone in the conference room with him, but there wasn't anyone else there. He rubbed his knuckle into his temple to refocus. He knew the answer was somewhere in the reports he was looking at, not in some old cartoon movie.

Kelly sat there, staring at the columns on the notebook page. Two near identical and one different. Kelly kept looking at the lists of injuries. The dissimilarity in the placement of the bodies. He knew he was looking at something significant, but he couldn't quite tease out the detail he needed. He couldn't quite focus. The more he concentrated, the louder the rushing sound of the ocean in his ears became. He was trying to tease some nugget, some memory from a class he went to, from the recesses of his mind. The more he tried to focus, the harder it was.

I'm cracking up, he thought. Pressing his knuckle to his temple, he rubbed it hard in an up-and-down motion.

Then his head cleared. The noise of the ocean, the noise of diving into the water, being under the surf, receded into the distance. It was all clear to him. "Call yourself a detective," he said to himself in disgust.

"You can't pin this on me. I'm a hobbit, not a cop," Bilbo said.

"Well, as partners go, you haven't exactly been pulling your weight," Kelly replied.

"Ha, don't blame me, I've never been to a police academy."

"Some partner you are."

"I've gotten you out of tougher scrapes." Kelly never understood why Bilbo chose to affect the accent of a TV cop show detective from New York, but he did whenever they were working a case.

Kelly had pulled out his phone and started to text Harris when Chief Almeida walked in.

"Where's Jo?"

"She said she had something she had to do, and then she'd bring back lunch."

"You didn't go with her?" There was a question within a question that the chief didn't quite ask.

"She said she'd go on her own. I decided to look at the files. Doc Redruth's report came in."

"Anything of note?"

"There is, and I don't think you're going to like it."

"Go on, Detective," the chief said evenly.

"I was comparing the autopsy reports from Nick Steuben and Richie Sousa to Doc Redruth's report." Kelly was speaking with care. He was entering uncomfortable territory.

"And?"

"They don't match up. Nick's and Richie's are near identical in terms of the injuries, body placement, and cause of death. Mikey, on the other hand, likely wasn't strangled to death. The hyoid bone was still intact. He appears to have been killed from a blow to his head. Doc mentioned that it was probably a rounded object, like a bat. On top of that, he had a fractured right forearm. He was malnourished and didn't see the dentist often."

"What are you getting at, Detective?" The chief's voice was chilly. No one likes being told they'd screwed up.

"Chief, Randal James Hampton didn't kill Mikey Parker. His injuries are consistent with child abuse, not what the others went through."

"Jesus. There's no way. It had to be Hampton."

"My guess is it was your good friend, his father."

"Jimmy Parker . . . I've known him for years. He'd never . . . he could never. I don't believe it."

"Don't believe it or won't believe it?" Kelly asked.

"Does it matter?" Almeida shot back.

"When did he first report Mikey missing?" Kelly said.

"I think it was right after Richie Sousa went missing."

"Are you sure, or is it possible that in the middle of the search for not one but two missing kids that things could have gotten confused? Or that Jimmy Parker took advantage of the situation to deflect the blame away from himself?"

"Jesus," the chief said again.

"After all, he was the one who shot Hampton, and you covered it up."

The Bunker,
December 1981

He drifted off to sleep again, but this time it was different. He woke up when his dad's truck bounced and jostled him out of his warm, safe nap.

They were bouncing over the field he had walked across. The fog was thinning out, and the headlights splashed across the Monster's car. Albie could see the bobblehead hula dancer on the dashboard.

"Albie, stay in the truck while Mr. Parker and I go inside," his dad said right after he parked.

"Dad, I don't . . ."

"Albie, listen to me. We won't be long. Just stay here and lock the doors."

"Okay."

"You ready, Jimmy?"

"Yep." Jimmy held up his hand, showing Albie's dad his gun. It was a revolver like the police carried. Both men got out of the truck, pushing the doors shut, and went over to the bunker's recessed entrance. Albie saw that his dad had a gun, too, one of the ones that the guys in the war movies always carried. An automatic, he thought it was called.

He watched the two men go to the door and pull it slowly open, then go in. They didn't shut it behind them. Albie sat in the dark truck for a few seconds.

"What if the Monster is hiding his car and he gets me again?"

Albie got out of the truck. It was better to face a spanking from his dad than have the Monster get him. Albie hobbled as quickly as he could to the bunker's door. They had left it partially open. He slipped through the opening. He could see his dad and Mr. Parker up ahead. They were moving quietly toward the cave where Albie had been held by the Monster. Albie could smell the burned spices again and hear the weird music playing. The two adults stepped into the room and moved slowly forward. Albie stopped at the edge of the tunnel. He could see the Monster sleeping on a camp bed.

He was still holding the rope that he'd tied around Albie's neck, loosely in his hand. Albie also noticed he wasn't wearing any pants or even underpants. Normally just thinking about an adult in their underpants would have made Albie laugh, but not tonight.

"Wake up, you son of a bitch!" Mr. Parker yelled.

The Monster jumped to his feet.

"You killed Mikey!" Mr. Parker screamed, and then his gun roared, and a fireball seemed to leap from it.

The Monster collapsed back on the camp bed with a third eye in his head.

"Jesus, Jimmy, we were supposed to bring him in alive."

"Fuck that, he killed my son. Hurt your boy. How could you even think we'd let him live? He deserved what he got."

"What are we going to tell Joe?"

"I dunno."

"Tell me about what?" Officer Almeida asked from the darkness behind Albie.

"Jimmy shot the guy."

"Hello, Albie. Are you okay?" Officer Almeida asked him.

"I'm kinda hurt, sir. Cold too."

"Albie, I told you to wait in the truck."

"I couldn't, Dad. I saw the Monster's car. I was scared he was hiding, and he'd come get me again."

"Again?" Almeida asked no one in particular.

"It's okay, Albie," his dad said.

"Jimmy, what happened?"

"I shot him, Joe. That son of a bitch killed my Mikey, and I shot him."

"Jimmy, you've got a record. You shouldn't even have a gun."

Albie watched the adults talk. He couldn't figure out why they seemed angry with each other. He was cold and sore and just wanted them to work it out so he could get home to Mommy.

"I don't care, Joe," Mr. Parker said.

Officer Almeida stood there, not saying anything for a minute, chewing on his lower lip. "Jimmy, where'd you get the gun?"

Albie didn't understand why that mattered. Sometimes adults didn't make sense.

"I won it in a poker game with some guys off a fishing boat."

"Local boat?" Officer Almeida asked. Albie wasn't sure why it mattered.

"No, they were out of Gloucester."

"Gun's not registered?"

"No. You know I have a record. I can't register a gun. Also, it might be hot."

Albie didn't understand why having a record mattered. He had a record of the Muppets singing Christmas songs. Did that mean he couldn't own a gun when he was bigger?

"Okay. Give me the gun." Mr. Parker placed the gun in Officer Almeida's hand.

Albie almost warned him not to take it. Mr. Parker had said the gun was hot. He didn't want Officer Almeida to get burned.

"Jimmy, show me where you were standing."

"Right about here," Mr. Parker indicated.

"You were the only one who shot him?"

"Yep."

"Okay. As far as everyone is concerned, you two waited outside until I got here. Albie too. Then you saw me go inside, and you left to take Albie to the hospital. I'll take care of the rest."

"You sure, Joe?"

"Yep, with Jimmy's record, this is the best way. Now take your boy to the hospital. Call your wife when you get there. I'll take care of all this."

"Okay, Joe, whatever you say."

"C'mon, Albie," Big Tom Kelly said, "Officer Almeida's right. We should get you checked out at the hospital. I know your mother's worried sick."

"Okay, Dad." Albie was glad to go. He never wanted to see this terrible place again and didn't understand what Officer Almeida and Mr. Parker were talking about.

CHAPTER 15

The air in the conference room began to feel heavy, like the air right before a sudden summer thunderstorm. Then, deflated, Joe Almeida sat down at the table, looking closely at Kelly. Bilbo stood in the corner. Normally he played bad cop, but now he was letting Kelly take the lead.

"You look just like your dad. I knew it was you the minute I saw you."

"Thanks. I get that a lot."

"Did you see this case and ask to come out here? Come out here looking to rake me over the coals for the choices I made thirty-five years ago?"

"No, this was the last place I ever wanted to come back to. We were shorthanded, and the lieutenant gave it to me. There's no arguing with Dickie Savoy."

"That's it? Just dumb luck?"

"Pretty much."

"So now what?"

"Now I'm going to drive out to Wauwinet and talk to Jimmy Parker."

Bilbo was standing at the door, tapping his foot with uncharacteristic impatience, waiting for Kelly.

"Kelly, he's in puppet land upstairs," Almeida said, tapping his index finger against his temple. Kelly wondered, looking at Bilbo Baggins in the doorway, if Parker was the only one in puppet land.

"Randal James Hampton was an evil man, take it from me," he said. "But Mikey deserves some measure of justice, even if it's thirty-five years too late."

"We really did believe it was Hampton." Almeida put extra emphasis on the word *really*.

"I know. Time's wasting. You want to tell Jo where I went when she gets back?"

"Sure."

"Thanks." Kelly got up and left the conference room as he whispered to Bilbo, "Let's roll."

CHAPTER 16

Outside, the chief heard Kelly's black Crown Vic start up and move off. Almeida's mind was thirty-five years away, thinking about a brave little boy and the very real monster that he came into contact with. He was still sitting there, gazing out the window, when Jo Harris blew in like a hurricane fifteen minutes later.

"What the fuck sick game are you two playing at?" She slapped a photocopy of a newspaper article on the table in front of Almeida.

"What's that, Jo?" he asked with the voice of a man who was long ago defeated.

"You gotta love small towns, Chief, and small-town newspapers. Everything is newsworthy. Even something like a school fair. I went to the Atheneum and went through all the microfiche from 1980 and 1981, looking for pictures of the victims. I was hoping to find Albie."

"Uh-huh. Solid detective work. Always knew you had the talent," Almeida said with a detached voice.

"I found pictures of the other kids, but one picture stood out. It showed a fat kid eating cake, a daub of frosting on his cheek. The caption read, 'Little Tommy Kelly, Albie to his friends, enjoys a slice of cake at the bake sale.'"

"Good work, Jo."

"You knew it was him?"

"Not at first. I knew the State Police were sending a detective. I didn't think much about it. Then I saw him, and I knew. He looks just like his dad, Big Tom Kelly."

"You knew he was Albie, and you didn't fucking tell me?"

"His middle name is Albert, after a friend of Big Tom's killed in Vietnam. The family always called him Albie instead of Tommy. The kids called him Albie because he was fat. Fat Albie, like Fat Albert."

"Why didn't you say something?"

"Jo, what was I supposed to tell you? That the detective you were working with was a victim in a thirty-five-year-old case that we solved? That he was raped, beaten, and barely escaped with his life? The man who you recently spent the night with? That wasn't for me to tell you."

"You were still protecting him."

"I felt . . . I *feel* horrible for the Kellys. After Albie was found, after he got out of the hospital, this place, like I said, people turned on them. Lots of people said that it was unfair that Albie lived, and the other boys didn't. Some people said it to Mary Kelly in the supermarket, other times it was in church. Some people sent the family notes. Some kids egged their house and car. This island, this place collectively wronged them, on top of what happened to that boy. It wasn't right. He was such a brave kid. The Kellys were good people. They didn't deserve the shit they got. None of it."

"What else didn't you tell me?"

"I didn't shoot Hampton."

"Big Tom Kelly?"

"No, Parker. They got there before me. Parker shot Hampton just as I got there. He had a record, and the gun was hot. He would have gone to jail again."

"So you helped him out?" she asked sarcastically.

"I took Parker's .38 and sent them to take Albie to the hospital. Then I went over to where Hampton's corpse was, squatted down, and fired a round from my own .38 at the door."

"But the bullets, there's no way they would match."

"It was 1981. Most .38 rounds were lead roundnose 158-grain bullets. Same basic bullet in each gun. No one was going to make a ballistics comparison, even if the bullet hadn't been mangled by the heavy metal door of the bunker. Hampton was dead, and no one on-island was going to dig too deeply into who or how. No one off-island was going to look too closely either. The Staties were out of the loop. It was done."

"So your career was built on a lie."

"No, my career was built on my not talking about any of it. Just like Jimmy Parker's business was a success, and Al Johnson got to retire and live his dream. No one wanted anything other than to forget the bad business."

"And make sure that people still wanted to come out here for the summer, to buy land and build million-dollar homes. Right? Jesus, this stinks, Chief. Where's Kelly?"

"Don't hold any of this against him, Jo. He was eight. All the lies, he didn't have any part of it. And as for not telling you, I'm not even sure how he could have."

"Where is he?"

"He went out to interview and probably arrest Jimmy Parker."

"What for?"

"Because Kelly figured out that Mikey wasn't murdered by Hampton and that he'd been abused for years."

"By his father?"

"Most likely."

"And he's going out there to bring him in?"

"Or kill him," Almeida said matter-of-factly.

Harris didn't say anything but instead turned on her heels and ran for the door.

March 1982

Albie was standing on the deck of the ferry. He was next to his mother, looking out toward town. Albie watched the cars driving up the street by the Whaling Museum and town hall. A few people, small like ants, were walking around in the distance. The sun was out, but it was chilly.

They were leaving the island. Albie should have felt sad, he knew that. He was leaving the only home he'd ever known. He wasn't sad, though. Standing up on the deck, he felt something else as the breeze ruffled his hair. He felt something in his chest loosening, unlocking. Bilbo was standing in the parking lot, small hobbit hand raised in a frozen wave goodbye.

His bruises had healed. He still slept with a light on in his room. He wet the bed sometimes, like a little kid. He knew he was too old to do it, but his parents didn't say anything. They just had him change his pajamas and stripped the bed. His mom would give him a hug and lie next to him, holding him until he fell asleep.

Many nights when he woke up after dreaming about being in the Monster's cave, he was glad to see either Mommy or Daddy sitting in the reclining chair they'd moved into his bedroom. If it was Mommy, he knew that he could wake her up and ask her to hold him. He'd be safe and warm and loved. If it was his dad, he knew he'd be safe. Even if the Monster was still alive, he knew it would be too scared to come for him. His daddy had been a hero in the war. Albie had seen the medals. His dad would protect him from anything.

Peter Colt

That had been in the beginning. Albie went back to school in the new year. He was nervous and didn't know what to expect. He knew that everyone knew he'd been taken by the Monster. In his daydreams, they treated him like a returning hero. Nothing could have been further from the truth. It wasn't that anyone was outright mean to him. No one called him "Al-pee" or teased him. No one said anything to him at all after his first day back when his teacher made the class welcome him back.

The other kids just left him alone. He wasn't asked to play kickball or football anymore. No one wanted to talk about Star Wars *or sit with him at lunch. Albie didn't get invited to any birthday parties. In many ways, Albie felt like he'd died in the Monster's cave and come back as a ghost. That was why no one could see him or talk to him.*

He didn't have to worry about sitting next to anyone on the bus because his mother drove him to and from school daily. Every day like clockwork, when he walked out the doors of the elementary school, she was waiting in her car for him. She wouldn't let him out of her sight.

Albie's chest grew tighter with each passing day. It would have been easier if someone like Louie Delvecchio had teased him or said anything. It would have been easier if he had someone to be angry with or to fight. Instead, it was the whispers that got to him. The kids in school were always whispering around him. His parents were always whispering. The few times he went to the supermarket with his mommy, he heard people whispering but no one would look at him.

When no one in school would talk to him, Albie would imagine he was hanging out with Bilbo Baggins. Maybe they were having second breakfast. Bilbo would be smoking his fragrant pipe, and they'd compare adventures and close calls that they'd had. Albie loved it when the dwarves gave Bilbo his dagger, Sting. He loved that it glowed blue when there were orcs nearby. He wished he had that in the cave with the Monster. He really loved the scene where Bilbo saved the dwarves, floating them down the river in barrels. Bilbo was clever. As his schoolmates closed him out more and more, Albie began to spend more time in the fantasy world he created with Bilbo. It didn't hurt to live in his imagination.

Then one night his parents sat down with him while he was playing with his Matchbox cars on the floor.

"Albie."

"Yeah."

"We have something to tell you."

"What, Mommy?"

"Sweetie, we're moving."

"To Surfside?" Albie couldn't think of any other part of the island to move to.

"No, sweetie. We're going to move off-island. Daddy's been offered a job on the mainland working with your Uncle Bob."

"Okay." Six months ago, he would have cried and felt horrible. Now he just felt the tightness in his chest. Moving away didn't seem so bad.

The horn on the ferry blew loudly above them, startling Albie. When the second one blew, he was expecting it. The ferry began to pull away from the pier, and Albie walked to the port side so he could see Brant Point. He and Mommy always threw pennies overboard as they passed Brant Point. It was a local tradition that meant they'd return safely.

"Mommy?"

"Yes, sweetie."

"Can I have a penny to throw overboard?"

"No, honey. I don't ever want to come back to this godforsaken place again," his mother said bitterly.

Albie didn't know what to say, but he was learning that sometimes you didn't have to say anything. He looked out across the harbor at the small lighthouse, the one he thought he was walking toward that cold night three months ago. The gulls wheeled overhead, riding on thermals and screeching out their particular song. The chilly ocean breeze ruffled his hair, and he watched Brant Point slide by as the ferry headed for the mainland. Albie felt something unlock in his chest as he left that terrible night behind him on the island. He knew he never wanted to come back either.

CHAPTER 17

Harris ran down the stairs and outside to her car. She had trouble getting the key in the ignition, her hands were shaking so badly. She couldn't tell if it was anger, frustration, or fear. Would Kelly really be going out there to kill Jimmy Parker? After all he'd been through, was he thinking straight? She forced herself to take a couple of breaths. She got the car started and whipped out onto Fairgrounds Road, tires screeching.

She flipped on the red-and-blue flashing lights, and when she came to intersections, she blared the siren. She turned onto Milestone Road and then cut an oncoming car off as she veered left onto Polpis Road. The Ford slipped sideways in a patch of sand left over from snow-melting duty, but Harris reflexively corrected the car and shot down the road.

Her heart was pounding, and she was still trying to process all of it. Tommy Kelly, State Police detective, was Albie. It made no sense, and it made perfect sense. Kelly's revulsion at reading the autopsy reports, the case notes, wasn't because he was a dad. He was reading about childhood friends being hurt, reliving his own trauma. A hell she couldn't imagine. She mashed down on the accelerator. She was going out there to stop him or save him, she wasn't sure which.

CHAPTER 18

Kelly stood on the steps of the house and picked up the brass door knocker, striking it three times on the brass pineapple. He waited and eventually heard footsteps from inside. Bilbo stood beside him in his peasant hobbit clothes.

"Albie, do you want to be good cop or bad cop?" Bilbo asked in a thick Sam Spade accent.

"It doesn't matter. Let's just play it by ear."

A woman in plum-colored scrubs opened the door.

"Can I help you?" she asked in a Jamaican accent.

"Is Mr. Parker in? I need to speak to him, please," Kelly said, holding up his badge and its companion ID in their case so she could see them. Bilbo Spade held out his credentials too.

"Yes. Come in." Kelly followed her inside, conscious of the weight of his pistol holstered on his hip. He followed the nurse or home health aide, whichever she was, down the hall. Parker was in the front room where Kelly had last seen him. He was watching the TV, but the sound was off, sparing them the chatter of a cable sports show. Parker stared at the images of the Red Sox on the screen, his eyes taking them in but not really seeing.

"Don't tire him out. He didn't sleep well last night," the aide said to Kelly. He might be a State Police detective, but she was his nurse. Their lines had been drawn.

"Is that uncommon?"

"He doesn't sleep well most nights. Excuse me," she said as she left the room.

Kelly sat down on the edge of one of the chairs by the couch. He leaned forward and tried to glean some sort of spark behind Parker's watery eyes. Bilbo leaned against the doorframe, unlit match clenched between his teeth.

"Mr. Parker, it's me, Detective Kelly from the State Police. I'd like to ask you some questions." Kelly stared at the old man, who just blinked at the TV without acknowledging him. "Sir, I was hoping to ask you some questions about your son, Mikey."

The old man's eyes shifted slightly.

"I was assigned to his case, and some questions have come up . . ." Kelly trailed off. "I don't believe your son was abducted by or killed by Randal James Hampton."

Nothing from the old man. *Puppet land,* Kelly heard Almeida say in his head.

"Fuck it," he said under his breath. "Sir, Mikey's remains show signs of long-term physical abuse that are consistent with child abuse. Did you or your wife beat and starve Mikey? Did you beat your son to death, Mr. Parker? Was that why you were so quick to shoot Hampton? To cover up for what you did?"

Parker's jaw started to move, like he was chewing on some unseen thing, or he was trying to find the words. Kelly realized his hand was on the butt of his pistol.

"Was it like seeing a ghost when I walked in? Big Tom back from the dead?" The old man made a gurgling noise in the back of his throat. Bilbo nodded with approval at this line of questioning.

"I'm pretty sure you're supposed to read him his rights before you question him, Detective," Laura said from the door. She was leaning, her hip against the frame, blond curls splashing over her shoulders. Her face was set in anger.

"Albie, it's the dame," Bilbo said.

"That's only on TV. If he was in custody, then I would, but this is a noncustodial interview."

"I don't think it matters much. He clearly isn't capable of cooperating with your investigation. He isn't capable of much of anything anymore."

"You know that Mikey wasn't killed by Randal James Hampton, don't you?"

"I do. Just like I know that you're the little boy that got away from that monster. Albie, isn't it?"

"Yeah, my parents stopped calling me that the minute the ferry pulled into Hyannis. I've been Tommy ever since. How do you know that Mikey wasn't killed by that man?"

"Mikey was six years younger than me. It didn't take much to figure out what was going on when my parents were talking in whispers in their bedroom."

"What happened? Did your father lose his temper? Hit him one time too many?"

"No, not him. Dad wouldn't hurt a soul."

"If your dad wasn't abusing him, then who was?" Kelly decided not to bring up the fact that her father had murdered Randal James Hampton. Laura didn't say anything.

"Laura, if you don't tell me what happened, everyone will assume your father killed Mikey."

"Everyone always blames the father, don't they?"

"Sure, it's pretty common." He glanced over at her and saw that she was staring straight ahead, her face very still, almost frozen.

Then, slowly, her lips started to move without making any noise, until she said, "It's funny how when people think about abusive parents, they automatically rule out the mother. I can't bear the thought of anyone thinking Dad hurt Mikey. He covered for her for so long and blamed himself for it all. She did it, and she should take the blame for it."

"Your mother killed Mikey?" Kelly asked, coaxing the words out of her that he wasn't sure he wanted to hear.

"She was an anxious woman, my mother. She worried about everything, and the solutions she had weren't practical but involved spiritual answers. God was her answer for everything. God told her not to spare the rod for fear of spoiling the child. She didn't spare anything. She was already getting worse, unraveling before Mikey . . . before he died.

"She used to punish us for sinning. Her God told her what to do, and she definitely didn't 'spoil' Mikey. Me neither, for that matter. I just didn't get the rod. Wouldn't do for a young lady to have bruises that would be easily seen. She never hit me where the marks would show. She made me kneel on corn kernels and pray for forgiveness. Ever kneel on corn kernels, Detective?"

"No, I can't say I have." Kelly felt his jaw stiffen as she kept speaking.

"I don't recommend it. Kneeling on corn kernels wasn't for Mikey, though. Mikey was a boy, and she thought he was being possessed by evil spirits. He used to have fits, and she was convinced that it was demons. Because epilepsy made too much sense. Why turn to medicine when you have belief? She used to beat him. Badly. But do you know what the weird thing was?"

"No, what?" he answered, almost certain he didn't want to know.

"Afterward, she'd be all lovely and sweet. Make him his favorite meal, grilled cheese and tomato soup. Then a day or two later, or even the same day, she'd go back to beating the piss out of him. I didn't get the lovey treatment afterward, but it wouldn't have been worth it."

"She killed him?"

"He had a fit, and she tried to pin him down. She tried to subdue him, which included hitting him a lot. Not slaps but with her fists. She managed to pin him, but he ended up elbowing her in the nose. She let go of him. He ran outside and hid. It was after dark. She sent Dad to find him. She made me pray for forgiveness until Dad came back with Mikey. You said you never knelt on corn kernels."

"No, I never had the occasion to."

"At first, it's just uncomfortable. After a few minutes, it hurts, and after ten, it feels like your own body weight is driving nails slowly up into your kneecaps. You try to shift your weight, to lean to one side, give one knee a little relief, but that just makes it so much worse on the other knee."

"Your dad went out to find Mikey, hoping to spare you?"

"Yes. It seemed like it was forever. It was less than an hour, but I was in agony. It hurt so much I peed myself." Kelly watched her face flush with the long-remembered shame of it. "I didn't dare tell her. She liked to punch Mikey, but for me it would have been my grandfather's old leather belt or more time kneeling. So Dad hurried out in the night to find Mikey. When he brought Mikey home, I was never so glad to see them in my life." She laughed bitterly.

"What happened then?"

"She took Mikey and dragged him into his room. She must have thrown him on the bed. She was hitting him, but he was struggling again. She got on top of him, pressing his face down, trying to pin him, trying to drive out the demons that existed only in her head. Then, after a time, he stopped moving."

"He suffocated?" There was no point in telling her that he died from a blow to the head, that the struggling on the bed just sped the process along.

"Probably. I don't know for sure."

"Then what?"

"Then Mikey was gone. A few days later, Dad told me that Mikey had been taken by the same bad man who took Richie Sousa. He was just gone. A few months later, we had a small funeral. We buried an empty coffin. Jesus, it was a small one, specially made for kids. Who came up with something like that? Then when the bones turned up in Tom Nevers, I knew. Dad must have buried him out there."

"And that was it?" Kelly asked.

"That was it."

"Your dad was trying to protect your mom."

"He knew that if we called the police, Mom would go to jail or an institution. He was an ex-con and didn't want to gamble on child services taking me away from him."

"I can see why he would worry."

"What now?"

"Albie, she's gotta go downtown and talk to a dick," Bilbo said. He had changed his clothes and was now wearing a pinstripe suit and fedora. His naked, hairy-toed feet stuck out from the cuffed pant legs. You could dress a hobbit up . . . Kelly snapped his attention back to Laura Parker with some effort. Kelly was aware of the rushing sound in his ears and that he was having trouble concentrating. It was so bad that he was listening to a hobbit in a pinstripe suit.

"I'd like you to come in and leave a formal statement."

"What good would that do now?"

"I think we owe it to Mikey. It would mean that the case would be closed, which means it would be over. For all of us."

"And Dad? What would happen to him?"

"Nothing. He's not competent to answer questions. Moreover, I don't see anyone looking to charge him with anything, least of all me."

"And me?"

"No one is going to charge you with anything. You were a young girl, the victim of your mother's delusional abuse. There's nothing to charge you with. Even if they found something, there isn't a jury in the commonwealth that would convict you. Either of you." Kelly tried his best to speak in a gentle tone.

"What will you do?"

"Take your statement. Write a report that tries to make sense of this whole mess for my boss."

"Then what will happen?"

"The report will go to the DA for review, and then it will be filed away. I will go home and work on the next case they send my way."

"You must really hate being here, huh?"

"We should go." Kelly knew there was no point in trying to answer that question.

"I wasn't going to let you take him to jail."

"I know. I don't blame you."

"Okay, let me grab my coat and tell his nurse I'll be out for an hour or two."

He nodded, and she walked out of the front room. He stood up and looked at the old shell of a man. Kelly tried to think of something poignant or witty to say like in the movies, but there wasn't anything. He just felt empty. Parker looked pathetic. There was no glory, no joy to be had in the moment as far as Kelly was concerned.

He stepped out into the hall and waited for Laura. Looked at the pictures on display. Not the normal happy family pictures, just a collection of moments in time. He stared at them, trying to see into their lives. He found his mind was wandering and kept having to claw his attention back to the pictures. The hobbit wasn't helping either. Laura looked happiest playing field hockey. Running, the wooden stick in hand and the ball against the curved end. She came downstairs and stopped long enough to put on a coat.

"Okay, Detective Albie, let's go clear the air about my dad," Laura said softly to Kelly, who looked up from the pictures.

"Sure, let's do that."

Outside, Harris's Ford came to a halt on the crushed-shell driveway. She jammed the shifter into park and hopped out. She saw Kelly and Laura Parker leaving the house.

"Kelly!" she said sharply.

"Jo, hey."

"Kelly, is everything okay?"

"Yeah, everything's fine. Laura Parker is going to come in and leave a statement."

"About what?"

"It's a long story, but the short version is that it wasn't Mr. Parker who killed Mikey, but Mrs. Parker. Laura witnessed it."

"And Mr. Parker?"

"There's no point in charging any of them with anything. I just need a statement so we can close this dumb case and set the record straight about Mikey."

"What happened?"

"C'mon, Albie, wrap it up with your girlfriend. We've gotta get the frail downtown," Detective Bilbo Kojak said.

"I'll meet you at the station and bring you up to speed . . . about everything."

"Kelly, is Mr. Parker really okay in there?"

"Mentally, no, but he's with his caregiver, and this won't take long. We can talk after."

"Sure."

"You okay?" he asked her.

"Yeah . . . no. It's a lot to take in all at once."

"I can see that," he said reasonably. He wasn't sure where he stood with all of it himself. Then to Laura he said, "Ms. Parker, come on, I'll drive you over. Jo, I'll see you at the station."

He held open the passenger door of Black Beauty for her. She got in, and he closed the door.

CHAPTER 19

Kelly ended up driving into 'Sconset and then down Milestone Road to head back to the police station. Bilbo kept telling him which turns to take. Kelly liked scenic 'Sconset with its high hedges and old homes. He liked Milestone Road, as it was the only place on the island where you could drive somewhat fast.

Laura Parker wasn't saying much, only answering his questions in monosyllables. She was, to his eye, a woman deep in thought. He didn't press her. He knew intimately how hard it was, confronting demons from the past.

For Kelly, it was hard to picture her happy. Her early life wouldn't have offered much reason to be. She had seemed happy only in the field hockey pictures, especially action shots of her on the field.

"Ask her about that," Detective Bilbo said.

"You played field hockey in high school?"

"Yes."

"Were you any good?"

"Yes, we won the championship."

"I don't know much about it. It's kind of like floor hockey or street hockey, like the hipsters play on roller blades?"

"Except it's played on grass and people run."

"The stick is different, too, right? Has a different shape?"

"Yes, it's all one piece of wood. No plastic or laminated wooden blades. It's shaped like a J. There's a flat side that you dribble with and shoot with. The other side of the blade is rounded, the whole thing is a couple of inches thick. I still have mine from when we won the championship."

"You were proud of being in the state championship, I bet."

"When I was a teenager, it seemed like it was important," she answered.

"That makes sense."

"Sure, things like that, prom, the winter formal, who's dating who. All that stuff seems so important when you're a teenager. Then you grow up and face real problems—real loss—and that stuff seems so trivial."

"You experienced all that a lot sooner than most. Your mother's abuse. Her killing Mikey . . ."

"I did."

"But the state championship was your special moment. Your moment to shine?"

"Exactly. It was my chance to show them that I was good at something." Her smile flashed.

"But Mikey ran off, and you had to kneel on the corn kernels. That must have been excruciating."

"It was. I told you it hurt like hell."

"And you peed yourself," Kelly reminded her.

"I did." Her face flushed at the thought of the memory. "My knees were killing me. When I got up, I had trouble walking."

"Sure, I'm not surprised. You must have been worried about being able to play the next day."

"I was. I was so fucking angry at her."

"Angry and humiliated, pee drying on your thighs. Irritating your skin," Kelly said almost absentmindedly.

"It was the worst. I went to bed holding my hockey stick, praying that I would be able to play the next day," she offered in a small voice.

"Is that what you killed Mikey with? You hit him in the head with the rounded part, didn't you? I mean, we both know he wasn't choked to death. Your mother's fists couldn't have damaged his skull like the wounds indicate. So it had to be you."

She didn't answer right away. Kelly's attention was divided between the road and glancing at her. He half expected her to smile, the way she always seemed to, but she didn't.

"How did you figure it out?"

If Kelly had been expecting hysterics, he had the wrong woman. She continued in her flat, almost dazed voice. It was the voice of the girl who had to kneel on kernels of corn, Kelly thought.

"I was certain you thought it was my dad. I was sure you were going to kill him when I saw you with him in the front room."

Kelly didn't bother to tell her that he'd been thinking about it.

"I was waiting for you to get your coat, looking at the pictures of you playing field hockey."

"That was it?"

"No, I noticed that the back side of your stick, you know that part that looks like the bottom of a *J*."

"It's called the head."

"Yeah, I noticed the back of the head was rounded. The doctor told us Mikey had been struck in the head with a bat or a fish billy, something rounded based on the damage to his skull." Kelly paused.

"Go on," she urged.

"Then it occurred to me that your father was unlikely to protect the woman who murdered his son, much less go to such great lengths to do it. But his daughter, his little girl who he might have felt guilty about not protecting from her abusive mother . . . well, that's something else altogether."

"Yes, it is. Mikey was my stepbrother. My parents met before we moved out here—each already had a kid. Like the Brady Bunch."

"But not happy," Kelly said.

"No, Detective Albie, not happy at all."

Kelly noticed she was pointing a small automatic at him. A .380 Ruger. A good, simple gun. Small, easy to hide.

"Is this the point where you tell me not to make any sudden moves?"

"Yep. Just drive. I think we'll skip the police station."

"Albie, this isn't good," Detective Bilbo, master of the obvious, said.

"Where to, then?" He was trying to sound casual as his mind raced.

"Drive. I'll tell you where to go."

"Then what?"

"I'll shoot you."

"Just like that? You won't get away with it. Hard to hide a body and car out here."

"I won't have to. I'll call the police and tell them you tried to rape me. I'll rip my blouse open, hit my face so I'll look right by the time they get to us."

"No one will believe you."

"Don't be so sure. Just because you're a cop? Ha! This isn't the 1950s. Your profession has a lot of tarnish these days. People will believe me. People know me here. You, you're just a damaged little boy who grew up to be a damaged cop, who fucked over a poor, lonely woman the way you were fucked over. That's all anyone will see."

Kelly shrugged for want of anything clever to say.

"Why'd you kill Mikey?"

"I was so happy when Daddy brought Mikey home that night. My knees hurt so much and . . . I could barely walk. I could smell my own pee. I had a game the next day, and I wasn't sure I'd be able to play. I was so angry with him."

"That's understandable. Must have been frustrating."

"Even when she was hitting him, I thought . . . good. The shithead deserves it. Do you think that makes me a bad person?"

"No, that makes you human."

"Do you believe that?"

"Sure, you were a kid in horrible circumstances. Resenting your brother because your mother punished you for something he did. It's understandable."

"She got done hitting him and brought him downstairs. She was all lovey, making him his favorite, grilled cheese and tomato soup. She didn't even say anything nice to me when she let me up from kneeling. But Mikey, she was treating him like a fuckin' prince. She always did."

"That must have been rough." Kelly could see that once again Laura was lost in her story, the demure motel worker gone.

"He was her little shining star," she continued. "It was infuriating. No matter how much she hit him, she treated him like he was so special. Me, she told me I was wicked. I deserved it. When Mikey was around, I was just an afterthought, someone who screwed up, someone who needed to be punished."

"That must have been infuriating." Kelly was mindful of the muzzle of the pistol pointed at him. He was even more aware of how few options he had. "Wanna tell me what happened?"

"That night, after everyone was asleep, I crept into Mikey's room. My knees still hurt. Even though I'd changed, I felt humiliated from having peed myself earlier. I still feel humiliated. Then I thought, I'll show her."

"You brought your hockey stick?"

"He was sleeping and looked so peaceful. I raised the stick over my head and hit him. I don't know how many times; I know that I thought to use the rounded side. Then he was gone. Just like that, I had showed that bitch. I had taken her precious little prince away from her. Then I went to bed and slept until morning, when I woke up because she was screaming. It was the best day of my life."

"That's why your dad buried Mikey in Tom Nevers? Why he shot Hampton? Not to protect your mom but to protect you?"

"That's right, Daddy was finally protecting me. He loves me," Laura said in a small voice from the passenger seat.

"I know."

"He's a good man. He couldn't protect me from Mommy."

"Or from yourself."

"Albieeeeeee!" Detective Bilbo screamed from the back seat.

Kelly pushed down on the gas pedal, and Black Beauty shot forward. "Slow down!"

Kelly kept his hands on the wheel and spoke fast. "If you shoot me, we'll end up in a wreck and your plan won't work."

"Why not?"

"I've been recording you. Digital recorder in my jacket pocket."

"Wha—" She never had a chance to finish the question. Kelly snapped his right hand off the steering wheel, grabbing for the gun. She jerked it away from him and he lunged sideways, one hand on the wheel, reaching for it again. His fingers brushed against her hand. She jerked back. He kept clawing for the pistol.

The gunshot next to him in the confines of the car sounded like a bomb going off. His mind dimly registered tiny, warm, wet raindrops against his face. Blood and brain matter. Kelly reflexively jerked away from Laura, jerking the wheel with him.

Black Beauty, powered by lovingly maintained Detroit V8 muscle, pulled hard to the left as Kelly instinctively pushed his foot down on the accelerator, trying to brace himself in response to the gunshot in the close quarters of the car. Black Beauty shot across the bike path, hit a small earthen berm, and rolled, coming to rest on its roof in some wild, tangled bushes. Kelly bounced around, his head smashing against everything, the airbag punching him in the face. When the car finally came to rest, he'd already begun to slip into an inky, dark pool.

CHAPTER 20

Kelly was back in the Monster's cave. He was trying to find his way out; Bilbo was beckoning to him to follow him. Except when he got to the door, the cave started to shake like he was inside a giant paint can on a giant paint shaker. Then he tumbled off the roof of the projects in Worcester with the ill-fated track star spinning to the earth next to him. When he hit the pavement, there was a light shining painfully in his eyes, and his head hurt from the inside out.

He managed to slowly open his eyes, the unpleasant fluorescent lights shining painfully into them. His head ached, and it slowly dawned on Kelly that he couldn't think of a single part of his upper body that didn't hurt. He heard a steady beeping somewhere above and behind him and saw that there was an IV in his arm. He was pressed into a bed by crisp white sheets.

The hospital. He was in the hospital, his slightly scrambled brain pieced together. He looked over at the chair, expecting to see either of his parents sitting in it, like he had so many nights after he escaped the Monster's cave. Instead, it was none other than his boss, Dickie Savoy.

"Don't look so surprised. The air unit flew me out in one of the helicopters. They were only too happy for the flight time."

"How long have I been out?" Kelly managed to croak.

"A little over a day. You're concussed and bruised, but the doc thinks you should stay under observation for a couple of days. Do you remember anything?"

"Water?" Kelly croaked.

"You remember water?"

Kelly shook his head, regretting it instantly.

"Oh, you're thirsty." Savoy stood up and took one of those institutional plastic cups with a lid and straw that you see only in hospitals. He held the straw to Kelly's lips, and he drank for a few seconds.

"I was driving Laura Parker in to leave a statement."

"Then what?"

"Something clicked, and it occurred to me she killed her little brother with a field hockey stick. I asked her about it, and she pulled a gun. I got her to admit to it, and she made it clear she was going to kill me. I grabbed for the gun, and in the struggle, it went off."

"Yes, and then you wrecked the car."

"Fuck," Kelly muttered.

"Tom, where'd she get the gun?"

"From home, her bedroom or wherever her coat was. I didn't search her . . . she was cooperating . . . a witness. By the time I figured out she'd killed Mikey, we were already in the car."

"We recovered a little Ruger .380 that was registered to her."

"Jesus."

"Why didn't you search her?"

"Cooperating. Witness." Kelly whispered the two words. He was an idiot. He should have searched her, or had Jo do it.

"Tom, do you have any proof?"

"Monster," Kelly said before he drifted off to sleep again. In his dreams, Luke Skywalker was there in his tan *Empire Strikes Back* costume, shaking his head ruefully at Kelly. The look of disapproval was clear. Then, as happens with the magic of dreams, Luke's face transformed into Bilbo's.

Detective Bilbo Baggins walked in.

"Hello, Albie. How are you?"

"I think I'm going to be okay."

"You gonna eat that?" Detective Bilbo asked, pointing to the remains of Kelly's last hospital meal.

"No, go ahead." They'd been partners for a long time, and Kelly knew what Bilbo was after.

"You did good, Albie. You solved the case."

"Thanks. I should have seen it sooner. I screwed up."

"You can't blame yourself. You've been under a lot of pressure, being back here, reliving it all. It made it hard to see things clearly."

"Thanks, partner."

"No need. You needed me, and here I am. That's how it's always worked, when everything gets too hard, hurts too much, I show up to show you the way."

"Has it always been that way?" Kelly asked.

"Yes, it has. Ever since that monster hurt you. When your mind can't cope, your brain pushes a button, and I show up to help you through it."

"You're in my imagination?"

"I'm part of your mind."

"You're not real?"

"I'm not *not* real. I'm just part of your mind, like for emergencies."

"Am I cracking up?"

"No, kid. You'd be cracking up if you had to deal with this stuff and I wasn't here."

"Oh, that's not much better."

"Either way, it's time for me to split. Gotta go, kid."

"Where are you going?"

"I've got other cases to solve. I'll always be here if you need me."

"You're leaving?"

"I can't solve all your cases for you. See you in the funny papers, kid."

Albie heard the door close behind his hobbit friend.

Kelly woke up some time later. Dickie Savoy was still there. He asked for more water, and after he drank, he began in a halting voice to tell Savoy about the Monster that terrorized the island in 1981. He told the story slowly and left nothing out, except the details of his own personal assaults. He glossed over that with a couple of terse, technical terms. When he was done, his boss looked at him and said kindly, "Okay, Tom, get some rest. We'll work it out."

"Boss?"

"Yeah, Tom."

"There's a digital recorder in the wreckage of that Crown Vic or in my jacket. I taped her."

"Good. Good man," Savoy said.

Kelly would have asked him if he was going to be okay, but, exhausted from the effort of telling the story, he'd drifted off to sleep again. He dreamed about his mother in the months after his ordeal. How gentle and kind she was, making him his favorite foods. This time his mother brought him grilled cheese and tomato soup, and Kelly thrashed violently against the sheets he was trapped in.

When he woke up again, it was nighttime. Savoy was gone, and it occurred to him that the last time he was in this hospital, this same building, he'd been eight. Now he was back. Both times he was here because of what the Monster had done. He closed his eyes and went to sleep.

Morning filled the room with sunlight. The nurse came in and checked on him. She asked all the perfunctory questions and made the determination that he should have breakfast. Savoy came in while Kelly was finishing his scrambled eggs and bacon.

"How was it?"

"As hospital food goes, not bad, but the coffee leaves a lot to be desired."

"I figured as much," Savoy said, placing a large paper cup down in front of Kelly.

"Thanks, boss. I really appreciate it."

"I've been talking with Chief Almeida, and I also have been on the phone with the superintendent."

"Oh. How much shit am I in?"

"The superintendent is not pleased, but it could be a lot worse. It's a fuckup, but it wasn't, thank God, a custodial death. That and you didn't cause the agency any embarrassment. You'll get a letter of reprimand

and have to undergo some retraining that you'll get paid overtime to attend. You probably won't be getting any promotions anytime soon, but it could be worse. It probably didn't hurt that you're married to his academy classmate's daughter."

"Probably not. It could be worse." Even Kelly wasn't sure if he was talking about his marriage or current career prospects.

"Tom, why didn't you tell me? I would have sent Jacques out here."

"Ah hell, boss, I don't know. I wasn't really looking to share that stuff with anyone, much less you."

"Okay, that's fair, but you could have trusted me with it."

"I know I can. It's just something that I was never going to talk about to anyone. Ever."

"Chief Almeida told me about how brave you were then, and how the people out here reacted."

"It was thirty-five years ago, a lifetime."

"Still, the fact that you were able to come out here and focus on the case. Get anything done . . ."

Kelly shrugged. There wasn't anything to say.

"What's going to happen to Chief Almeida?" Kelly asked after a moment.

"I'm not sure. That seems like a Nantucket problem, but I suspect he was thinking of retiring soon anyway. This will probably speed that along."

"I think his wife is sick. Cancer."

"Yeah, that probably has a lot to do with it."

"So, for all intents and purposes, the case is over."

"Yes, you ID'd the remains, found out who was responsible, and took the case as far as it could go. Unfortunately, your only witness who wasn't in puppet land just blew her brains out in your car. All we have is your recording, but that should be enough to keep you out of trouble. And the other cases from 1981? No one, especially the people here, wants anything other than for those to stay dead and buried. In fact, I think they would prefer it if there was nothing connecting Mikey Parker's remains to the 1981 cases."

"So that's it, then?"

"Pretty much, unless you want to make a fuss about it or write a true crime book about it?"

"No, I think I agree with the locals on this one. Let sleeping dogs lie. My guess is that they will assume and gossip that Laura Parker was distraught about the discovery of her brother's remains and took her own life."

"Makes sense. You will have to leave a statement for the local cops and talk to Internal Affairs."

"Great," Kelly said with no enthusiasm. IA interviews were like trips to a dentist who didn't believe in Novocain.

"Look on the bright side: This wasn't an in-custody death. So at least you have that going for you. And you're alive, bruised but alive."

"Story of my life. Thanks. Did anyone tell Jeanie?"

"Yes, Jacques went out. He let her know you were in a crash. He told her you were banged up but otherwise all right. He said the boys took it well."

"I'm sure she didn't."

"Jacques said her response was . . . atypical," Savoy said dryly.

"Probably pissed about not getting the life insurance or the line of duty upgrade."

"Yeah, well, that's true love for you. I'm heading back to the mainland. I will see you when you get back to work."

"Sure. Thanks."

"See ya, Kelly," Savoy said and left.

Kelly wasn't really looking forward to going back. Even though he was going to give his statement to IA here, that wouldn't be the end of it. There would also be the Accident Review Board, and at some point, Savoy would have to give him his letter of reprimand. Kelly would have to read it and sign, acknowledging its receipt. It would go in his permanent file and mean that a promotion—not that he was looking for one—was off the table now. At least for the foreseeable future. In short order, someone else would screw up pretty badly and they'd take the attention from Kelly's screwup. Also, he was going to have to face Jeanie, who would no doubt find some way to add this to the list of his many failings as a husband and father. At least he could count on that.

Kelly managed to get up and go over on shaky legs to the little closet. Inside he found a plastic bag that held his wallet, phone, coins, the half-dollar he liked to fidget with, and the items that had been in his pockets. He knew that either the local police or Bruce Green would have taken and stored his duty weapon. His clothes were in the bag, except his MSP fleece jacket that he'd been wearing. That, covered in blood, was in an evidence bag at the police station.

He made his way to the hospital bed on jelly legs. It was as much for having spent almost thirty-six hours in bed as it was from the concussion. He made it to the bed, ignoring the cold draft from the open back of the hospital johnny. After adjusting himself as best as he could into a comfortable position in bed, he pushed the power button on his phone.

Nothing happened. He tried again, and then it occurred to him that it had been 50 percent charged before he left the station. It was dead now. He dropped it on the little table that was next to his bed. At least he had an excuse to put off talking to Jeanie.

"Hey," Jo Harris said from the doorway.

"Hey, yourself," he said amiably, if a little weakly.

"I was going to come by sooner, but Savoy said he wanted to talk to you. I got the feeling it was private."

"More or less."

"How are you feeling?" she asked, walking into the room.

"A little worse for wear, but I'll survive."

"Well, you gave everybody a pretty good scare."

"Sorry about that." He paused.

"No matter, I'm just glad that you're all right."

"Thanks. Jo, I'm sorry I didn't tell you about what happened when I was a kid. I wasn't trying to keep it from you . . . I just don't know how to talk about it."

"It's okay."

"It isn't, but believe me, I wasn't trying to be dishonest."

"I know, Kelly. I also get it. It's a lot to trust someone with, especially someone you don't know well."

"Even people you do know well. I never told my wife or any of my friends."

"I get it."

Kelly wondered if she did. It was a lot, and he wasn't sure he understood any of it.

"Thanks."

"No worries. I heard that MSP is sending Internal Affairs out to take a statement from you."

"Yeah, I'm not looking forward to it. Plus, you guys need a statement."

"After you talk to your IA guy. Then one of the other detectives will take it."

"Makes sense."

"Now what will happen?"

"Not much. I will answer IA's questions and get a letter of reprimand in my jacket."

"No, I meant will you be all right?" she asked.

"I think so. I didn't commit a crime, or scandalize the MSP, so I should be okay."

"Business as usual?" she asked wryly.

"Business as usual," Kelly agreed.

"What a mess."

"It is, was. Jo?"

"Yeah."

"Don't be too hard on Almeida. He might not have done the right thing in 1981, but he was trying to. That should count for something. He's still the same man you looked up to last week. A good man."

"But he helped them cover up the murders. He lied. He helped Jimmy Parker protect his murdering daughter and abusive wife."

"There's no way we'll ever know if how they handled things would have had any bearing on the case. They caught the guy in the end. As for Parker, he thought he was helping him. The town, the whole island, was grateful to Parker. He killed a vicious predator."

"That's some circular logic."

"Sure, but like I said, most of the time you knew him, he was a good man. Go easy on him. No one is perfect."

"I might be," she said with a smile, and Kelly was grateful for the joke.

"I'm glad one of us is."

"You do all right, Kelly."

"Thanks."

"I'm guessing that you won't be in a rush to come back here."

"Um, maybe not, but the boat goes to the mainland too."

"Is that some sort of half-assed invitation?"

"It is an invitation. Yes."

"Well, Kelly, you do grow on a girl."

"Been awhile since I heard anything nice like that," he said.

"I'm sure I can come up with something nicer."

The Internal Affairs detective came into his room while Kelly was sitting among the remains of an uninspiring lunch. Even in one of the wealthiest communities in America, hospital food was still hospital food. Which is just a notch above what they serve on most domestic airlines.

"Detective Kelly? Is this a bad time?" a tall man with thinnish red hair, gray at the temples, asked from the doorway.

"No, I'm not going anywhere."

"I'm Brian Dolan from IA."

"I figured." Dolan was wearing a blue suit with black shoes and a regulation bulge on his hip, where his service weapon was holstered.

"Um . . . I was told your supervisor talked to you."

"Yes."

"You have a right to a union rep or counsel."

"No, not now." Kelly was pretty sure that if Savoy was wrong that he could get a lawyer to shred the statement taken at the hospital bedside of a recently concussed detective.

"Good, this is just a formality. Do you mind if I sit?"

"No, go ahead."

"They flew me over in some little puddle jumper."

"Not fun?"

"I don't love flying, even less so when I am sitting in the copilot's seat."

"Yeah, I can see that."

"Do you mind if I record this?" Dolan took out a small digital recorder. The question wasn't really a question so much as a nod to courtesy.

"Sure. Go ahead." There was no point being difficult; the fix was in. Being difficult would just make it worse for him in the end.

"Great, thanks." Dolan pushed the record button and put the recorder down on the table.

"Okay, can you tell me about the events leading up to your car accident?"

"I was assigned a homicide case after the local police found human remains that appeared to be several decades old."

"The Nantucket Police Department?"

"Yes."

"You were sent out?"

"Yes."

Dolan asked several more establishing questions and then asked, "Detective, how did the deceased come to have a gun in her possession? Specifically, a Ruger .380?"

"I don't know. I believe that she retrieved it from somewhere in her house."

"Why?"

"I can't speculate as to what she was thinking."

"Was she in custody?"

"No, she was accompanying me voluntarily to the local police station to leave a formal statement."

"Concerning?"

"The remains that were recovered and the investigation. She was the stepsister of the deceased."

"Why didn't you frisk her before putting her in your car?"

"Because at that point she gave every indication of being a cooperating witness. She wasn't in custody, and there was no sign that she was armed."

"Huh, well, apparently she was. What happened next?"

"We drove to the station via Milestone Road. I was discussing the case; it became apparent that she had murdered her younger stepbrother in 1981. She pulled the gun and threatened to kill me. I tried to take it away from her. A struggle ensued. At some point midway or a bit past it, I was startled by a gunshot in my car at proximity. I instinctively flinched, and the car left the road surface. Then I woke up in here."

"That's it?"

"That's it."

"Okay, just a few more questions."

"Sure."

Dolan spent the next hour asking the same basic questions in different ways. Kelly wasn't sure if he was being thorough or if he wasn't the smartest detective. Finally, Dolan stood and stretched. Then he picked up the recorder and turned it off.

"I can't say what's going to happen to you, but they won't hammer you."

"That's good."

"You'll get a letter in your file and probably some retraining. You'll get gigged for the accident, too, but none of this is fatal. Thank God she wasn't in custody."

"Yeah, lucky break," Kelly said dryly.

Peter Colt

"Okay, kid. Good luck." Dolan left without shaking hands. Kelly wasn't upset in the least.

The nurse had managed to scrounge up a phone charger for him before Dolan had arrived. The upside of the interview was that his phone had charged enough for him to call Jeanie. The bad news was that he had to call Jeanie. Kelly was contemplating this when Joe Almeida walked in.

"Hello, Joe," Kelly said.

"How are you doing, Kelly?" Joe asked.

"Starting to feel a little like Ebenezer Scrooge."

"Cheap?"

"Visited by a bunch of ghosts," Kelly responded.

"Am I the third?"

"The fourth, actually, but I am really hoping that the guy from IA is not the Ghost of Christmas Future."

"That would make me the Ghost of Christmas Past," Almeida said.

"I think we could each claim that title."

"Are things going to be okay with your job? IA and all that?"

"Yeah, it would seem that the fix is in. Or at least that's what my lieutenant, also known as the Ghost of Christmas Present, indicated. It wasn't an in-custody death and won't be in the news for long. In short it won't be a scandal, so the MSP's image won't be tarnished."

"Good. It wasn't your fault," Almeida offered.

"Did you know about Mrs. Parker?" Kelly asked.

"Abusing her kids? No. She was always nice, quiet, very religious but without pushing it on anyone."

"Guess she saved it for the kids."

"Seems so. No, we all believed that Hampton killed Mikey."

"Makes sense, in an Occam's razor sort of way."

"Kelly, if I knew or even suspected . . . things would never have played out the way they did."

"I know, Chief," Kelly said resolutely.

"We made a mess of it."

"I have been lying here in this hospital bed, going over it in my head. I don't think that the decision to keep the lid on the abductions was the right one, but I don't think it altered the course of events one way or the other."

"Except Mikey Parker."

"Except Mikey."

"You think that Laura Parker would still be alive right now?"

"I don't know. Maybe."

"I do," Almeida said gravely.

"There are no time machines. The die was cast thirty-five years ago."

"Well, that certainly doesn't help."

"No, I guess not, but you can't undo it. You can beat yourself up, or you can accept it and move on."

"Like you did?"

"I had a lot of help. Mom and Dad never made me kneel on corn kernels. They never hit me. They also had me talk to a child psychologist, which in 1982 was unheard of. Dad tried to toughen me up and, in his own way, he was a son of a bitch about it. But in the end, I learned to accept it, learned to accept all of it and live with it. I couldn't change what happened. I can only move forward."

"Are you telling me that if you can do it, I can too?" Almeida said with a forty-watt smile.

"Something like that."

"Thanks, Kelly. See you around." Almeida stood up and started for the door.

"Chief."

"Yes," he said, turning.

"Give Jo some time. She won't get over it, but she will figure out that she likes you even with feet of clay."

"Thanks, Kelly. Take care."

"You too."

April 2016

Kelly stood on the top deck of the ferry. It wasn't the MV *Nantucket* or the much-maligned MV *Uncatena* that he remembered from his childhood. This was a much taller one, still white with a black stripe along its hull, the MV *Eagle*. He looked down Steamboat Wharf, noted where it turned into Broad Street. He watched the ant-size people and the cars that looked like they belonged to a model railroad as they moved around the island.

He wasn't sure what to feel. He was leaving the island again, but it was different this time. Thirty-five years ago, he'd been a little boy, recovering from injuries both physical and psychological that had been inflicted upon him. He had slipped into a world where he was spending time with a character he'd seen in a cartoon that wasn't for kids.

Now he was an adult, forced to reexamine the whole thing. He thought he should feel something, but in the end, he was just leaving a place. He thought that there would be the same tightness in his chest, but it was gone. Not forever, he knew that, but it wasn't a constant companion. Now it would just be consigned to the occasional nightmare or event that would jog the unpleasant memories loose.

The call the night before to Jeanie had gone as predicted. She didn't believe in babying her soon-to-be ex-husband. She was consistent at least. In an uncertain world, he could always count on Jeanie being Jeanie. The boys were glad he was all right and really wanted to know if he'd rolled Black Beauty.

"Totaled it. Unlike *The Dukes of Hazzard*," he said.

"Dukes of what?" they asked. Kelly explained the reference, racing against their impending boredom. They were consistent too. They told him they loved him, and he thanked God for his boys for the thousandth time.

Jo Harris had driven him to the ferry. Sitting in her unmarked car, she said, "Is that offer of a place to stay off-island still good?"

"Yep. I can throw in meals too."

"Wow, Kelly, don't go all mushy on me."

"Me? Never," he said, and then he leaned over and kissed her. What the hell, it wasn't like they weren't already fodder for the island's twenty-four-hour gossip cycle.

"Okay, get out of here before you ruin what little reputation I have left," she said with a laugh.

He got out, shouldered his bag, and made his way to the gangway. He gave his ticket to the guy collecting them. Kelly walked up the gangway and stopped by the railing. Jo was standing outside her car. She waved briefly at him, then got in her car and drove off.

The blast from the ferry's horn startled him out of his reverie. Then the second blast sounded, and the ferry started to pull away from the wharf. He looked at the yacht club and the million-dollar homes as they slowly receded into the distance.

He crossed the deck and watched the fancy hotel named after a pale pachyderm slide by, and the coast guard station on Brant Point. As the ferry rounded Brant Point, he fished two pennies out of his pocket. He could hear his mother's voice in his head saying that she never wanted to come back.

It wasn't that Kelly had any burning desire to return. He just didn't want to be held hostage by the fear. He didn't want to give in to the horrible things that happened to him when people called him Albie. He threw the pennies in the ocean as the ferry rounded Brant Point. He also threw them in for Mikey, Richie, and Nick. Then, as an afterthought, he took out his fidget half-dollar coin, the one that reminded him of Albie's magic quarter of invisibility. He threw that overboard too.

He'd paid the ferryman his fare and then some.

Acknowledgments

I say it all the time: I am just a guy who writes manuscripts. There are a lot of other people who take what I write and turn it into a book. I am deeply indebted to them.

First my wife, Cathy, who lets me slip into my office for hours every night to write. My good friend CME, who reads the first draft and cleans up my spelling and grammar—were it not for her efforts, I am not sure anyone would have ever given me a book deal. There is a small number of friends and family who read the manuscripts and offer feedback. In my mind it's not ready until it's Aunt Ginny–approved.

This book absolutely wouldn't exist if it weren't for the tireless efforts of my agent, Cynthia Manson, and editorial director Megha Parekh, who saw something in the manuscript worth turning into a book. I am indebted to Clarence Haynes for his keen editorial eye, as well as Sarah Engel and James Gallagher. There are also a lot of people at Thomas & Mercer whose names I don't know who worked very hard to get this book in your hands.

Lastly, I want to thank fellow writer Roberta Gately for taking the time to read the manuscript and offer much-needed feedback.

About the Author

Photo © 2024 Elizabeth Bean

Peter Colt is the author of the Andy Roark mysteries. He was born in Boston, Massachusetts, in 1973 and is a graduate of the University of Rhode Island. Peter spent twenty-four years in the army reserve, with deployments to Kosovo in 2000 and Iraq in 2003 and 2008. He is currently a police officer in Providence, Rhode Island, where he lives with his family and two perpetually feuding cats. Colt's hobbies include cooking, camping, and kayaking. He also writes a near-weekly Substack. For more information, visit www.petercoltauthor.com.